TR[illegible] SON

Volume II

GEOFF CARTHY

THE CROWN AND THE ARROW SAGA

PART 1

Also by Geoff Carthy:

A Traitor's Son Vol 1

Forthcoming:

The Thegn Vol 1

The Thegn Vol 2

GEOFF CARTHY

A Traitor's Son

Volume II

Part One of The Crown and The Arrow Saga

STORIES*into*LIGHT Publishing

A Traitor's Son Vol II

ISBN of paperback edition
978-1-7392612-3-8

Geoff Carthy

First edition 2025

Published by Stories into Light 2025

In memory of

RON CARTER

1927 - 2023

CONTENTS

1. Fyrdsman

(Godwin)

"Bound to be dirty then."

Comtyn had been spared total destruction, and it turned out that a messenger from Edmund had saved Bosham. The hamlets in between were less lucky, but Caewin and Saehild were the only deaths. Aelfric, Ealdorman of Wessex, would not make war on Mercia over a village idiot and an errant niece.

Prince Edmund did not sanction Brihtric's reprisal, but neither did he act against him. He told the Mercian to take his men back to Scorham and find boats, to catch up with the fleet. It would no longer be at Sanwic, for the King had ordered that it should sail on, and up the Tamys. Brihtric plainly thought little of this tactic, but was not going to argue with Prince Edmund. He led his men back east, and as they left they muttered their complaints about the lack of blood. Godwin wondered how much they'd welcome blood when it was tough Danes they were hewing at, big men who hewed back, rather than ancients and children and women.

Edmund shaped up his troop to leave the burning village in the opposite direction, inland towards Wintancaestr, and ordered Godwin to come with them. It was only Brother Snell's intervention that swayed Edmund into allowing Godwin first to help dig a grave, and then with Cudbert, Sel and Eg to lower his mother's body into the ground. He could tell through the winding cloth that she had been lightened of her chainmail as well as her dignity. Her sword was gone too, and her cloakpin brooch. Some Mercian ceorls now had them, prizes of this revenge mission.

Snell spoke words Godwin barely heard, they threw soil onto her, and Odylia threw a flower. To Godwin's surprise Edmund too picked up a handful of earth. "She didn't deserve the husband God gave her," he said.

Edmund would have taken Cudbert as well as Godwin, so Godwin said he was released from the oath made to Wulfnoth, and should stay in Comtyn to lead the rebuilding. Sel and Eg too, the one bound to Cudbert, the other's scrawny limbs of little use to Edmund for a year or more.

"Weren't just to your father I made a promise." Cudbert said. "Was to your mother too. And I don't renounce it, specially not now."

"There are too few men left here. Mother would see that. I'll return when I can." Every word had to be forced through the fog of numbness that surrounded him.

Odylia boldly stepped up before Edmund. "My father helped Godwin's father. My father is just as guilty, so I owe you as much as Godwin does."

Edmund looked down at her. "You only confess now you are safe from Brihtric."

"I ain't confessing. I done nothing wrong. But I got no family here, and I can serve you. I know how to splice rope and steam wood. I can cook and mend and clean. I know herbs that heal cuts and relieve aches."

"I've got an ache you can relieve," one of Edmund's men called out.

Odylia showed Edmund the poultices she'd concocted for the wounded horse, and Edmund let her come. Whether for the sake of his men's cuts, or for their aches, Godwin wasn't sure.

He wasn't interested in the twelve men's names, but he heard them as they rode. A man called Long Ercenbert seemed to be the captain. He stood taller than most, though not heavier. Godwin had no contact with him, as routine orders were given by his second-in-command, Deorleaf the Mown.

Deorleaf was a short man with flinty grey eyes, who carried most of a square beard. He got his name from the fact that his left check was bald and pink where hair would not grow from scar tissue. The rest of the beard drew attention to it. Perhaps that was the point, to show off how close he had come to death. "The Waelasman who dealt me this has a full beard on his head, but no head on his shoulders," he said when he saw Odylia looking at him.

Godwin caught other names, Wystan and Marceus, without being sure to whom they attached, and Geareth the Haystack, who was obvious. The youngest was Fordred, a tall youth of about sixteen years, who rode a stocky brown pony too small for him. A thin beard did not hide his resentment towards Godwin and Odylia who both had better horses, though Odylia's was wounded and might not make it through the day. She hadn't asked permission to take Linden, who stoically bore both her and the pain. Godwin kept his peace. She'd earned a loan by treating the mare's wounds, but mostly he still felt guilty about what he'd done to her at Brimclif.

Sunk into a black bog of guilt, grief, remorse, anger and fatigue, he cared not a frogfart that none of the troop would talk to him. His father was the notorious traitor, yet there he sat on his grey, a better mount than any of theirs. When they stopped to rest the horses and share some bread, they mocked him, calling him "thegn" and "sire." He should not have retorted that he was indeed a thegn now his father was gone, as if he thought himself proud and above them, but their insults and their spittle had penetrated his numbness. The Prince immediately slapped his face so hard his mouth bled. "Comtyn no longer has a thegn," he announced to all. "No son of Wulfnoth once-Cild shall even be headman, by the King's word."

The slap was for his own good, he knew. But it came too late. Edmund's men had seen his pride.

He wanted no-one to speak to him; he wanted to speak to no-one. One day, his father had sailed away; in consequence, his mother was killed. He and his sister were effectively orphaned. His father's greatest treachery was not to his King but to his family. Following that, Godwin didn't give a tadpole what these men thought.

In the evening Edmund called a halt. A fire was lit for roasting fowl taken from runs in one or other of the razed villages. Half a chicken and more each, washed down with looted wine, a fine feast for these men who'd been rushed so speedily out of Lunden. Filled and warmed, they sat around the fire and sang, argued and told stories.

Godwin and Odylia were given food and drink, but the men allowed them no gap near the fire, so they had little alternative but to share their blankets. "I'm sorry about your mother," she said, and when Godwin didn't reply, she added "I never knew mine."

A simple truth, but not helpful. "You should run back to Bosham while you can. I know you've got folk there, no matter what you told Edmund."

"What folk I had, they was in Walberswick. None'll want me, not after what my father brought down."

"Comtyn, then. Find my sister, she'll return there. She needs someone to look after her."

"Won't be me," said Odylia. "I don't owe you nothing."

Godwin felt no urge to argue. He'd saved her from forced marriage to old Gewis, for which she should be grateful. But he'd threatened to kill her, and he'd cost her brother an arm. Who knew how that all weighed in the scalepans in her head?

She rose, ending the conversation, and his eyes followed her when she walked into the darkness under the trees. He became aware of movement near the fire. One man stood, then another. A third, Fordred, was pulled up by the second. They slunk towards the trees where Odylia had gone, and Godwin had to push off the blanket and pull on his boots. Had these men no pride, no shame?

He crashed after them, calling "Leave her!" and "Odylia, come back." She won't have gone far, he thought, for in the darkness there was no need.

He was suddenly confronted by three faces, lit by the fire behind him. Fordred was flanked by two older men. Were they three brothers? Just beyond, Odylia rose from her squat still holding the clump of leaves she'd wiped herself with. Godwin wished she'd get the chance to stuff the leaves into one of these men's mouths.

The tallest of the men started laughing. "You had her? Not want to share? Fordred's going to share, after he gets first stir. Aren't you lad?"

The older of the others joined his laughter with forced gusto. Fordred himself was less confident. Odylia stood her ground. Her hands moved behind her back. Her knife, the one Eg had grabbed at Brimclif, she must have reclaimed it from him. She would defend herself – hadn't Godwin been told she was wild? – but she'd inevitably be disarmed. Then it was only a question of how many more men would be called here after she'd been triply raped.

"She's not yours to share. She's not here for you."

"But she is. Why'd our Prince have her along except for us? So back off, or we might decide you're for sharing too."

Godwin drew his sword, wishing Cudbert were with him. Three days he'd ridden, to protect his people from Mercians. These sounded like Wessex boys, and yet his task wasn't finished. "Run back to Comtyn, Odylia, like I said."

The men faced him, and drew their own swords. They had their backs to her.

"I ain't running from no-one." She leaped forward, a blade in her hand, and stuck it into the right shoulder of the tallest of the three men. He yelled and dropped his sword as she leaped back.

The other man turned and faced her, leaving Fordred standing before Godwin. These were Edmund's husceorls, he thought, hand-picked for the mission to intercept Brihtric. Even the youngest of them, he'd be a fighter, not simply brash like Arni.

The stabbed man rose with his sword in his left hand. "Ye'll pay for that, ya little cunt." The pair stomped towards Odylia, as she backed off holding her dagger in front of her.

Feet came crashing through the undergrowth. "Halt this!" It was Ercenbert, with Deorleaf and three others. "What the fuck do you think you're doing? Wystan?"

The stabbed man pointed at Godwin and said "We saw this little bugger follow her into the trees. We feared for her. Tried to protect her, she got the wrong idea and fucking stuck me."

"Wystan, you're f…" Ercenbert started to say, but he heard footsteps striding up behind him, and a weary "What's this?" It was Prince Edmund. Ercenbert stopped and shook his head. He wasn't going to call out Wystan as a liar, Godwin realised, not in front of the Prince. "It's under control, Lord. You three, get back to the fire. Wystan, get that wound seen to. And no more of this, whoever's to blame. Bunch of fucking pigs."

Odylia followed Godwin back to their spot, and as they pulled their blankets tight, Godwin watched Ercenbert talking to Edmund. Both looked in their direction, and Godwin wondered what explanation Ercenbert might be offering. Edmund nodded, and came over. He squatted alongside Godwin, and offered a small silver flask, unstoppered.

Godwin sniffed it and recoiled. A wasp had got inside each nostril and stung him, and his eyes immediately filled.

"Sip," said Edmund. Godwin braced himself, and let the smallest drop touch his tongue. It stung like mustard, but with a gentler heat. He took more, and swallowed, and choked on the sweet fire.

"What is it?" he asked when his throat let him.

"Some call it burned wine. Some, wine spirit. Some, water of life. Others say it's a mix of the Archangel Gabriel's spittle and Satan's piss. What it truly is, I have no idea. It was a gift from the Frankish King. Have more. It is good for bringing sleep on cold nights."

Godwin sipped again, and coughed again, but felt a glow deep inside. Edmund chuckled as he reached for the flask, but before Godwin could hand it back Odylia took it, supped more than her share, and suppressed her coughs more successfully than he had.

She returned it, and Edmund laughed again. "My fault," he said to her. "I should have made it clear that nothing like that was to happen. I apologise." He dipped his head to Odylia. "It won't occur again. And you, Godwin… Three of them, fighters all. Choose your battles carefully."

"Brihtric had twenty-three."

"As I say, choose your battles carefully. You'll fight for a girl. And you stood with your mother. Will you fight for a man, Godwin?"

"Does he choose his battles carefully?"

"Oh yes," Edmund chuckled. "Of necessity." He took his own mouthful of the burned wine. "The men will wonder why you stepped in. They're talking now that you think yourself one sainted holy fucker who thinks there's a seat reserved for him at the high table."

"When they put themselves so low, all tables are higher."

"It's no way to make friends."

"I don't need friends."

"What you don't need is enemies. So fuck this girl loudly tonight, to let them know why you protected what's yours."

"She's not-"

"She is now, so have another drink, the pair of you, and get to it. That's by royal decree." He looked at Odylia. "It's for your safety too. Understand?"

She nodded.

As the fire was allowed to die and the men bedded themselves down, Odylia gave Godwin even less choice than Edmund had. He lay there unfeeling, as if half in the black soil below and half in the dark cloud above, as she untied his cords and bared his lem, which had no care for Godwin's trials. She squealed and moaned louder than Gret did; but whether her moans came truly from her shieth or falsely from her throat, sounded for the ears of Wystan and others, he could not say, and did not care.

Godwin had been to Wintancaestr before. He'd gone with his father to conduct business and to meet with other Thegns, and with his mother and Saewin to visit his grandfather and aunts. Once, they'd even met Ealdorman Aelfric himself. And he'd gone with other villagers, to help at the market, to drive sheep or pigs, to buy cloth or tools. It was the grandest place he could imagine, with its bustle, its noise, its smells.

The city was dominated by two great structures, and two palisaded compounds. The great cathedral, built of yellow stone from distant parts, stood wide and squat, with a low square tower and a steep roof of baked clay tiles that glowed as red as a squirrel in the evening sun. He and his family had joined two hundred and more worshippers when they'd been there of a Sunday, and he'd wished he could go every sabbath.

The Cathedral had a huge organ built by Bishop Aelfheah before he was appointed Archbishop and sent to Cantenberh. Its music, with the choir singing, was truly the sound of heaven, filling the nave, and filling his head. It was said that it took threescore men to work its bellows, which Godwin could believe, for it was loud enough to be heard in villages miles away downwind. Nearby priests would hold services outside so their congregation could hear angels sing. He tried to tell himself that God was just as present in Comtyn, that Brother Snell was no less favoured in His eyes than the Bishop of Wintancaestr, but there was no doubt that he felt more uplifted in the cathedral than in the little village chapel. Perhaps it was not God who made the difference, but people.

The other grand structure faced the cathedral across the market plain; the great hall where Kings held their Witangemots. In recent years the nobles were more likely to be called to Lunden, but the ancient role for this hall was what gave Wintancaestr its name. Save the Cathedral itself, it was by far the biggest building Godwin had seen, bigger than the minsters at Cicaestr and Suthamtun. Its huge triangular gable rose to an apex as high as trees, like a cliff, and its solidity had withstood Danish fire more than once. The roof was new enough that the dense thatch was till coloured gold. From a distance it appeared to almost touch the ground, like a skirt. Only on getting close did it become clear that the hall showed not just its ankles but its calves, for the walls were more than head-height, with a line of windows shaded by the thick overhanging eaves.

Making a square with the Cathedral and the hall was a high palisade fence with two gates. Behind the gate closest to the main hall was a further collection of halls, huts and houses that were homes to the King and Queen when they were here, and all their family and servants and visitors; and Ealdorman

Aelfric's halls too. Behind the other gate was an even larger collection of halls, stables, cookhouses, stores, smithies and workshops where countless soldiers could garrison, although currently only a hundred or so men were quartered there. This was where the citizens had run for safety, as many as could fit, when the Danish army last descended not seven years back.

They passed through the gate, and Godwin saw something he'd not perceived from outside – that the fort and the palace compound were separated by another palisade, and the King's halls were behind another gate there, a fort within a fort.

Edmund's troop turned towards an earth-floored hall where they joined the other royal husceorls who weren't currently in Lunden with the King. Odylia was directed to a separate building where lived the women and girls who cooked food, who cleaned, and mended clothes and shoes and limbs. Little separation was enforced, and many women sat and worked alongside the men. Godwin saw signs – clothes and handlooms and combs – that many slept in the men's halls. Odylia saw this too, and the moon had barely risen before she made her way to his bed to warm him. He decided he preferred Gret's softness to Odylia's bones, the handfuls of breast she offered to Odylia's crabapples, and definitely Gret's thick waves of hair to these hanks of black seaweed. But she wasn't lazy, and her sheith was tight, and he had no other friend, so he forgot Gret and any reason to feel guilty.

They'd arrived on a Saturday. Sunday mornings were for worship, with services held in the compound. The Cathedral was filled with citizens, leaving little room for fyrdsmen, but Godwin asked Ercenbert for dispensation, saying he had family in Wintancaestr whom he'd likely be able to find among the worshippers. Ercenbert gave grudging consent, so Godwin joined the congregation. He walked down the aisles, but spotted no face he knew save that of Ealdorman Aelfric, whom he had no reason to approach.

He left before the service finished, to stand just outside the door where he could see everyone as they emerged. Elders and children, thegns, ceorls, traders, landowners, matrons, young women with full bellies leaning back, and old couples with sticks, bent forward.

And then a face he knew. So like Saehild was his aunt Leah that he wanted to shout "Mother!" as he shouldered through the crowd. There too was uncle Lensing, and cousins, and his grandmother. And behind them, talking to Ealdorman Aelfric, was Ecfrith his grandfather. It was Ecfrith he must approach, but Leah he was drawn to.

"Grandfather," he said, and the old man turned. Godwin knew he'd made a mistake as soon as Ecfrith recognised him. When an old man bares his last remaining yellow teeth at you, you know you're not wanted.

"Who is this?" said Aelfric.

A growl came from Ecfrith's throat. "This is Wulfnoth's son. This is the sorrow and the shame my family suffers."

"Your niece was killed," Aelfric said. "His mother."

"She made her bed," Ecfrith said.

Faces turned. Whispers passed. Questions, and muttered answers.

"Be gone!" Ecfrith snarled. "You are not my kin."

Godwin turned to Leah. She stared at him, her lip curled.

They disowned him too. Why? He was not his father's son.

But he was.

There was a routine to each day, supervised by Ercenbert and Deorleaf. Breakfast was followed by weapons training, sweaty and dangerous, fighting with and against sword, axe, and pike. Blades were not always wood, and rarely a morning passed without some man being deeply cut or having a bone broken. He learned that those most likely to be injured were not the weak, but the tentative.

They formed up in shieldwalls, and Godwin saw how the front rank of shields and the second rank of pikes protected each other. He learned how and when best to swing a poleaxe or a glaive in the wall, and how to twist the blade when withdrawing it, so as not to cut his own men. Groundwards if the blade is low, skywards if it's high. He charged a wall to get inside the line of points, then defended a charge. When the fighters close, as they will, watch for the man who stoops to cut under your shield. Attack him over yours before his blade breaks your ankles. Defend not only yourself, but also the man to your left, whose sword arm is most vulnerable. Trust the man on your right to protect you. Do not fall. You won't get up. Worse, you will let down your fellows.

He practiced holding the wall tight, kneeling behind his shield as round-tipped arrows thudded onto the wood. A man beside him died from not crouching swiftly enough: round-tip or no, he swallowed the arrow, and it saw daylight out the back of his neck. Then they had to hold their shields high, as shelters against falling arrows. As he cowered, Godwin wondered what to do against a smart commander who ordered half his archers to shoot low and the other half to make rain. A fyrd needs archers of its own if only to counter the enemy's bowmen. Or a raiding party to get among them. First one, then the other. Coordination was all.

Afternoons were for small groups, covering forest crafts, firelighting, snaring, biwacts, stars and wayfinding that men needed when away from garrisons. Most knew some of these skills, but Godwin found the overall level of ignorance and clumsiness shocking.

Not every man learned everything. For some there was horsecare, and pigeons; for others, surgery, making splints and staunching blood; for others still, building shelters and bridges, and siegecraft skills: making ladders, towers, and turtlebacks of hazel wattles and leather.

Godwin was pitched into weapons drills with a dozen others, all older than he. Fordred, who it turned out was Wystan's younger brother, revelled in using his weight and strength to overpower Godwin with the heavy wooden practice sword. With each attack he'd yell "For Wystan," and drive Godwin back. "He's going to lose his arm."

Stay away from me, Godwin thought. Arms drop off in my wake, Arni's, Wystan's, nearly Cudbert's. He defended himself as best he could with his shield, and countered with "Because he let himself be stabbed by a girl." But that increased Fordred's fury, and as Godwin tired, and Fordred found gaps, banging the side of Godwin's helm with a thud that made his head reel if he lowered the shield, then hammering his ankles when the shield was up and he couldn't see where Fordred aimed. He was exhausted, bruised and bloodied, and the beating only stopped when a fyrdsman Godwin knew only as Trebert stepped in. He was a big, lean man, and unusual among the fyrdsmen because of his shaven face and short cropped hair. For some reason, when he told Fordred to desist, Fordred obeyed.

Trebert spoke with Lytleman the arms master, who told Godwin to go to the infirmary. "Get your girl to see if you have any broken bones," he said.

Odylia's healing skills were being applied and enhanced in the infirmary. She took off his shirt, and prodded and pressed him all over. He failed to cry out, so she concluded that his skeleton was more or less intact.

She made a poultice of marigold and comfrey leaves for the worst of his cuts, held a cloth soaked with wolfsbane juice to his bruises, and gave him a boiled willowbark infusion. It was more than he expected. As a lowly fyrdsman, he hadn't thought to get more than an evening of enforced idleness.

"You're faring better than Wystan," she told him. "He's still fevered. I see him in the infirmary, though they don't let me go close. He's shittin' himself that I'll finish him off."

"He's not recovering?" Godwin said. "From a dagger stab? What kind of leech do they have?"

"The dagger was dirty," Odylia confided. "*Really* dirty."

Godwin thought back to the dark woods. She'd groped behind her back for the dagger, before she even covered herself. She had leaves in her hand. He realised what she'd done. "The soiled leaves," he said. "You wiped the blade."

She bit one side of her bottom lip like she'd been caught stealing a scone. This was not a girl to wrong. Wystan was right to keep her clear of his bed.

"These herbs you've given me, this drink… you stole them, didn't you. From the apothecary."

She unbit her lip, but nodded, looking up with big eyes from under her eyebrows.

"You mustn't. I didn't save you, not once but twice, to see you whipped. Especially not for my sake."

She gave up her air of false innocence and glared at him. "You didn't save me. That Brimclif Headman would have felt what Wystan did, only not in the back, and not in the shoulder."

He believed her. She'd have done Gewis in. Then she'd have had to make her own way home. What prospect for a girl travelling alone and penniless? "We got you out. And what about Wystan's brothers? They might have killed you."

"They'd never have got what you get," she said softly, her mood changing like a flipped flatbread. Godwin wondered if any part of her was sincere. She put her hand on his groin and found other ways to ease his pains, and the moist secret part of her was sincere enough.

Next day it was back to the training. It was little easier with any of the husceorls. The others didn't hold the personal grudge that Fordred did, but everyone knew Godwin as the son of Wulfnoth the traitor, and, pleased to have someone other than themselves stood under the shitseat, they gave him no let. If they wanted tears, they didn't get them.

Trebert made efforts to get himself paired with Godwin, and although he was stronger, older and more skilled, at least he was fair, and stopped when Godwin was beat.

Unfortunately, Fordred made equal effort to pair up with him. In a year or two, Godwin would be bigger, and would have the beating of him, but a year or two was beyond the fence of a boy's patience. "I don't know how much more of this I can take," he said to Trebert.

"You're not thinking. Don't fight by his rules, fight by your own."

Edmund had told him to choose his battles. "How?"

"He can beat you face to face. So where do you match him? Where do you best him?"

In the archery butts. Godwin didn't have the range of men who could bend stiffer, longer bows. But at shorter target practice Godwin hit the straw figure as often as anyone. He pictured not a Dane but Fordred standing there, until he noticed that he shot better when he was not angry.

So the next time they went to practice their bowmanship, he challenged Fordred to an archery duel. "Fifty paces, Fordred. Two arrows each." One for range and wind, one for the kill. "Bodkins, not roundheads."

Fordred just said "I'd hit you and be hung as a murderer."

Godwin shouted loud enough that all around could hear. "He's a coward! A whimpering coward with no skill. Is there a one of you who'll stand in for him? I take any challenge!"

No-one stood. No-one valued Fordred highly enough.

Fordred looked around in hopeless desperation. Even his brother curled his lip as if to say "You got yourself into this, you get yourself out." When someone thrust a bow at him, he had no choice but to take it and step forward.

Those behind Godwin on one side, and Fordred on the other, fell back. The drama attracted people like flies, and soon the pair were stood in a long corridor of spectators, men and women, old and young. Trebert had a bow for Godwin, not too heavy, for range was not an issue here. He had four arrows, two of which he stuck into the turf at Godwin's feet. "When he shoots, stay side-on to him. A smaller target."

Cudbert had told him the same, long ago.

Trebert also had a heavy sack, from which he pulled a hauberk of chainmail. "There are rules. Put this on. And we use flathead arrows." Flatheads delivered worse wounds, but were less able to pierce mail.

He stepped out fifty paces, and marked Fordred's spot with two more arrows into the ground. He threw down a hauberk, then returned to Godwin. "Don't worry. If you are hit, I have bandages. And the girl …"

Odylia appeared at his side, holding up a small hemp bag by its drawstring. Godwin assumed it held a poultice.

"Breathe in and hold it," Trebert said. "Out, slowly. Relax your shoulders. He's not a person, he's a straw target. You hit those every time."

Fifty paces away, Fordred gripped his bow like it was a hatchet. It took him three attempts to successfully nock his first arrow. He'd not hit the side of a house like that.

As Trebert made his way to a point halfway between them, and as Odylia moved outside the likely arc of Fordred's arrow, Godwin turned his face to the breeze. He didn't hold his finger up lest that give Fordred a clue. He judged that he'd have to aim on a line to a poplar tree beyond Fordred and half a body's width to his left, for the wind to drift the arrow in. If he respected his opponent's aim he'd try to step to windward after letting loose, but to plan this would throw his own aim off. And, and since it was Fordred, he'd be just as likely to step into the arrow's flight as away from it.

He nocked his arrow smoothly and took his stance. Inhaled. Breathed out through pursed lips, slow enough to flicker a candle flame but not kill it. He stretched the string fully to get a feel for it. Fordred was doing the same. But his stance was poor.

Trebert stood immediately in front of the row of spectating fyrdsmen and took a shield from one of them. He held it flat at waist height. "Set yourselves," he called. "Arrowheads down. Do not raise your bows until I release this. You have two arrows each."

He had talked tactics with Godwin beforehand. "If you rush, you might loose your arrow before he does, but you will miss. Let him make that mistake. Watch his arrow. Watch the shape it makes in the wind. Yours will make the same shape, so allow for it. Other than that, ignore his arrow."

"Hard, if it's stuck in my head."

"This is not a test of aim, it's a test of self-control. You have both, my friend."

Godwin looked not at Fordred, but at the tall tree beyond. Fordred was a straw man. He didn't want Fordred dead, or even wounded, not much. But straw men need no mercy.

Breathe in. Breathe out. Do not extinguish the candle…

Everything slowed, like he was freezing in snow. He reacted to Fordred raising his bow, and realised that he'd missed Trebert dropping the shield. Yet there it was, on the grass. In one motion he lifted his own bow and drew back the string with his fingertips. He aligned the arrowtip to the middle of that poplar.

Fordred's hand came away from his string. No, you don't release the string by moving your hand, but by relaxing your fingers. If the arrow had been accurate he'd not have been able to dodge it, but saw it flying high and left.

His first shot would probably miss too. But not his second.

Fordred stooped to pull the other arrow from the ground. Before nocking it, he looked up at Godwin taking careful aim.

He dropped the arrow and bow to the grass, and ran into the crowd, past his brother, fleeing laughter, jeers and hisses as he had fled Godwin's yet unshot arrow.

Godwin altered his aim, and let fly.

He had never shot better. The arrow sank deep into the soil between the curve of Fordred's abandoned bow and its string.

Odylia came to him, her face flushed with excitement. She stood on tiptoe to kiss his cheek.

Trebert returned to slap Godwin on the back. "I cannot wait to tell the Prince!"

He had the ear of the Prince?

Fordred, Wystan and their brother were furloughed to allow Wystan to recover at their home village. Godwin became just another fyrdsman, reviled more than most, but not excluded.

The following Sunday a new priest took the service, and Godwin was surprised to recognise him as Trebert, whom he'd killed the day before. Trebert had killed him too, twice, and both had bruised ribs and skulls and knuckles. They'd commiserated about their wounds afterwards, and laughed together.

A priest. That explained his shave and his cropped hair, rare among fighters but common for clergy.

After the service, Godwin went to him, saying "You a priest, and you didn't even offer me last rites when you took my head off."

Trebert was delighted to see him, and clapped his shoulder in greeting, then apologised as Godwin winced.

"I never thanked you properly for helping me. I am truly grateful. Most of this lot seemed to take the view that the sins of the father should be visited upon the son."

"I don't think it's a theological matter, Godwin. But since it's Sunday, let's make it one. Your biblical quote wasn't Jesus' word. And anyway, it was about sins against God, not Brihtric or even the King. And the visiting would be done by The Lord himself, not some lout like Fordred."

"Should I have been calling you Father?"

"Just on Sundays."

"Well, Father." Godwin had a thought. "Fordred's furlough. Wystan going home to recuperate. Was that anything to do with you?"

Trebert shrugged. "I thought the Holy Spirit was stronger here for their departure."

Godwin nodded. "I'm in your debt." He wanted to know more about Father Trebert. "You train with us. Are you part of the fyrd?"

"When do men value their souls the most?" Trebert said. "Yes, I am with the fyrd. I hope you don't need last rites, but if you do, it's me who'll likely be giving them."

"I'll try not to put you to work," Godwin said. "Do you expect to fight?"

"Who can say? But that's why the Prince wants me. Not for souls, any priest could do that. Not for the reading or writing. Any reeve could do that. But if ever all is lost, he wants the last men at his side to be fighters, not men of learning."

"The pagans won't spare a man in a habit."

"The opposite. They'll ransom a prince, but a priest? I'd choose to die fighting."

"As long as you're alive, there's hope," Godwin said.

Trebert spat at the ground. "Did you hear of Father Tomas? Taken prisoner, and returned with his lungs pulled out through his ribs behind him. They told him they were making angel's wings to fly to him heaven. Hope? He begged for mercy's sword."

It was a sunny morning, and instead of training, the fyrdsmen were told to paint shields, either their own if they had one, or from the collective store. Two pails of green paint were set in a field, and each man queued to take his turn with one of the four brushes the paintmakers had brought. In a couple of days, the word went, they'd be putting white crosses over the green. Good, easy work.

The sun was just past its high, and Godwin was near the front of the queue with two shields, neither belonging to him. He was drowning in the warm linseed smell of the paint, when Deorleaf pulled him away. "The Prince wants to see you," he spat. "And he sends me. Me! I don't know what he wants, but if he isn't pleased… well, he'd better be, that's all."

Godwin returned the shields to the stack waiting to be painted, and followed Deorleaf across the yard. "Lytleman wouldn't have let him kill you, you know. Fordred, I mean."

Godwin made no reply.

"It was making you stronger. And we wanted to see how long it would take you to beat him."

"We?"

"Me and Ercenbert. I lost the bet. I said not this year. He said sooner. He said you'd find a way."

"So how much does he owe me?"

"Fuck all. Should have run your own bets. Other thing you should have done was let them have her. Saved you a lot of bother. There's other girls, and she's one skinny rat."

He led them past the stores and the apothecary where the skinny rat would be stealing potions and learning more of her herblore, until they came to the inner palisade. Four ceorls guarded the gate to the royal compound. On seeing Deorleaf, they moved aside.

Another two stood by a modest house. One opened the door and put his head in to call something Godwin couldn't hear. On getting an answer, he opened the door wide. Deorleaf started to lead the way, but the guard put his palm to his chest and shook his head. Deorleaf swore at him to no avail, and Godwin proceeded alone, wishing something would happen to stop everyone hating him even more.

Then he was inside the single large room, hung with tapestries, furnished with chairs, carpets, tables, and a bed covered with furs. Light came through the cream and orange glass of the fractured leaded windows, while lamplight and a fire further illuminated the room. It made the chain Edmund wore around his neck, his rings, his fasteners and his brooches glow from within. In the thick yellow light even his silver looked gold.

"Young Godwin!" Edmund smiled the friendliest smile Godwin had received from anyone save Trebert. "How are you getting on?"

"I think I'm learning, Lord." Learning to bide my time.

"I'm sure you are. You have a sharp mind, you won't stop learning." Edmund gestured at a cushioned chair with armrests, inviting Godwin to sit. His father had had one, made of oak, but he was forbidden to use it. He had disobeyed of course, when no-one looked. The oak was now ash.

Edmund poured wine into a cup and gave it to Godwin. It all seemed very ordinary for a moment, and Godwin had to hold in his head that he was here sharing a drink with the Prince of England, Edmund Ironside, leader of battles, bulwark against the Dane. Why?

"But that's not what I was asking. Weeks ago you watched your father sail away, knowing he can't come back. You saw your mother killed. So again I ask: how are you getting on?"

He recalled sitting next to his father on that log. He saw his mother on her knees, sprouting arrows. "Do you miss her?" his father had asked, and he'd said he didn't. Godwin suddenly felt a boiling inside him and a fount behind his eyes. He struggled to press down the pain, but knew his face had crumpled. He started to say "I", but when he heard his own croak, he stopped lest he crack completely. He had to stand up and walk away.

He was at the door, and Edmund said no word. He wouldn't stop him leaving.

He breathed in deeply, forced his shoulders down, and pulled his face back into shape. He looked at the cup of wine still in his hand. How had he not spilled any? "I miss her."

He turned, to see Edmund nodding. "My mother died when I was twelve. I miss her still. But I still have my father."

"I am not like my father," Godwin said unbidden. This was what everyone thought, that he was a traitor in waiting, not to be trusted.

Edmund laughed. "Praise the Lord that we do not have to be like our fathers." He beckoned Godwin back to the chair. "Drink," he said.

Godwin drank from his cup.

"Is there more you want to say?"

Godwin shook his head.

"There is more I want to say." Edmund too drank. "Brihtric. You will want revenge."

"No!"

"Liar. And shame on you if you do not. All I ask is that, if and when the time comes, you talk to me first, because a good time for you may not be a good time for me. You owe me your life, and I will hold you to that. I promise that when it is right for both of us, I won't stand in your way."

Edmund wanted Brihtric dead.

"How goes your training? What are you learning?

Did the Prince want a blademan? Was this why he'd been called? "I'm learning to fight," Godwin said. "To be strong."

"Good. No-one expects you to be a warrior overnight, your body isn't grown yet. But your mind… your mind is sharp, as I said. And your spirit. I like your spirit."

"Thank you, Lord."

"Your girl, she is happy?"

Godwin shrugged. Odylia seemed content in her improved situation. Better Wintancaestr than Brimclif. Better himself than Gewis, that old letch of a Headman, or Fordred and his brothers who surely would not have been satisfied with one assault. She had food, and was practicing a valued skill. Two if you counted thieving. "She doesn't complain."

Odylia surely wasn't the reason he'd been called.

"There is probably one thing you don't realise, Godwin," Edmund said. "Strange to say it, but you are the only person in Wessex who has witnessed a sea battle. You and the girl – she was there too, am I right?"

Godwin said "And Cudbert, Sel and Eg. They were at Comtyn, when you came."

Edmund laughed again. Godwin felt easier for Edmund's laugh. "I stand corrected. You five know more about sea battles than anyone else this side of Watling Street. We don't use ships to fight at sea, we use them to carry men to fight on land. Few have fought in them, fewer still have led them, and even they, once the fighting starts, have to look to their own boat, their own crew, their own lives. Who has got to sit on a cliff like a god watching a battle unfold? So, Godwin, what I want to know from you, is what happened that day. How did a small group of twenty boats defeat three times their number?"

"There was a storm."

"Are you saying your father's boats were protected from it? Did they sail on a pool of calm, with their own gentle breezes?"

"They were lucky."

Edmund shook his head. "If they were lucky, then Gothor was unlucky. Gothor Cild, he led the boats that chased your father. He is gone. But I don't believe in luck, good or bad. I believe in opportunity, and I believe in foolishness. I suspect your father took the first, and Gothor was guilty of the second."

Godwin saw where Edmund's mind had turned. He wanted to know the lessons of the disaster, to glean what he could from the treachery.

He described the events, from the moment they had sighted the Dertemuth boats, to the handful of men crawling out of the sea and into Brimclif.

"And in your view, from your vantage point, why were fifty better boats lost, while twenty worse ones sailed away?"

"They weren't worse. They were different. We had a Danish boatwright, and he didn't build them for speed, but for working against the wind. No boat can chase them, no matter how fast, if it can't go the same direction. Gothor sailed too close to the shore and never got upwind of… my father's boats." He nearly said "our boats." "Father's fire arrows had the wind behind them – even if Gothor had had fire of his own, and I don't think he did, he wouldn't have had the range. Once they were spotted, once the Bosham fleet launched and out to sea, further out than Gothor, Gothor was doomed. So it seems to me."

Edmund nodded. "I understand that he stayed close to shore the better to surprise Wulfnoth. So as not to be seen."

"I say he should have come at night then. And when the wind was off the land. As it was, his boats had nowhere to go."

"If he'd been further out, he'd have been spotted sooner."

"It wouldn't have mattered. Their positions would still have been reversed. My father would have been caught between the cliffs and a fleet four times as large." His father would be dead, by sword, by drowning, or by execution. "Would my mother still have paid for his crime?"

Edmund nodded. "I fear so. And yourself. Some think you should be brought to London and beheaded, as an example."

"I'm grateful that I'm not, Lord."

"Your debt will never be paid off, you realise that."

Godwin let this sink in. He was Edmund's now. Once a thegn's son, now a thuw. Yet he'd be even more hated when word spread of this meeting.

"This is helpful," said Edmund. "This we can use."

"There's another thing…"

"Go on."

"I think my father was prepared. He had his braziers ready, and fire arrows made. His crews weren't in mail, because drowning is a bigger danger than arrows. Each man had a shield. Boats knew what to do. He had flags, and the captains understood what the signals meant."

"How much do you know of how the Vikingr fight sea battles?"

Godwin blinked at this question. "Nothing, lord."

"The thing is, the Vikingr don't fight sea battles now, not like you saw, because no-one will face them. They have no practice. They fight boat on boat, and they have larger swifter ships, so it's just a question of boarding and outnumbering the unfortunates. The only tactic that's been used against them is to line up boats together like a shieldwall. This is what Brihtric will do, if Sveyn sends boats up the Tamys. Myself, I don't think that's likely, but we have a fleet, so use it we must. So we make a wall of boats, then either the Danes will try to burst through, or more likely, they'll put ashore where they can, and march around our boats where they will. They could choose to march on Lunden-"

"And we will face them."

Edmund shrugged. "We will have a fyrd. Will it be big enough? But that's a different matter. They might not march on Lunden, they could choose to lay waste the East Saxons, or Cantware, and we can do little to stop them. We'd have to split our fyrd to protect both the north and the south shore, so it would be half our strength against all of theirs. Our boats can take men to one side or the other, but we'll always be chasing them."

"And they will lay waste where they can, until the King pays more gafol."

"That's the heart of it. Everyone knows this, especially Sveyn Forkbeard. What we need is to go onto the offensive. To surprise the Danes both on land and on sea." Edmund looked up at the roof of his hut, then he turned his eyes onto Godwin. "I shouldn't be telling you this. You will not pass it on to anyone. And no talk about the sea battle. That goes for the girl too. I don't believe there isn't someone here in Sveyn's pay." Edmund grinned at Godwin. "Some say it's you."

Of course they do. "Would it help if I wrote down what I saw, and what I thought?"

"You can write?" Edmund was surprised.

"Brother Snell taught me, and my mother. Latin and English. She was from a good family here in Wintancaestr."

Edmund nodded "Ah yes. I recall Aelfric saying as much. Have you seen them?"

This is how bad things are, Godwin thought, when Prince and Ealdorman are discussing your family. "Only in church."

"Write your account of the battle. Tell me your thoughts. I want something by sunset tomorrow. You can add more later if you need. Go to the cathedral for parchment, quills and ink."

Deorleaf had disappeared, and Godwin made his way alone back into the fyrd compound. He was not ten yards in when he was pushed to the ground by one of three ceorls who had walked up behind him. He looked up resentfully, and when he tried to rise they pushed him back down and kicked him until he gave up trying to rise. They walked away sneering "Prince's bumboy."

If he wasn't the traitor's son he was the Prince's toy. There was no winning. He didn't even mind the abuse so much, it was the sheer stupidity that angered him. One day, any of those three, or Fordred or Wystan, might need him to defend his sword arm in a shieldwall.

He went to look for Trebert, who'd be able to get writing materials. He didn't say what he wanted them for, save that it was the Prince's command, and Trebert didn't ask.

He told Odylia about the meeting with Edmund, and his questions.

"Did you mention the tide?" she asked.

"What tide?"

"It was past the high. Easier to launch the boats on the ebb. Quicker to get out past the shoals. If it had been low tide, things might have turned out differently."

"That was lucky, then."

"No. The boats were ready to launch early that morning."

"That's good."

"And wetting the sails?"

"What?"

"They were going to wet the sails against fire arrows."

"By Bevis. Was that from Hemming?"

"Yes."

"Anything else I might have missed?"

"Lots, farm boy."

She was being useful so he let the barb enter. But he was thinking about the lack of waves on a farm.

Midmorning of the next day, he started work. Trebert had arranged a quiet chapel in the Cathedral for Godwin to undertake his work, and found parchment, ink and a quill. It was slow and painstaking, for he was not practiced in his writing, but he couldn't ask for help. Odylia was with him, and together they reconstructed what they'd seen, and drew lessons from it. He enjoyed the thinking and the discussion more than she, and while he wrote she became bored. Mid-afternoon, she wanted them to fuck, probably just because they were in a chapel. He had to fend her off. "It's not you who has to produce something for Prince Edmund by sunset."

"You just make sure you produce something for me by midnight."

Both missions were accomplished.

Early the next morning they were violently shaken by Deorleaf. "You two, outside, now. I said now!" He went to a dozen other beds around the hall, rousing men, letting women sleep on. Odylia was uncertain – had he really meant her too? Ercenbert turned back, seeing her sitting motionless and confused. "Yes, I said you!"

They hurriedly pulled on boots and cloaks and went out into the dawn-grey morning. Ercenbert was waiting impatiently until the troop was gathered. The men assembled were not the same dozen as had come with Edmund to Comtyn. There were only two from that troop: Deorleaf, who would be in command, and Geareth the Haystack. There was skinny old Ingwald, fat Plum Plaemond, Freth who was small and nervy, longstanding drinking mates Tidwyn and Ecgulf, and a few others. Godwin thought he could match most of them with a sword, even Geareth who was slow and had no stamina. Ingwald as a fighter was a joke, and Freth had the combat instincts of a rabbit. And why himself and Odylia? All in all, they weren't a fearsome bunch.

He leaned sideways and whispered to Odylia "Whatever they've got lined up for us, I doubt it's dangerous."

"Bound to be dirty, then," she muttered back.

2. Rameslege

(Edward)

"That's a girl. Or an elf. One or t'other."

The weather was set fair. The sea would be calm, Wilmaer told him, and the roads were good, so Edward was impatient to be away from Lunden. Rye, all but an island at high tide, with miles of reedlands around it, offered scope for adventures that Lunden could not. He wanted his brother, Wilf, Fulton and himself to play together like they used to. Alfred and Wilf had been fun to be with back then, even though they were younger. Ecfrida was to come too, which mostly pleased him, as long as she and Cynethe didn't dampen the boys' time together. It would have been nice to have had Goda along too, but with the pox hitting Hendi harder than it had hit Goda, it was right to let her stay with her friend and the nuns.

They set out across the Tamys bridge, the one the King had proudly ordered to be rebuilt a few years before. Edward recalled when it was opened, the great ceremony with flags and drums, and how he'd walked between his mother and father from the north tower towards the south. He'd been five years old, but no-one was sharp enough to grab his arm when he decided to run ahead to be the first to complete the crossing. He'd felt foolish when his father told him afterwards that the carpenters who built the towers would have crossed many hundreds of times before that day. He recalled how, when they walked back, a horse had reared and bolted, and leaped off the edge into the river; so now there was a decree that horses must be led across, not ridden. Looking back on it, Edward decided the rider had been drunk. Horses weren't that stupid.

At Suthringework they transferred to two boats that would sail them to Meddestane. He was with Fulton, Ecfrida and Cynethe; Emma took Alfred and Wilf in the other, along with the monk Ordulf and his novitiate Sibyhrtoftel, who was only ever called Sibbi. Edward knew Sibbi from Latin lessons. They used to talk to each other without Alfred being able to understand, which had been fun until Alfred lost his temper and his mother ordered them to stop their teasing. Edward said it was to encourage Alfred to learn. Fulton took six strokes of a strap.

The oarsmen were not needed, as a kind breeze blew with the tide. Between river and fields all was flat, marshy, and inhabited only by fisherfolk and reeders who lived in huts on thin sticks rising out of the mud. Beyond, the downs of north Cantware could be seen, and on the other bank, the undulating woodlands and fields of Eassex.

They passed a church, which Ecfrida told him was at Ulwic, on land gifted a hundred years ago by their great great grandfather to a Flandra abbey, a similar gift to the land at Rameslege now promised to Fécamp.

They reached Aerith before noon, and an hour later the sailors cheered as they saw the fleet assembled at Tilberh. Hundreds of boats were tied together in long rows three or more deep, making a single floating island one third of a mile long. Fulton was awestruck. "Have you ever seen so many boats?" he asked in wonder.

"No-one has," Edward told him. "So six to guard Rye would not be missed."

His mother had reassured him before they left that Rye was safe from Viking raiders. "No Danish boat will leave my father's havens," she said. "Nor come from Flandra, because

Count Baldwin has his own problems with Vikings."

"What if they come all the way across the east sea?"

Emma had smiled. "They go to East Anglia, or Lindesege."

"What if Sveyn Forkbeard sends boats? Or an army?"

"Rye is too small and insignificant to interest him. And its tides and shoals are treacherous. The last men he sent south were defeated by your brother, remember? He will not strike there again, not so soon. We will be safe, trust me. Otherwise, we would not go."

Edward wondered if Edmund was there in Tilberh, watching them sail by. They were no longer on an estuary, they were at sea,and the prow sliced through waves and sent up spray to sting their faces. The shores on each side were half a mile away, and then a mile, and Edward felt a sudden terror, not due to the swelling waves, but because they were past the fleet that might defend them. If a longship should appear, they would be eaten like the leviathan swallows a sprat.

They saw no longships, just three distant fishing smacks.

He'd only ever sailed short voyages before this, in more sheltered waters across the Solent. He found the boat's roll and pitch bracing, and the wind too, though Fulton looked pale after they ate. Across on the other boat Alfred was leaning over the side, puking. He chided himself for the pleasure the sight gave him. "Are you all right?" he asked Fulton, who didn't answer.

The steersman pointed to two low headlands on the southern shore. "The Meduwaen mouth. Hold on to your lunch if you can," he told Fulton, "It will calm soon."

The sea became river again, like the Tamys, but instead of Suthringework, there was Hrofcaestr with its palisaded fort watching over them from a low hill as they rowed past. The river's meanders meant that the oarsmen were needed, but it was easy work, with flat water, and rest when they turned away from the wind.

They came to another town. "Meddestane," the steersman said. There on the riverbank were Theo and Wendel, sitting on horses, with four more hitched nearby: a striking piebald palfrey presumably for his mother, two bay rounceys for himself and Ecfrida, and a pony like those gifted to him by some Wessex ealdor when he was younger, for Alfred. Three covered waggons awaited too, all bigger than the pair that had carried them over the Tamys. As soon as they landed, he looked inside to see new straw palliasses, and folded hides, poles and bars to enable them to be tented. Even when loaded with their boxes there was enough space to sleep should they not reach the hospitality offered tomorrow night at Cranbroka.

Next morning, as they made ready to leave Meddestane, a man with half a beard rode up at the head of small troop of armed ceorls. He was tall, and wore a leather surcoat over his bright mail, with a sword at his left thigh and a helm slung off his belt behind his right. He bowed respectfully from the saddle, and introduced himself as Deorleaf, called The Mown, of Ceorring. "We are sent by Prince Edmund. Twelve of his best men, to escort you to Rye and see you safely back to Lunden, or wherever you wish to travel onwards."

"Best men?" Edward muttered to Fulton. "He looks strong enough, but we can run faster than most of the rest. Look at the fat one. The old guy with the red face. Two of them are just boys." He pointed to a youth on a grey. His face put him at about fifteen years, although he sat in his saddle like a man. Alongside him was an even younger lad on a brown pony. "Look at that one! He's no older than you and me."

"He?" said Fulton. "That's a girl. Or an elf. One or t'other."

Edward looked closer. Fulton was right. Sharp, delicate features, long hair falling out from under that cap, the merest suspicion of tits.

"Quite a pretty one, mind," Fulton added.

Edward supposed so.

Deorleaf was still speaking. "We will ride four ahead, four behind, and four alongside the waggons where we can, or between them if we can't. These two are spares." He indicated the two youngest members of the escort. "This lout is called Godwin. He'll stay close to you. If you want to talk to me, he'll carry a message and I'll come straight away. And that other kid, she's Odylia. She don't look much but she carries potions and has some skill. Temper like a vixen, so any robbers on the road better watch out."

"If we need them to keep us safe, we are in desperate trouble," Emma told him.

Deorleaf bowed from the neck. "Of course. The truth is that Prince Edmund thought some ceorls around his young brothers' age might be easier on the lads, and-"

"You do not call them lads" Emma snarled, all the more frightening for not shouting.

"Apologies, my lady. And your Lordships." He nodded in their direction. "Prince Edmund thought they don't want big hairy men around them all the time. This pair was the best we could do."

Emma indicated Fulton, Wilf and Cynethe. "Friends and companions they have already. If danger finds us, big hairy men is exactly what they want."

Edward looked at Fulton and shook his head. Now they had to put up with these two for company. Edmund seemed to be able to find a way to interfere, even from Tilberh. Perhaps this Godwin would have the sense to keep a distance. Perhaps the girl would play with Alfred and Wilf. Girls like smaller boys, don't they? It makes them feel maternal or something. Or Ecfrida and Cynethe might adopt her.

It was a two day journey to Rye, broken by a night at Cranbroka, where the food was worse than Meddestane's, but the floor was clean, and the straw mattresses, they were assured, freshly stuffed.

The second day brought light but ceaseless rain. They sat inside the waggons under the awnings, heaving and bumping over the rough track, holding the frame to brace themselves. It sapped everyone's energy, and the damp air was joyless. Ecfrida decided that riding her horse under a waxed cowl was preferable to being jerked and jolted in the waggon, cooped up with Emma, Arsindis and Cynethe. She rode between the boys' waggon and her own. When Edward checked to see if the rain had eased, she was talking to that young ceorl, Godwin. Whatever he was saying, it made her laugh. The girl Odylia rode two horselengths behind them. She didn't look happy. Who would, riding in that rain?

Buffeted and jolted, they rolled across the Weald to the fields and woodlands of Rameslege, until at the crest of a low hill they saw their destination. Rye stood on a sharp mount that rose like a beacon out of wetlands extending dank and misty to the east. A patchwork of salterns surrounded it, scores of them on either side of the sluggish river as it wandered to the sea. With summer past and the salt collected, the pans were flat and brown

The drizzle eased as they approached, but the sky remained only a shade lighter than the grey sea. Edward wondered if, with all that water and mud, the place was anything other than dank even when spring breezes blew fresh and summer sun shone warm. If this land was for Fécamp, Fécamp was welcome to it.

They were greeted by Rye's Headman, Vale. The hall they had use of was warm and comfortable, with feather mattresses, not straw, that still felt warm to the touch –

Edward guessed they had been dried in front of one of the two lit fires. The board laid on by the Headman was generous, too. Alfred complained, of course, but Alfred did not like fish. What was he expecting, by the sea? But even Alfred jollied up in front of the fire, and afterwards the boys fell to discussing what they'd do over the next few days. Edward wanted fishing, for that was peaceful and calming. Alfred wanted to hunt wildfowl with the bows and arrows they'd brought. Or if Edward wanted nets, why not try netting birds?

Edward told him there would be time to try everything.

"So fowling first," said Alfred.

"No, fishing first."

"I'm not going fishing with you."

"Well I'm not going fowling with you, and mother says we have to stay together, with Theo and Wendel both."

"I have a suggestion, if I may?" It was Godwin who spoke. He'd been sitting with Odylia, close enough to hear the argument.

Both brothers turned to him, Alfred surprised at the interjection from a ceorl, Edward hoping for a face-saving solution.

"How about bowfishing?"

Next day, Emma supervised Ordulf and Sibbi as they began their labours measuring out fields and salterns with the rods they'd made, marked ditches and dykes, and counted livestock. The boys went with Godwin and Odylia to one of Rameslege's ponds stocked with carp. They promised that if they caught more than four, they'd go elsewhere, for eels, although Alfred said that whatever they caught, he wasn't going to eat it. But he concentrated fiercely, standing still on the bank as he aimed. He even quietly held the coil of cord as others took their turns, and patiently waited between shots for the waters to still and the fish to calm and return to the surface for the grubs they threw.

Edward stood next to little Wilf, watching as Godwin showed Alfred the technique of shooting through water. "Wait until the fish is side-on," he said, "So it's a bigger target. You have to aim below the fish, because the water will deflect the arrow upwards. The further away you are, the shallower the angle, and the more it will deflect. Another reason to wait for the fish to come close, so you can aim straight down. Mind your foot!" He lifted Alfred's bow arm just slightly, and Alfred didn't mind. If Edward had done that, Alfred would have squirmed away.

A few yards along the bank, Odylia was instructing Fulton. It seemed she had bowfished before. But then, Edward recalled, so had Fulton. He thought her pretty. The sly dog was only pretending to be ignorant!

Edward turned to Wilf alongside him. "Are you taking all this in?"

It was a successful day. Alfred fell into the water and came up laughing. He refused to go back to Rye, but Edward insisted. They returned with four carp and two eels, and Alfred, changed and warmed, ate his fish stew as if it was lamb.

Alfred loved Godwin. Edward had to admit that the youth had a reassuring air about him, a directness that told you where you stood. He was a boy who, for some reason, you wanted to please. No, please wasn't the right word. You wanted him to respect you. Edward was very aware that Alfred looked at Godwin with the same eyes that he looked at Edmund. It was not surprising, when he considered it, for Godwin was in some ways a younger version of the Prince, confident, intelligent, funny. And not so brash as Edmund, which was a bonus.

Ecfrida seemed fond of him too. They were of an age, and seemed to converse easily. Edward couldn't hear what they were talking about, but Godwin's relaxed air put her at ease, and Cynethe too. The pair had been drawn to him like two moons, and they weren't even giggling in his company, but talking easily, and laughing naturally. Whatever his words, they weren't mere flattery, and Edward wondered where he'd learned his charm. Was he more than a mere ceorl in Edmund's service?

What was his relationship with Odylia? Edward observed her cold expression when she saw him talking with Ecfrida, and this time it couldn't be blamed on rain. She wore a contemptuous grimace too when Godwin was with Cynethe. Ecfrida was as highborn as could be, Cynethe as beautiful, and Godwin seemed equally at ease in the company of either. Edward sided with Odylia: it was not right.

He wasn't sure why he didn't like Godwin, and he said as much to Fulton later that evening, when they crept into a vacant waggon they'd made a castle of.

"I don't like him either," Fulton replied.

"Do you mean that?"

"What I mean is, I do like him, but don't like liking him."

Yes. Edward understood. "Why is this?"

Fulton considered. "It's boys like him that make boys like me feel smaller than we are."

"I know what you mean," Edward replied. But Godwin didn't seem to be making Alfred feel smaller than he was. The opposite, if anything. "We're not small," he added. Then he realised that saying "We" put himself alongside Fulton and all the other boys who felt small.

But he, Edward, was a prince.

He jumped down from the waggon, leaving Fulton to wonder what he'd said wrong.

Edward conceded that the day had been more fishing than fowling, so next morning they ventured out by coracles of willow and leather to an island that stood in the tidal flats no more than a foot above the high tide mark. Theo and

Wendel stayed on the Rye side of the water, satisfied that Godwin could guard them against any Danes who might invade their little principality. So the five of them, Odylia, and two dogs loaned by Vale the Headman, had the tiny island to themselves.

Godwin was expert, and took down a goose in flight. The others could hardly hit birds standing in the mud, or swimming lazily. Alfred missed a swan, his arrow falling so far short that the bird didn't even know it was under attack. Edward managed to hit it, to his inordinate pleasure. The swan couldn't fly but it wasn't dead, and the dog sent to retrieve it slunk back on the losing side of a battle with the big bird's yellow beak.

They were going to leave it to the crows and the eels, until Alfred demanded Godwin's sword and strode through the mud to the stricken swan. He couldn't miss that long neck, and blood rolled down its white feathers like berries on snow.

"No fish for me tonight," he yelled, and lifted it proudly to carry back to them. It was as much as he could do to get both arms around the swan's body and struggle through the mud managing the weights of bird and sword together. His foot slid off a tussock, and he fell onto his side, dropping the swan into the mud.

He looked up at them, eyes wide and uncomprehending. The sword was planted point down into the ground, leaning like an old fencepost, with a red smear covering half of the shiny blade. It took Edward seconds to realise that this was too much blood to be the swan's, by which time Godwin was away, striding to Alfred, crouching beside him. "Bring the bowstring," he called.

Odylia unstrung the bow and ran to him. He tied it around Alfred's leg, circling twice and pulling tight before knotting the ends. "Fulton!" he shouted. "Run to Wendel. He must go back to Rye. We need water, and bandages. Find Ordulf."

Fulton ran. Odylia picked up the sword, and, shrugging, took out her knife and gutted the swan there and then. Godwin squatted in front of Alfred, who leaned over his shoulder. He hooked his arm around Alfred's good leg, and stood.

That was when Alfred screamed.

Godwin got him to a coracle, and managed to paddle the little craft back to Theo. Odylia took charge of the other coracle, and Edward let her. She knew boats. Godwin said "We'll use the coracle to carry him," so Fulton, Theo, Wendel and Godwin took the moaning Alfred as gently as they could back to Rye. Edward and Wilf followed, trailed by Odylia and the swan.

Emma cursed Theo and Wendel like they were swine, and she cursed Godwin for letting Alfred have such a weapon. Edward tried to say that it was an accident, and how could Godwin refuse to lend Alfred his sword when he demanded it, but she only stopped when Alfred himself groaned that it was his own fault. By then Odylia had covered the wound, a long and deep gash angling down to bone through the muscle of his thigh, with a poultice. Ordulf bandaged it.

Odylia prepared an infusion with ground willowbark, garlic, crushed cornflowers and dried herbs from drawstring bags she kept. But she said she was no leech. Ordulf knew no more than Odylia, and Hessy, the woman sent for by the Headman who was known for her midwifery and healing, offered a potion that looked little different to Odylia's. All three agreed that it was good that Alfred was not feverish, and agreed too that if his flesh started to burn there was no more they knew to do.

Emma told Wendel to make ready the best of the waggons. Alfred was to go back to Lunden.

"Is that wise?" said Deorleaf. "It's an arduous journey. Four days, in a waggon."

"You have two," said Emma. "Send your best rider and your best horse to Meddestane. I want a boat there tomorrow morning, to take us to Lunden and the royal leech."

Deorleaf was decisive. He ordered Freth to go, and told Wendel to get the waggoneer to hitch up four workhorses, not just two. He told half his troop to ready themselves at once, for Emma and Alfred could not travel unguarded. "Is Wilf to accompany you?"

She looked at Alfred, and nodded.

"Do you want Odylia?"

"Arsindis has more knowledge than these peasants," she spat. But she ordered Odylia to quickly grind and mix more of her concoction for the journey.

"He must drink water too," Odylia said as she handed over a pouch.

Edward thought his mother was going to slap her. Instead, she ordered Deorleaf to come with them, so with five of Edmund's troop plus Wendel, there was an escort of seven who, within the hour, departed.

Theodric and the other six from the troop remained as Edward and Ecfrida's guards. They comprised the fat one they called Haystack, the old man with the red face named Plum, and a pair who seemed inseparable, Ecgulf and Tidwyn, who looked to Edward less like trained husceorls and more like shieldwall fodder. Then there was young Godwin, and the girl. Hardly a fearsome gang, but Rameslege was peaceable, and Deorleaf and his men would return in a few days. Edward decided he was safe.

With Alfred's bounding energy disappeared and Emma's leaden observance gone, Rye was more relaxed. Theo, now deprived of Wendel's company, befriended the men of

Edmund's troop, especially Haystack. Edward, aware how selfish was the thought, considered that he and Fulton would now have a better time here.

That evening, after their meal, Edward was talking with Ordulf about the terrain he was measuring, and his assessment of the value of a marshland hide near the shore against a grassed hide inland, or a treed one. "You see, it's not the area of land that matters, it's how many people can live off it …"

Edward looked around the room as he half-listened.

"And then, consider if it needs more people to work it than it can sustain…"

When he noticed Cynethe sitting alone, silent and glum, he had to check the hall. Surveying the place like Ordulf surveyed land, he saw that Ecfrida and Godwin were absent.

And Odylia was rising to leave too.

Then Fulton rose casually from next to him and went out the same way as the girl. Surely this was not coincidence. He ignored Ordulf's "Then there's gafol for the scire and the King…" and stood up. He glanced over at Theo, merrily drinking with his new friends, and followed Fulton outside.

Dim light came from other huts, from lamps and reed-candles where folk had not yet gone to sleep. It was enough to see that no-one was nearby. He heard nothing more than the horses shuffling sleepily in their stable. He walked on, and the waggon he and Fulton had made their own came into view. The other was the one Emma and Ecfrida had travelled in, parked beyond the buildings because setting all three next to each other had obstructed the villager's own pathways around the place.

He went past the stables. Yellow light glowed through the hemp and between the skins that covered the waggon. Voices came from inside. He hesitated. He didn't want to spy, because, suspicious of Ecfrida and wary of Godwin, he might not like what he saw. But Fulton? What was he up to? Why had he followed Odylia? Did she know? Was she expecting him?

Keeping close to the stable's timber wall, he edged sideways as quietly as he could. There was a shape, too big to be Odylia. "Ffff," he hissed, which Fulton had once told him was the best sound for carrying a short distance and no further. A pale face turned to him. Fulton's hand beckoned. He moved alongside, and now he could see what Fulton was looking at: Odylia, standing next to the waggon.

"What's she doing?" he whispered.

"Spying on them."

"What are you doing?"

Fulton took a few seconds to answer. "I was following her."

"Why?"

"Why do you think?"

"But… her?"

"Why not?"

There were all sorts of reasons why not. Odylia was scrawny and… he couldn't think of the other reasons right then. He just didn't understand it.

They watched. They listened. The two voices in the waggon lowered in tone. There were silences. What was going on in there? Ecfrida mustn't… She's the King's daughter. Should he put a stop to it? Was it his job?

Odylia's hand came round behind her back, and lifted her tunic. She'd taken a knife from there when she'd gutted the swan. She groped for the handle and freed the blade. Edward didn't know if she planned to stab Godwin or Ecfrida, or both. He looked at Fulton in the dark. Fulton was looking back at him, understanding what had to be done.

They stepped forward and before Odylia knew they were there, Fulton had her right wrist and was twisting the knife from her grip, as Edward tightened his arms around her. She struggled and squirmed, but she stayed silent as he lifted her bodily so her kicking feet were clear of the ground. Fulton caught her ankles. She was surprisingly light, hardly more difficult to carry than Alfred had been last time they roughhoused, a couple of years ago.

The boys were younger than she, but bigger, and they carried her like a sack to the other waggon, and forced her under its cover. "See she stays here," he told Fulton.

He returned to Ecfrida's waggon. All was hushed within, save soft rustles. He coughed, and the hush became empty silence. "Frida, send him out," he said. "And I'll say nothing to father." Then he had a better idea. "Godwin, come out now, and I'll say nothing to Edmund about how you violated his sister."

There were movements. Whispers. Godwin emerged.

Edward was pleased how quickly he came, not just for his obedience but more importantly because it showed that Godwin hadn't needed to dress himself. "Go," he ordered. "You'll not talk to her again."

Godwin stood over him, taller, stronger. More confident. He was the kind who made other boys feel small. Edward had to force himself not to step backwards, for Godwin could surely kill him were he so minded. He was powerful enough. But not stupid enough, not by a stretch. He marched wordlessly past Edward back to the hall.

Ecfrida stepped down from the waggon. He couldn't see her eyes, but her body spoke her fury eloquently enough. She slapped his face hard, and tears stung his eyes. What hurt most was that surely he'd done her a service, protecting her from herself.

There would be no profit debating the point.

She retreated back into the waggon, saying "Fetch me Cynethe."

"Fetch her yourself," he spat, and returned to Fulton thinking up sharper retorts, like how about he fetch Cynethe for Godwin?

Fulton had lit a candle and was seated on a box, with Odylia cross-legged on one of the palliasses brought for the journey. Edward hauled himself up, and sat opposite Fulton, looking down on her. He could have her flogged for drawing a blade. He could have her beheaded! It was a strange feeling, this rush of power. He wasn't sure he liked it, trusted it, or wanted it. "What was that about?"

She glared up at him. "He's mine. She's got no right."

"Betrothed?"

She glared again.

"We can always ask him," said Fulton. Edward liked the way Fulton seemed to read his mind.

Odylia shook her head.

"What were you going to do? Who were you going to kill, her or him?"

She dropped her gaze, and seemed to sink lower into the mattress. "I don't even know. Both. Neither. Maybe I just wanted to join them."

"Join them?" said Fulton.

"I could have had her too."

"Had her?" said Edward. "What do you mean, had her? Stabbed her?"

She laughed. "That was his job. There's other ways of having a girl."

Edward could not comprehend her meaning. "I got him out," he told her. "She won't talk to him again-"

"Neither will I," she said.

"-not while I'm around. And soon we'll be back in Lunden, and you and he will be back to Wintancaestre."

"Can't wait," she said. Then she looked up at him with vixen eyes. "You know who he is, don't you?"

"He's no peasant, I think. His father's a headman, at least. Maybe a minor thegn."

Odylia grinned. "Very good. But which thegn?"

"Tell me."

"Why should I?"

Fulton said "Because your Prince commands."

Odylia's murderous intent was the anger of a jealous girl who happened to carry a sharp knife. It didn't warrant punishing. But he'd felt that fiery ball of power in his hand, and he wanted to play with it. "You could be flogged, you know. Or worse."

"For what?"

"For threatening the Princess," said Fulton.

Her eyes hadn't left Edward. "You'd be telling everyone your sister's a whore."

"Hey!" said Fulton.

"It's all right," said Edward. Odylia wanted to play too. "Ecfrida is a whore. What do I care who knows?" He knew he had even more power than this. "It doesn't matter what you did or why. You don't need to have done anything. Just a word from me…"

"So tell us," said Fulton. "About Godwin."

She wasn't brash now. "He kidnapped me. He had a knife to my throat. I earned the right to have him by that."

"You're holding back, you bitch." This was a new and unfamiliar Fulton, a Fulton who knew how to act the bully.

It was a heady feeling, the two of them playing this game together. He didn't feel so small, and was sure that Fulton didn't either. "Tell us about Godwin."

"Not much to tell," she said with a shrug. "He's from Comtyn."

Comtyn. Where had he heard that before?

"He's father's the Thegn there. Or he was."

"Wulfnoth Cild," Edward breathed. "The traitor."

Odylia nodded.

"How do you know?" said Fulton. "Why should we believe you?"

Edward was glad that Fulton knew not to take a braggart at face value.

"I don't care a finch's fart if you believe me or not."

"You were asked how you know," Edward snapped. "So speak."

Odylia sat cross-legged on the palliasse, and leaned back against the side of the waggon. Only her eyes moved, searching the underside of the awning as she took herself back. "I come from near Bosham. It's part of Wulfnoth's thegnship. My dad was a fisherman. Is a fisherman. Was a fisherman. So he knew the boatbuilder there, a Dane called Hemming, who-"

"A Dane?" Edward said.

"Yes. Hemming was captured after a raid. He was spared if he'd serve Thegn Wulfnoth, so he was leading the work to build boats for the king. The Thegn told my father to oversee him, until we all set sail for Sanwic…" She continued her story, telling how Wulfnoth planned to steal the bots, how Godwin accused his own father of being a traitor, and tried to leave. But his friend and his friend's father were caught, and Godwin kidnapped her to save them. She was left behind in England with them. They had to walk home, where Brihtric had destroyed her village. He killed Godwin's mother, and would have killed Godwin too but for Edmund's arrival.

The two boys were open-mouthed at the adventure. "Fuck me," Fulton said when she finished.

Odylia arched an eyebrow. "Only by royal command."

Fulton looked at Edward, his question unspoken, but Edward had no idea what the question was, let alone the answer. Odylia had suddenly started a new game, one with rules he didn't know.

She was suddenly in charge. "You going to let me go now, or keep me here all night?" Her voice was no longer combative, but more like the tone he himself used when teasing Goda.

Still the question on Fulton's face.

"You can if you want," she said.

"Keep you for what?" said Edward.

"Perhaps something like this." She tilted her head at an angle and shifted onto her knees, leaned forward, and kissed his lips. The ball of power in his hand was now a small cabbage, and he did not know how to respond. Disappointed, she moved across to Fulton. She kissed him. Fulton had family, including his pregnant sister, and he had friends apart from Edward. He had seen rituals such as this. He may have experienced them. Fulton put his hand behind Odylia's head, and Edward saw her settle herself for a long kiss with him. He watched how their heads moved together, how one of Fulton's hands moved to her shoulders and the other slid around her waist. One of her hands went behind him and the other gripped his thigh.

Edward reached out and pulled her back. She came without resisting. She transferred her kiss to him. Her lips were wet. Her tongue was in his mouth, and he became that cabbage for a moment, then lest she pull away, he held her, and let her tongue find his, and play. What was he supposed to feel? He pulled away. "Is this how you'd have a girl?"

She laughed. "Sort of." She returned to kissing Fulton.

"Show me," Edward said.

She turned to him. "Really?"

It was all so strange, fascinating and puzzling. "Yes."

Again she laughed. Her hand went to Fulton's waistcord, and untied it. Fulton looked at him as if seeking reassurance. He nodded his fascination and curiosity, and Fulton lifted his behind from the seat to let Odylia pull down his braies. His pintle stood up, hard already. How had she done that without even touching it?

She knelt beside him and bent her head. To his amazement she did to Fulton what Fulton had done to Stigand. He didn't understand how this related to the way Odylia might have "had" Ecfrida, but that no longer mattered. Seeing her mouth enclose his friend's pizzle, this was beyond fascinating. He wanted to see exactly what she was doing, how her lips encircled the head, how her fingers gripped the shaft. He felt his own hardening. His breathing was as shallow as Fulton's was deep. Fulton's eyes were closed; Edward's had never been more open.

He didn't think, he just pulled Odylia away and bent his own head down. He gripped that shaft. It was so hard. He opened his mouth, relishing a taste on his tongue that he'd never before tasted. He felt a hand squeeze his own stiffness through his clothes. He fumbled to unbuckle his belt and push down his leggings, never freeing Fulton from his mouth. The hand returned. It was small. Odylia's. He pushed it away and pulled Fulton's hand there instead.

Odylia giggled, but he was immune to any thought, so full was he of sensation. Honey flowed through him from mouth to balls, and on, and back, like a tide, so much more intense than his own secret morning pleasures. The wonder of it swelled his skull and rolled down to his very toes.

The waggon rocked. Odylia was leaving, and he was glad. He wanted this to share with Fulton alone.

Odylia said "Ah."

She hadn't gone. Someone had arrived.

"So it's all right…" Ecfrida's voice. "…it's all right for you to have a peasant, but not me?"

Edward's head whipped up. A silver thread of saliva still linked his bottom lip to Fulton's purple shining helmet. His own pizzle instantly wilted in Fulton's hand.

Flames burned his cheeks from within. How quickly the furnace of desire turned into the cauldron of shame.

3. The Battle of Tilberh

(Emma)

"The most pathetically organised defence."

The road was no more comfortable going north than it had been coming south. The rain held off, but the mud survived to worry the horses for their footing. Sitting with Alfred, Wilf and Arsindis in the waggon did not help anyone's comfort, so Emma rode alongside. Three ceorls were in front, and three were with Wendel behind. Deorleaf had ridden ahead to find accommodation, and a boat.

Alfred perked up at first, sitting in the fresh air wrapped in blankets between Wilf and waggoneer. The motion quickly tired him, so Wendel lifted him into the bed of the waggon, where a thin palliasse was a miserable cushion against the jolts. Emma praised him for his bravery, for not moaning or crying though the pain in his leg must be terrible. He complained of feeling chilled, and recalled that soon he'd again be sick from rolling waves.

She had a pouch of dried valerian root, a pinch of which in water, Odylia said, would make him sleep. It did not. She offered a prayer for God to help the valerian, but God decided Alfred was strong enough awake.

They stopped overnight at Cranbroka. Alfred would not eat, but water was boiled so he could drink Odylia's concoction. Emma added three pinches of valerian, two prayers, and a gold coin for Cranbroka's church, and Alfred dozed next day all the way to Meddestane.

Here, Deorleaf awaited them. He was with the Thegn, who

bowed and offered anything for the Queen's comfort as if she, not Alfred, was in need. Deorleaf explained that there was a boat to take them to Tilberh, where another would get them to Lunden. But tides and the dark meant it could not leave until morning.

"And how did you get a message to Tilberh?" Emma demanded.

"Your Majesty, there is no faster way to Tilberh than the boat you'll be on." Deorleaf refrained from shrugging, but his pained expression asked, what more can I do?

"So what you're saying is, no boat will be ready for us when we arrive. It will be hours, a day, or more, until there's one to get Alfred to Lunden."

"Edmund planned to be in Tilberh. He will order you a boat, surely."

She did not want to be beholden to Edmund. "If a boat can get us that far, it can get us all the way. Tell the boatman. He will be rewarded. Tell him he does not want to say no."

In the morning she smelled Alfred's leg, and felt for any burning that were the first signs of blackwound. There were none, but she was impatient to be in Lunden with her leech and her apothecary. In their hands, Alfred would recover. He was not a weakling.

She ordered more valerian infusion to be made up and poured into a stoppered flask. Then she breakfasted, and forced Alfred to eat spoonfuls of bread and milk.

It was still early morn when they followed Deorleaf down to the riverbank stade where a boat was tied. It was a small vessel, with four oars, a mast hardly more than two men in height, and a sail that would not cover her bed. The boatman's two sons and two hired boys would crew it. She closed her eyes and asked God to put a breeze behind them, and promised money for the Abbey at Wiltun, for those boys did not look strong enough to row for long against the wind. Meddestane had been a good day's sail from Lunden, even blessed with that following breeze. She feared slow going. But she could always change her mind about Tilberh. With all those battle-ready men there, surely there must be leeches amongst the retinue?

She clarified with Bass, the captain, that he knew he was required to go all the way to Lunden. "Ain't but been there," he said. "It's too far for me and the boys."

"We sailed here in a day. You can moor overnight, you will be given food and a place to sleep, and four silver pennies."

"Ah, but we lose two days not catching fish, maybe more. We need eight."

"Fish are cheap. The Queen's grace is more valuable."

"With all respect, we can say grace but we cain't eat it. How about seven?"

"Five. A sixth if we are there by sunset."

"Agreed." He offered his hand, but Emma turned and left it empty.

She got one of Deorleaf's men to transfer their two chests, their capes, some food, and the straw mattress onto the boat, and instructed Deorleaf to return to Rameslege with the waggon. The troop would be needed for Edward and Ecfrida's return trip, and the waggon too.

She settled Alfred on the paliasse and sat next to him. Arisindis, Wendel and Wilf squeezed themselves onto a single bench just forward of Bass at the steeroar. The four boys rowed steadily, and unreefed the sail whenever the turns of the river brought the wind to help them. Hrofcaestr passed, the Meduwaen widened its mouth, then they were between the headlands. God must have at last heard the prayer or seen the coin, for he looked kindly on Alfred and sent a near easterly wind. They raced the seawaves.

Alfred was the colour of a winter cabbage, but pale was better than red and sweating, Emma thought. She gave him water with valerian but he puked it into a leather bailer. She held his hand, but did not say "My little man," though she wanted to, and perhaps would have but for the four boys looking on. She didn't need to add to her son's hardship. Only once did he speak, to say "Fuck, it hurts." She barely noticed the obscenity, so justified was it, so fitting, coming from Alfred's mouth..

She settled herself down, feeling seasick, knowing that there was nothing for it but to sit, to endure, and to resist the temptation of taking valerian herself.

The boat was probably overladen and too deep in the water. She looked at the crew of runty fisher-boys: Garulf, Bass's eldest, Matti his second son, and the two other youths whose names interested Emma even less. There was no point asking them to row now and add to the speed the wind gave – better to keep their energy up for later, when they were on the narrower, more sheltered Tamys with its big meanders.

The coasts remained distant on either side. She checked behind, lest bad weather was catching them from the east sea.

Three square sails punctuated the horizon like warbanners.

She stood, holding tight to a mast stay. She brushed away the tears the wind drew to her eyes and blurred her vision. Two more distant squares. Three. Four. How could seven shapes so small be so terrifying? "Bass," she said.

He stood. He shaded his eyes and squinted. "Shit," he said. "Row, boys. Row you hard."

"How many do you count?" Emma asked him.

"Eight," he said. "Ten. I don't want to know if there's more."

"Have you ever seen that many together?"

"Not since the furies after Saint Brice's Day."

Emma winced. It was in the first year of her marriage. Sveyn had been busy taking control of his Norwegian provinces, and England had enjoyed a few years with only minor Viking raids. After his victory over the Norse, Sveyn looked back across the sea, and had his fleet take Wihtware, to use the isle to launch raids on the south coast. He withdrew after a gafol payment of twenty-four thousand pounds of silver.

Emma recalled Aethelred's anger and humiliation, and his urge to lash out. He enjoined Saxons to rise and kill all the Danes living amongst them, and set the thirteenth day of November, the feast-day of Saint Brice of Tours, for the cleansing. It was her first view of how ill-considered his decisions could be. Eadric had counselled against the order, and he was not alone. Aethelred cited instances from the bible, when the holy had slaughtered pagans by God's will, but Archbishop Aelfheah said many Danes were converted, and even a King is not a God.

Some Danes abandoned their homes as Aethelred had hoped, but most of his subjects ignored the command and confined themselves to settling scores, and exacting debts or enforcing their cancelation. There were fires, and many homes and cattle stolen, but no nationwide massacre.

Only the town of Oxenford had been truly zealous. Most of the pureblood Danish families had fled, but many who were intermarried or were of mixed Danish and Saxon stock decided to remain. They knew their bombastic thegn Aethelden for the fool he was, but they underestimated his rhetoric, and overestimated their neighbours, who were bigger fools.

When Saint Brice's Day dawned and the first murders began, a score and more families sought sanctuary in the church of Saint Frideswith. A certain Gunnhilde, rashly overconfident both of her status in the town and of her new faith in Lord Jesus, stood by the church door and tried to persuade the King's loyal people to show mercy. True

Christians stabbed her many times, threw her into the church, barred the doors from without, and set the building ablaze. Perhaps they thought their King would be especially pleased to see Sveyn's own sister killed.

The Forkbeard's fury was terrible. He took Wihtware again, and the south coast from Escancaestr to Polle suffered grievously. Wintancaestr, so well defended, was sacked, even at great and bloody cost to the Danes, because Sveyn wanted a personal vengeance. But Aethelred was not to be found. Sveyn fell on Oxenford with a thousand men, and Oxenford paid worst of all. He took his great heathen army into East Anglia, where Ulfcytel's fyrd put up a great fight and saved Norwic, so Sveyn took to boats and invaded Cantware. He only desisted on a gafol payment of thirty-six thousand pounds.

Emma looked again at the horizon. The leading longships, faster than a small and overladen Meddestane fishing boat built for stability, were closer. The squaresails were too numerous to count. These were not just freebooting Norse, this was surely an invasion fleet. But why attack Lunden? Does Sveyn not know about the fleet at Tilberh? Does he not have sparrows? Her eyes searched the shores, north and south, and found what she was looking for: a plume of smoke, just behind them on the north bank. Black it was, and blown to a low angle, but visible for miles. She scanned ahead, and sure enough, within a minute another plume to the west struggled into the air. Someone – Edmund or Brihtic – had planned well enough to set up lookouts and beacons.

Alfred was dozing at last, curled up to Arsindis's warmth. Best keep it that way. Wilf was under her other arm. Emma ordered Wendel to take a turn at the oar, to save some of the boys' energy, but Bass said these boys would row all day and all night together, and Wendel destroying their rhythm would slow them.

The estuary narrowed and curved to the south, hiding the ships from view. Bass steered the boat towards the Cantware shore, and urged his boys to pull harder. "Get in close, we have our shallow draught on them."

Emma saw his thinking: the Danish ships would be unlikely to divert for the sake of a single small boat, so if they could reach the tidal flats, they might be safe. But what then? On foot, they'd sink into the mud. With Alfred weakened, and miles from habitation… could she trust Bass and his boys? Even if they could get to Lunden, what would they find, if that fleet had arrived first? "No. We want the north bank."

Bass did nothing. "South shore's closer. We can find an inlet and hide in some reeds till they pass."

Wendel supported Bass. "Tilberh's going to see a battle. We're best off not being there."

"TURN NORTH!" she shouted. "I am Queen of England! This is a command to you, Bass. Here is Prince Alfred, sorely wounded. Do what I say, or his father will take your head, your boys' heads, your wife's, your parents', your sisters', and however many daughters you've fathered with them." She calmed herself as best she could. "Change course now, and I will explain to you both."

Bass's eyes showed a flicker of resistance, and he looked at Wendel, but Wendel was no longer his ally. Bass leaned on the steeroar, and told the boys to re-trim the sail.

"The King's fleet is at Tilberh." Emma told him. "You see the beacon smoke? They will be making ready to block the river where it narrows, to protect Lunden. There will be a wall of ships, and the safest place for us is on the other side of that wall."

Wendel turned to Bass, knowing he should have kept quiet earlier. "If we don't make it before they catch up with us, there are reeds and inlets on the Eassex shore."

"Aye, well, north makes better of the wind," Bass muttered.

The boys bent their backs, and the wind did help them. Emma looked fore and aft, trying to judge how quickly the squaresails were catching them. By the time the masts and flags of the English fleet at Tilberh came into view, the Danes were hidden behind the last bend. "It's gone narrower on them," Bass said. "They daren't risk straying from the centre, and they're stealing each other's wind."

"How far away do you think they are?"

"An hour. Less."

Even seen from a distance, Tilberh was a mess of activity, with sails flapping from cockeyed booms that clashed as the wind smacked whatever it found. Boats had their oars locked together, men's shouts could be heard even upwind, and horns sounded a code that Emma presumed some captains knew the meaning of. They seemed to have no plan for how they might detach themselves from the single giant raft she'd seen on the outward voyage, to re-form as a barrier of wood across the river, here where it narrowed to two furlongs or so. Not a single boat had yet put out into the stream. Could they assemble their defence in the hour or less before the Vikingr arrived?

In the chaos it was impossible to count, but she was sure there were fewer boats than before. Where were the others? Were they departed to protect Cantware after all? Or East Anglia?

One boat had come clear, a big one with twelve oars on each side, rowing toward them until it was within hailing distance. A call came. "Stop your rowing. Reef your sail."

"Stop rowing," Emma told the boys. "But keep the sail raised. They can sail too."

The boat tacked, and the two vessels sailed alongside each other. The Tilberh boat, more than twice their size, loomed over them. Archers stood as at a castle wall, arrows notched but, for now, pointed at the water. Its captain stood at the stern, looked down, and called out "Who are you to sail so boldy into…" and he faltered, for he saw he was addressing a woman. "…the King of England's realm?"

He thought she was the first of the invaders! Her laughter was a mix of disbelief and anger. "Fool! This is my realm. I am Emma of Normandy, Queen of England, mother of Prince Alfred who lies here wounded. We are bound for Lunden. Give me your name, man, and tell me who you serve."

"You lie."

"When your last sight is me watching your head roll, you will realise I do not lie. I say again, your name?"

"I am Dunn, Thegn of Bremesgrave, and I serve Brihtric, Ealdorman of Mercia."

"And Brihtric serves the King, and the King commands that his Queen and his Prince be taken safe to Lunden. You have the faster vessel, so take us aboard and get us to safety before those Vikings get close, or Bremesgrave will be Dunnsgrave."

Bass shouted for both Emma and Dunn's benefit. "We cain't go alongside. With these waves, that boat would smash us. Even if we could, it's too dangerous to try and get the boy across. He'd likely fall and drown."

He was right. They would have to simply carry on. At least they'd be behind the wall of boats, if ever it formed.

Dunn shouted again. "I am commanded to kill you all if you are enemy-"

"Don't be so stupid."

"-or to bring you to shore if you are not."

"Ashore in Lunden. There's to be a battle here, and we need to be far away. Let us pass, and tell Brihtric to close the gate behind us."

"I can't do that. You may be a Danish sparrow, sent to scout our defences."

"Idiot! Do I look like a sparrow? Does my injured son? I am countermanding Brihtric's order." She turned to Bass. "Ignore him. Sail on."

"Wasn't Brihtric's order," Dunn called.

She shouted up in frustration and anger "I don't care whose order it was, I'm your Queen, and I order otherwise."

"Even if you are the Queen," Dunn said, "Prince Edmund ranks higher."

She was horrified to see the twelve archers with arrows notched release their strings. With the wind, and both boats rolling, this was not a test of accuracy. Four fell short and punctured only water. Three flew high, and did likewise. Two thudded into the hull. One embedded itself into the mast. One hit Bass's son Matti's thigh. Emma did not her his yell, because the last arrow thunked into the inside of the boat just inches above Alfred's head.

Bass held up his hands at Dunn. "We come." Garulf took the steeroar and leaned on it to change course into Tilberh, as Bass bent to tend Matti's bleeding leg. Wendel held his sword hidden below the gunwale.

Emma sat next to Alfred, speechless. Edmund. If only he'd been on the boat, he would have allowed her to get Alfred to safety. She consoled herself by thinking how Dunn would scream, and how Bremesgrave would need a new thegn.

The closer they got to Tilberh, the more it appeared to be a place of chaos and mayhem. Boats seemed half crewed, with more archers than oarsmen aboard, while men ran hither and thither on the quayside to no purpose she could determine. Sails were up but furled, hulls jostled and clashed with their hemp basket fenders offering little protection. Emma couldn't see how they would get out into the river before the Danes passed.

Who was in charge of this mess? Edmund? Brihtric? Aethelred must be told, she thought. Or was he here himself?

She feared even more for Lunden if he was.

Her priority was still to bring Alfred to safety and to a leech. That meant getting inland, for very soon the Tamys would be a sea of blood. A few hours by boat had become a day or more by horse and wagon. She cursed Dunn, and Brihtric, and Edmund.

She cursed her husband for provoking Sveyn Forkbeard. Would he not learn?

She cursed herself for not seeing the danger.

As soon as she had Alfred ashore, she paid Bass his five pennies. "Although you did not take me all the way."

Bass said "My boy is hurt!"

"He'll live."

"That wasn't no part of the bargain."

"Take it up with Edmund. I will gladly support your case for compensation."

"We can't get home. We're about to be caught in a battle. We are fishermen, not fighters."

"When you are called to fight for your King, then you are fighters." She gave Bass a sixth penny, for she was not mean, and dismissed him.

She turned to Wendel "Find somewhere warm and safe for the Prince. Get a cart for him, and horses for me and you. Make ready to leave in ten minutes."

"What about Wilf?" he said.

Wendel would be more loyal for not leaving his son.

"What about me?" Arsindis added.

"Yes, yes. Do what you can." She turned to Dunn. Now she was ashore she wanted to stab him with the small seax she kept on her belt. But it wouldn't help. Wendel could deal with him later. "Take me to Edmund," she ordered.

"As he commanded me," was all Dunn offered. But he called out to one of his men "The two boys. See they are looked after." He wasn't taking risks with her, she saw that.

Even an idiot would have worked out that, Queen or not, she was surely highborn.

Dunn led her through a pair of bailey gates to a small hall that must be Brihtric's centre here in Tilberh. Two guards at the door knew Dunn, and spoke to him. He turned to her. "Prince Edmund is with the boats, by the river."

"I'll see Brihtric then."

"Brihtric is elsewhere."

They retraced their steps back to the river. Emma marched ahead of Dunn and strode to the centre of activity. "Hey," he said, hurrying after her. She looked anxiously to the east. The Danish longships had not yet turned the last bend, but they could not be far. And still no wall was formed across the river.

For all her disdain of Edmund's arrogance, she had believed him a good commander. Even the handful of boats that seemed ready were holding position just a few yards out. Get into the stream, she thought, not just to slow the Danes, but to leave space for other boats to move into. It looked as if someone had decided that Tilberh was the Danes' target, not Lunden, and must be protected at all costs. Madness. But if it kept them from Alfred, if it gave her time to get him away, she didn't mind.

Get away where?

Dunn approached a vessel where a man was shouting orders at a crew. "Are you in charge of this boat?"

"Aye, I'm captain."

"Who gives you orders?"

"Not you."

Angry and out of patience, Emma stepped forward. "He asked you a question. Who tells you what to do? A thegn?"

The captain continued directing men to their positions at the oars.

"Where is he?"

"Called to moot. Walk along, you'll see."

She left, now dispirited too. If they were getting battle orders so late, the Danes had caught everyone by surprise. Had there been no preparation since the fleet was called here from Sanwic?

"He'll be too occupied to see you," the captain called after her.

She wished she was a man.

Ahead, a watchtower stood at the top of a small rise, with a crush of fifty men and more below, all looking upwards, listening to an address from the top of the tower. These must be the commanders of flotillas, not individual captains, receiving their orders. She couldn't see who was on the tower delivering, but she soon found out.

The men started cheering, the cheering swelled, and a shout came: "Ironside! Ironside! Ironside!" They took it up, all roaring the name, louder and louder.

She growled and clenched her fists. Arrogant idiot. There will be time for hearing your men's cheers after the battle. If anyone lives.

The men were clustered too tightly for her to shoulder through to the centre.

A lookout on the tower called "Sails! They are coming!"

Another roar went up, and fell as if at an order.

"Then go!" The voice of Edmund Ironside, and she saw him in the shadow of the tower's canopy. "Remember your orders. You are brave and strong, and you fight for your King, for England, for your home, your wives, your families!"

The men roared again, and returned to the fleet. Emma was pushed backwards with no more than curious glances or quick leers, as if she was some sailor's lost wife or a whore they looked forward to mounting later.

At last she could step forward. There was Edmund. A man she recognised as his chief husceorl stood next to him. She couldn't recall his name. "Edmund!" she called.

Edmund saw her. "What the fuck are you doing here?"

Dunn tried to speak, but she shouted over him. She felt him shrink as he realised that she hadn't lied.

"I ask you the same question," she called. "This is the most pathetically disorganised defence I can even imagine."

"It was worse before I arrived, trust me." Edmund climbed down the tower's ladder.

She turned to Dunn. "Go back and see that Alfred is all right, before I hide my seax in your cul."

"Alfred?" said Edmund. But he wasn't slow. "Do as she says. Take Alfred to my hall."

Dunn scurried away.

"Don't stab him, please, he's a good man." Edmund walked to her and she to him, along a well trodden muddy path up a slight incline. She had to take care not to slip. "Alfred?" he said. "Where are Ecfrida and Edward? Not still in Rye?"

Emma nodded, wincing at the concern in his voice.

"Danes," he said. "They landed in huge numbers at Sanwic. I sent a rider to Rye this morning."

She'd been right when she'd seen the number of Danish longships. It was an invasion, not a raid. Edward was in mortal danger.

"My hunch is they will go in strength to Cantenberh, then Meddestane and Hrofcaestr. And Dofras. Rye is a backwater. Heremond will get there before any Dane comes near. Deorleaf may pick up word, and he will know to flee west."

Deorleaf was not there, she thought. If he doesn't know about the Danes, he'll have no reason to rush back. She felt sick, and knew she should have kept both sons with her.

"Why are you here? And why for God's sake bring Alfred?" He stopped at the top of the slope. From here, she had a better view over the quayside and the river. More boats had formed up, holding side by side in the shallows, a stout defence indeed – for Tilberh.

The Danish longships were still a mile and more away. It was an even larger fleet than she'd perceived, with yet more coming into view around the river bend.

"Alfred was wounded," Emma explained. "I decided to take him home."

"Wounded? How? How badly?"

In spite of herself she was mollified by his evident worry. "A sword cut. Deep, in his thigh. An accident. He's in pain. It's not burning, but he needs a leech. We'd be near Lunden by now, but you gave your order to Dunn."

"When your boat was spotted, we had no idea who it was. You can't blame Dunn for following my orders."

"I can blame him for not following mine. Now I need horses, a cart, and two spare men. We will ride to Berching monastery. Better Alfred endures a road than a battleaxe."

Edmund nodded, and turned to his husceorl. "Ercenbert, see to it."

"Thank you," Emma said. "And thank you for sending a rider south." He had at least executed some tasks efficiently.

The Danish ships were closer, packed densely along the river, near enough now to see the dragonheads with their fiery eyes, to count the oars, the brightly coloured shields, and the Vikingr helms behind them.

None of the English boats had yet gone more than two boatlengths from the shore, although the scurrying of men on the quayside trying to make ready had ceased. Emma looked anxiously towards the hall. Was Alfred there? Were the horses ready? "Where is Ercenbert?"

"Don't worry, you'll have horses. If the Danes want to attack Tilberh, we'll see them turn towards us, and you'll have time to get away. But I don't think that's their plan."

Not only were they not turning, but they had veered to the far side of the river, and were passing Tilberh well beyond the range of any arrows.

"Edmund, our boats were here to block the river, to protect Lunden. They'll think us cowards."

"Good," said Edmund. "How did the boy Godwin fare in Rameslege?"

Emma was taken aback at this unexpected question. "Godwin? He let Alfred use a sword too big for him. I'd like to blame him, but sadly I can't." He'd acted well to get Alfred back after the incident, according to Wendel and Theo. "A sharp lad." A good looking lad too, she thought. "Alfred took to him."

Edmund laughed. "I can imagine."

Ercenbert came towards them in swift strides. "We have two horses. A small cart. They're not much, but all we can find right now."

One horse for her, one for Wendel, the cart for Alfred and Wilf. It would do. Arsindis could make her own way. But with the Danes clearly passing by on the far bank, there was now less urgency.

"Someone fed them," Ercenbert added. "Alfred seemed to be hungry."

That was a promising sign.

Emma counted forty Danish longships progressing past them. She estimated two hundred English boats, but they were smaller and slower, lacking battle-hardened crews and fighters, badly led, and too disorganised to hinder the Danes. She kept her counsel. The Danes had only to turn, and they could charge into the English boats, and burst through. It wouldn't take long for the first fighters to get to land. They'd race up the slope, looking to destroy the towers and the halls, and anyone inside them.

If one ship began to turn its dragon's eyes to stare at them square on, she would gallop away with Alfred. Until Lunden was safe it would have to be north, as fast and as far as they could go.

Edmund said "Is Alfie well enough to be carried in a chair? Perhaps he can come here."

Alfred would be pleased to see Edmund. She nodded to Ercenbert. "Ask him. Have the horses close."

They stood in silence, watching the last of the Danish boats pass. Only now did the English look ready to put out into the Tamys as a fleet. Unable to block the river, they were no more than a guard of honour to usher the Danes on to Lunden.

She was disappointed in Edmund. It seemed he had dismissed Brihtric, probably for incompetence in losing those ships to the traitor, only to prove an even poorer commander himself. Edmund's bark was a mere yap, and his bite was toothless. He was like his father after all.

"The boy Godwin," he said. "Did you discover who he is? Did Deorleaf tell you?"

"No," she said. Why was he going on about Godwin? She wasn't really interested, but until Alfred arrived there was nothing aside from the floating chaos to talk of. "So who is he?"

"I told him," Edmund said, "that he is the only person we know who's been able to watch a sea battle without being in it, and therefore probably dying."

"What sea battle?"

Edmund again ignored her question. He said "In a few moments, we will be like him."

He was getting annoying. "What sea battle?"

"Godwin saw how Wulfnoth Cild destroyed sixty ships with only a score of his own. He watched from a clifftop."

There was clearly more to the story. "Really? How did you find him?"

"You could say he found me."

Before she could press for details a small voice called his name. "Edmund!" It was Alfred, on a chair being carried by two fat men whose eyes did their complaining for them.

Wendel and Ercenbert walked behind, each leading a horse. Alfred looked tired and pale still, but was at least smiling at seeing his big brother.

Edmund went to them, and let Alfred lean onto him in as much of hug as pain allowed. "How is the leg?"

"I'm going to have such a scar, Edmund!"

"That's m'boy," Edmund said, cupping the back of Alfred's head with one hand and squeezing his shoulder with the other.

Emma thought "Little man," once more, and was suddenly weakened by her pride in her son, and a strange and unexpected rush of warmth for her stepson.

She looked out at the Danish ships. None had turned. They were passing unhindered and sailing on towards Lunden, three and four abreast, crowding the southern half of the river in a convoy near a quarter mile long. There would be no battle for Tilberh, not today. She felt her shoulders relax. She hadn't noticed how clenched they were.

"On my back," Edmund said to Alfred. "Hold on tight." He crouched for Alfred to put his arms around his neck. He put one arm under Alfred's good leg and, before Emma realised his intent, he took Alfred to the watchtower and began to climb the ladder.

"Edmund!" she shouted, but Alfred was laughing even as he winced in pain.

Ercenbert climbed up too, leaving her with little option but to follow.

"Now," Edmund said when they were stood at the top.

Ercenbert pulled a red flag from a bag he carried over his shoulder. He unfurled it, and waved it in big arcs from side to side. The easternmost boat, the boat that was the first to be passed by the Danes, began to move out into the water. A second one followed a boatlength behind, then a third. More boats left, to form a line curling like a wave out onto the Tamys.

"Wind's good," Ercenbert said. The lookout turret flags whipped and cracked to the west. The English boats weren't so fast, but as they flowed into the stream, they filled the water behind the Danes.

"Look," Edmund said, pointing to the next bend in the river, where it turned sharply south about a mile away. Appearing from around the headland were dozens more boats. They had no sails, and rowed into the wind, towards the Danes. Dozens turned to scores, scores to a hundred and more, far too many to count.

Emma realised that her impression that there were fewer boats at Tilberh today than before was right. Edmund had split the fleet. "Brihtric?" she said.

Edmund pointed. "Can you make out that tower on the next headland? He'll be there. He saw our flag, or his hawkest-eyed lookout did."

"Why? Why split the fleet? They only have half a wall to batter through."

"Watch."

Now clear of Tilberh, the Danish boats spread across the river to form a tight arrowhead. She pitied the men ahead of them, in their smaller boats. "We must learn to build bigger ships," she said.

"We wasted our time and effort building ships at all," Edmund retorted. "My father was stupid to take on the Danes where they are at their very strongest. But perhaps we can make the best of it. Look, they have formed into an arrow. They want to punch through. But coming together has slowed them."

Emma realised that he was explaining to Alfred.

"So our boats can get closer," Alfred said.

Ercenbert nodded at Edmund. "Just as you said."

The flat base of the Danish triangle stretched a good way across the river. The English, in smaller boats with shallower draughts, and more confident in their knowledge of the waters, were spread even more widely behind them, and indeed, they were close.

A hundred then a thousand thin black arcs chased from the English boats and made gold at their fall. With the wind behind them, the archers could fire low trajectories. The huge and densely packed Danish squaresails were easier to hit than to miss, and for every firearrow that fizzed into the water, another hit a sail, a deck, a hull, spars, ropes, or a Dane.

"'Tis a beautiful thing," Ercenbert sighed, "when a plan ripens sweet."

The Danes bent their own bows to their attackers, but English commanders on the Tilberh side carefully kept out of range, yet close enough to keep their fire raining with the wind. Now other archers were shooting fire arrows from both banks, and from Brihtric's boats. These drew Danish arrows, but the Danes had no fire, and most sliced harmlessly through the sails, or thunked into the timber of a hull, a deck, or a shield.

Emma's lips curled into something like a smile. Perhaps one day, when Alfred and Edward were utterly safe, she might apologise to Edmund for not seeing how he'd drawn the Danes into a trap.

Brihtric's fleet closed in on the Danes from ahead, and Edmund's from behind. Outnumbered four to one, the Danes' own arrow power was divided, and weakened further as they panicked. They abandoned their bows and their oars to fight the fires and stop the burning sails from falling onto them. They lost control of their vessels, ships collided, and flames spread. Some abandoned the fight and found their oars again, and managed to turn for the shores south and north, to run aground and jump into the shallows and struggle through mud and marsh, to be welcomed into Cantware and Eassex with the spears and swords of the men lining the shore. Those ships still afloat were surrounded by English boats, and the English fighters chewed at the Danes like hungry rats.

The wind blew towards Lunden, taking the last of the battle out of sight past the next headland.

Danish smoke was all that assailed Lunden that day.

"It's a strange thing," Edmund said to no-one, but those around him listened. "We were children when it came to sea battles. We needed teaching. And who was our teacher?"

Ercenbert shook his head wryly, knowing the answer.

"Who was our teacher?" said Alfred.

"Wulfnoth Cild."

"The traitor?" said Alfred.

"Yes, the traitor. And the traitor's son. It's funny. If I hadn't saved Godwin from Brihtric's ire, Brihtric might not have survived this day."

"Godwin?" said Emma. "Godwin is the son of Wulfnoth Cild?"

Edward nodded. "He left his father, but not before he watched his father's battle."

Emma wondered if Odylia had more skill with herblore than she'd given her credit for, because Alfred appeared to be perking up. Herbs, or the excitement of the victory. Either way, the urgency of getting to Lunden had diminished, and Alfred pleaded to be allowed to stay for the feast. Food, a fire, and celebration would be better medicine than another trail by waggon into Lunden, or a boat and more seasickness.

Brihtric the Mercian sailed back to Tilberh, and leaped from the boat to the rousing cheers of the men, for all that most were of Wessex. He ran to Edmund and held him like a brother, raised his hand aloft and turned back to the crews to receive their cheers again.

Emma stood beside Edmund, thinking Brihtric, don't let it go to your head. The Danes won't fall into that trap twice. But Alfred was in his chair beside her, cheering too, and Lunden was safe for now, so Emma found it easy to smile for her husband's people, to wave at them, to feel a little hope for them.

Edmund told two of his men to lift the chair, and when he shouted Alfred's name the men cheered their young Prince as they cheered the older. She told Wendel to set Alfred onto his horse.

Brihtric had brought only a small portion of his fleet. Apart from the few that were lost, he left many to land on the estuary shores and scour the marshes, islets, and reedlands, and the willowbanks above the tidemark. They hunted Danes who had managed to get ashore.

He told Edmund that the carrion pickers, as he called them, were ordered to take no prisoners save those who were obviously – from their clothes, their jewellery, the quality of their weapons, or their demeanour – Danish leaders and nobles. These were to be brought as soon as possible to Tilberh. The rest were to be slaughtered without mercy. The pickers would work for a day, then he'd send out more to relieve them.

Brihtric had watched the foremost Danish longship, and though it burned, he saw that its surviving crew had managed to row to the north shore. It was there he'd sent his best men.

The sun was an hour away from setting, and the tide was rising, so Edmund mustered a score of boats and set out onto the water. He wanted to get to the beached and abandoned longships, the ones that weren't too fire damaged, and bring them to Tilberh. They could be mended, re-masted, fitted with new sails, and the English would have warships bigger than any they could build themselves. The men he took grumbled that they would miss the feasting, but Edmund was missing it too. This must be done now, he told them, in case the vessels float off on the ebb tide, or Danes return to row them away, or to burn them to stop their capture. Losing a ship to the enemy was, to a Viking, the greatest shame imaginable.

So it was that when a troop of Mercians came to Tilberh with a score of wet, roped, and bloodied Danes Edmund was not present to gloat alongside Brihtric. The Danes were pelted with mud and stones, and the troop who had captured them beat them again with their spear shafts.

Emma watched on as Brihtric questioned them. She couldn't make out the words, but it was clear from Brihtric's triumphal posturing in front of the fair haired man with the strong chin and the shoulders of a bull, that he had been identified as the leader of the Danish fleet. Strong as he undoubtedly was, he looked too young for the task, all the more so because he had been robbed of his outer garments and boots, and left only with a linen undersmock and wool leggings.

Hundreds of the English had gathered around. They stood together, arms around shoulders, chanting "Mercia! Mercia!" and "Wessex! Wessex!"

Brihtric held up his arms until the chanting subsided. "Let me present Kjell Ormsson," he declaimed, "who calls himself a Jarl of Jomsborg."

Emma had heard of the Jomsborgr from the east of Denmark, a warrior cult as feared around the Baltic and into Germanicus as the Spartans had been feared in ancient Greece. If Sveyn had summoned the Jomsborgr, she thought, he was deadly serious about his attack on Cantware. If it wasn't a full invasion, it was absolute terror to exact maximum gafol. And if they'd come direct from east of Denmark, they would have had no way of knowing about the English fleet and its position defending Lunden.

"He came under Thorkell the Tall," Brihtric continued, and

spat onto the ground. "He tried to sail to Lunden, to kill and to steal and to strike fear into English hearts. But we will have no fear of heathens who worship only blood and silver!" He let the men cheer again, and stood back as more mud was thrown. "We have a message for Thorkell!"

He went to Kjell Ormsson with his sword raised. Kjell did not flinch. He shouted something defiant, but the only word Emma recognised was "Valhalla."

Brihtric put his sword to Kjell's neck, lifted the hilt high, and pushed the blade down the front of Kjell's smock. Then with a downward slice, the blade ripped through the linen and left him barechested, with a long shallow cut in his belly that started dripping blood through a mat of golden hair. The men who'd brought him in got the idea, and cut through the bonds that tied his hands, freeing them so they could pull the shirt off him. The daylight was fading fast now, and some had found torches which they held around Brihtric, Kjell Ormsson and the captors. Others had found flagons and opened barrels, and ale was passed from hand to hand.

"What do we do with heathens?" Brihtric yelled as he repeated his move with the sword blade, this time down the front of Kjell's breechclout, ripping the fabric and leaving Kjell standing naked but for his leggings.

He would have looked ridiculous if not for the cut Brihtric had made down his stomach. Bleeding but still strong, exposed but upright, and illuminated by the flickering orange light from the torches, Emma thought him somehow noble.

The men's cheering had turned into a chant. They wanted more blood. There were many more captives to kill, and to go further with this one, Emma decided, was to miss the chance of a decent ransom. But as Brihtric's Mercians answered his question with chants that formed into a clear "Kill the Dane, Kill the Dane," she saw that he'd put himself onto a crumbling path that went steeply downhill and could not be climbed back.

Emma sighed. Such a waste. Kjell Ormsson was to die.

Wendel knew it too, and he tapped her shoulder, and indicated Alfred still sitting on the horse. The boy had a fire in his eye. Wendel's was asking, shall I take him away?

Emma said to Alfred "Had we been an hour later leaving Meddestane, that man would have caught us in our little boat. What would he have done with us?"

Alfred suddenly looked weak and ill again. "Killed us?"

Emma nodded.

He wouldn't have, of course, not if he'd been wise. He'd have paraded Queen and Prince at the front of his ship and dared any Englishman to attack him. And he'd have sailed unimpeded to Lunden. Then, who knew? Maybe respect and ransom, or perhaps the same humiliation Kjell had just endured, so much more shameful for a woman. Their Norman blood might have saved herself and her son, but there was no knowing the mind of a Jomsborgr. "Do you want to leave here?" she asked.

Alfred shook his head, as she'd known he would.

Two of Kjell's captors crouched behind him and tied his ankles together. Two more prodded his back hard with their sword points, drawing blood, and since he could not step forward, he was forced to his knees.

"What do we do with heathens?" Brihtric repeated.

"Kill them! Kill them!" his men bayed, drunk on victory and ale.

Brihtric moved beside the kneeling man, who followed him with his eyes. He lifted his sword high behind his shoulders. "He has no heaven, and he won't even go to his Valhalla, for that is only for heroes who die in battle!"

The man cheered and jeered again, and Brihtric said something to Kjell in Danish. It included the words "heaven" and "Valhalla", so Emma knew it was the same thought, spoken to taunt the man at the last second of life.

Kjell's shoulders slumped. Brihtric's sword whipped through the air. A good sword it was, heavy and sharp, and Brihtric was a strong man who wielded it well. A fount of blood, and Kjell toppled, his head connected to his shoulders just by tendons. Two more hacks and it was detached. Brihtric lifted the head by its blond locks and held it high, ignoring the blood dripping down his arm. The men's cheers would be heard in Lunden. He turned the face to Alfred.

Alfred raised a fist and cried out "Yes!" as loudly as shock and injury permitted. His boyish pitch carried over the men, and they called back "Yes!" to their young Prince. He saw their faces, and fisted the air once more. "England! And the King!" A thousand men from Mercia and Wessex alike cheered Alfred, and Emma had never felt prouder.

Brihtric showed the head to the remnants of Kjell's Jombsorg force. He pointed to two of the prisoners. "Those two, take them across the river and send them back to tell the story of Kjell Ormsson's downfall to anyone who gives a shit about him!" He shouted again: "What do we do with heathens?"

Emma nodded to Wendel, who led the horse away. Alfred looked over his shoulder, watching to the last as swords and spears bit into the Danish prisoners' flesh.

4. The Woman Grown

(Eadric)

"I don't want to be Queen of England."

Eadric had spent much of the journey home in pleasant thought and difficult speculation. What gifts might he present to Aelfgifu and Knut on their wedding day? Could he outdo Sveyn? Should he? Would Aethelred send anything? Or Edmund? Most difficult: what should be her dowry? There were lands near Northamtun that were in his gift. They would be appropriate, because had he not acquired them from her grandmother's side of her family?

He chuckled as he rode, and did not explain himself to Eadgyth, who travelled with him from Tamwerth to Coventre.

Less diverting were his thoughts about Nothman and Leofric. An hour or two of reflection together might have been valuable, and he could have talked more with them as they travelled back from Caestrfeld, but they had kept themselves distant before the parting of ways. He'd wanted to involve the brothers in refining his strategy for Aelfgifu, so they'd not feel it was counter to their interests, which, in the context of his wider ambitions, it was not. But surely Nothman had harboured ambitions with her beyond those of a man with pretty girl. If he didn't have the sense, Leofric certainly did.

He had to admit that he wasn't sure he could trust them. As allies, yes. But as sound and thoughtful ealdors to consult before taking action? Especially not Nothman. A shame that he was the older of the two. He was like to speak too loud, which was why Eadric had made sure Eadgyth did not travel with them on the return journey. As soon as Eadgyth knew anything, word would get back to Aethelred. The King had to be told, of course, but Eadric needed to call the dance, or the damage might never be repaired.

Then there was Aelfgifu herself, and the matter of when and how to tell her. It had to be soon, before whisper and rumour fed back from Weogorna. And it must be sweet with talk of riches and status, for the girl could be headstrong. She might run away, or sullenly resign herself, only to embarrass him in front of King Sveyn.

They dismounted at the door of his large hall. Aelfgifu approached even before a stableboy appeared, walking tall and demure, her face as pretty as a rosebud before it blooms, and as tight. She'd never been effusively affectionate; she behaved much as any daughter might treat a father demanding of respect: sometimes airily, sometimes playfully, or eager to please, or scared, but always easy to read. Today she had become a book that may not be opened.

A woman grown, he thought, acting for an unseen audience. Is this how it happens, not in slow transition but in a deliberate step, as if deciding that now is the time to put into practice the lessons she has been learning, all at once?

By contrast, she was unusually warm to Eadgyth, embracing her, asking if she had had a pleasant time in Tamwerth. She said with genuine sorrow, or lied with well-disguised pleasure, Eadric wasn't sure, that she wished Eadgyth could have been here to spend time with her. "We went riding, to the river. It was so lovely. Having been to Lunden and met your father and your brothers, I feel I know so little about your kin."

Eadgyth was taken aback, for the pair had never become close in the years that his wife had been, by marriage, the girl's godmother. Aelfgifu's warmth made sense, Eadric realised, if she had turned her eye to Edmund.

The girl was in for a surprise.

Later, as they ate, he asked how Nothman and Leofric had seemed, and how long they stayed.

"They only stayed the one night," she said. "They seemed tired when they arrived, and I feel that Leofric slept deep and well. But Nothman, I fear he slept poorly. He looked awful in the morning, as if he'd barely rested at all. Perhaps he was too cold."

"He's just spent over a week with me, mostly travelling. I'm sure he's used to cold. I hope you made sure they had fires."

Aelfgifu looked puzzled, as if she was trying to recall. "Did he have a fire? I think so. Yes, that must have been it. He was too hot. What do you think, Fleada?"

The maid stood behind her as usual. "I saw to his fire myself, my lady. And gave him a pot, for his comfort in the night."

The girls had a tightness to their mouths, suppressing something, Eadric was sure. Had Fleada visited Nothman in the dark? Nothman was the kind to lure such a lass, whether with charm or money. Fool girl if she succumbed. He had warned her, and she must know that if her belly thickens she'll be out, and back to Jorvik and her family. If they'd have her.

"He will catch up with his sleep in Weogorna," Eadric said, ending the matter.

The following morning, once Eadgyth had departed on a visit to the convent she endowed, Eadric asked Aelfgifu to come to him.

"I wish to tell you something," he said. He sipped his cider, but forbade her the same. No reason to fuel her unpredictability. "I see that you are growing. Maturing. It pleases me."

Aelfgifu sat, her face calm, her shoulder turned demurely away, her head held straight. Quite beautiful, he saw. And growing indeed. The visit to Lunden had changed her, in spite of the episode with Edmund. Or perhaps because of it. Had she realised how close she had come to throwing away something irreplaceable, to altering her destiny, inevitably for the worse?

"But first," he said "Let me ask you something. Were you a man, and were you a king, which king would you rather be, King Aethelred or King Sveyn?"

She was plainly surprised by such a question. "Is this a riddle? A joke?" she said. Then she composed herself. "Neither. They are both old men. Aethelred is my King, and I will not speak ill of him, but I would not wish to be him. And Sveyn is a heathen with a weak beard that isn't forked at all."

Eadric laughed. "The brothers. They fed you his secret." Then he was serious again. "If you had to decide?"

"Is a novice at some abbey an option?"

"I see your dilemma. Let me put it another way. If you were daughter to one, which would you rather be daughter to?"

"As I said, Sveyn is a heathen."

"That doesn't mean you would have to be so too. His father was converted, and his son is baptised. The son is known as Knut, but he has a given Christian name, Lambert."

"If I was King Aethelred's daughter, I'd have Edmund as a brother and Eadgyth as a sister." She giggled, a girl again. "Then you'd be my brother-in-law, not my godfather."

"Dear Aelfgifu, I am trying to get you to look at bigger matters than who your siblings would be. I want you to speculate on the powers in the land. Looking to the future, is God actually smiling on Christian Edmund more than on Christian Lambert?"

"I never imagine God smiling at all. That's why he sent Jesus, isn't it?"

She could be infuriating. He was trying to be serious, and although she reverted to her composed and demure posture, she was trying to tease him. Still a child.

He pressed on. "Danish influence grows in the Five Berhs, and in East Anglia. Where does English influence grow?"

She shook her head.

"You suspect the answer is 'Nowhere,' but you feel disloyal to speak it."

She nodded.

"In truth, English influence is growing in Wales, or it will do so shortly if Ealdorman Ledwyn takes my advice. And it grows in Normandy, largely because of Queen Emma. But I fear that in England itself, Angle-land, the power of us Angles and Saxons wanes."

Aelfgifu knew her history. "It waned before Alfred, then it waxed again. Danes were driven out of Mercia."

"Many of them, true, and those still here are blended. But what does it say about those victories a hundred years ago, that we now pay gafol to Sveyn, not the other way round?"

Aelfgifu spoke as if angered. "It says that Saxons are cowards who will not fight, and King Aethelred is not the man to make them brave. But Edmund Ironside is!"

"How spirited," he said, but he noticed that in spite of her raised voice, there was no new colour to her cheeks. "Edmund. Let us talk about him. A bard sang of him as the Ironside after a minor skirmish when two longboats made an untimely raid on Plymentyn when he happened to be there in force to settle some Cernwealas presumption. He was clever, he set an ambush, it was well done. And he recently had another minor victory in Eassex. But what real battles has he won? What campaigns has he mounted? What battles has his father won, to teach Edmund the art of war? Cotentin? Aethelred lost four fights there, and won a wife. I'm sure a thousand buried English souls are happy for him. If you think of Sveyn as the man who just sends ships to harass the English coast, then you forget Maldon."

"It was not Sveyn who defeated Byrtnoth," Aelfgifu said, in that superior tone educated girls seem to learn from their tutors.

"No, it was Olaf Trygvasson. And who defeated Olaf, at Svolder? Sveyn Forkbeard, and so he came to rule Norway, or all of it that matters. Be in no doubt that Sveyn is a warrior who wants to build an empire around the East Sea. He will have passed all he knows down to Knut, who-"

"Lambert."

"Please don't interrupt. For the moment he prefers to be called Knut, so we shall respect that. And he was definitely called Knut when he was looking on at Svolder as a boy. What has Aethelred taught Edmund?"

"Not to be Aethelred?"

"True. And let us be grateful. But little more than that, I fear."

There came a knock at the door, and Criba's voice called from outside. "My lord, a message for you from Lunden."

"Later!"

"It has your brother's seal."

He didn't know what was bothering the fraternal head, and didn't much care. "If the bugger was delivering it himself, he'd still have to wait. As will you."

He turned back to Aelfgifu. "Where were we?"

"I believe you were trying to tell me that if I want to be Queen of England, I will not be so for long were I to marry Edmund."

It was as if she was tired of her game, or his.

"You see," she continued, before he could make his next step in this dance he'd thought he was leading. "I always thought I was destined to be Nothman's wife. Or Leofric's.

Then in Lunden I realised that there is no-one in all the land more fitted to be Edmund's wife than I. An alliance between Mercia and Wessex is as sensible now as it was when you wed Eadgyth. Edmund is much more fun than Leofric, and infinitely preferable to Nothman, and-"

"And he is heir to the throne." He began to wonder if the incident with Edmund hadn't been more calculated than he'd suspected. "I see I should have talked to you about such matters long ago."

"It would make no difference. I don't want to be Queen of England."

Eadric was rarely lost for words, but had no reply to this. Any girl would want to be Queen of England, and Aelfgifu, with her spirit and her selfishness, had been fighting her way to the front of the aspirants. "You don't?"

"No. I want to be Queen of the East Sea empire. Yes, I will marry this Lambert, this Knut."

Again, Eadric was speechless. She knew already.

Leofric and Nothman had told her. One, the other, or both.

He'd been right to keep silent with them about the rest of his strategy.

Eadric looked at his goddaughter with new curiosity, and a certain pride.

"Nothman," she said. "It was Nothman who told me."

Of course it was. "You must tell no-one. Not yet. Does Fleada know?"

"She will be silent."

Eadric nodded. He even thought of thanking Nothman. His indiscretion had given the girl time to reflect, and fortunately she had wisdom enough to follow Eadric's will. Wisdom, or ambition. "So you will happily marry Knut?" He wanted to hear it again.

"Knut's moon is waxing. Edmund's will wane. That is what you were telling me, was it not?"

He nodded.

"You of all people know what's best for me."

"And for Mercia," he said.

"And for Mercia."

He called Criba in, and took the parchment. He broke Brihtric's seal and read the message.

"You smile?" Aelfgifu said. "Is it good news?"

He looked up at her. "That rather depends on where you live, and whose side you're on," he said. "My brother has won a great victory on the Tamys, which is good news for Lunden. But a mass of Vikings from across the East Sea have landed at Sanwic, and Cantware is awash with blood." These things she may now know, he thought.

He turned to Criba. "Tell Brihtric's messenger to convey my warm congratulations, but to keep himself safer in future." He hoped Brihtric would understand the meaning: no more fighting the Danes if he can avoid it.

"Father?" Aelfgifu said as Criba left.

She never called him Father. Godfather, sometimes. Lord. Never Father. "Yes, my dear?"

"What is my dowry to be?"

5. The Dokkse

(Fleada)

"It's not stealing if it's already stolen."

Aelfgifu became increasingly demanding of Fleada's time. She made her comb, braid and tie her hair in many styles and shapes, with different ribbons and pins. She made her bring clothes of varied colours, a blue cloak for her eyes, then a dark brown shawl that let her golden hair have attention, then a faded but once cherry-red jerkin that drew the eye to her breasts. "But this one is too dull," she complained. "I need a new one." She threw it to the floor and picked up the cloak, then cast it down too. "I don't want a mass of blue, I want a point of the brightest blue, set against the brightest red."

Sometimes Aelfgifu would let Fleada try on a dress or a cloak. Dressing up was fun for her, more so that it seemed to be for Aelfgifu. She realised that Aelfgifu trying to please a man she had no knowledge of was like guessing the colour of a flower in the dark, and not even being told if the guess was right or wrong. That's a game that can never be won, and can never be fun. She wanted to say as much, but being treated more as a handmaid than a friend these days, she could not.

She was dispatched to the dyer for freshly coloured fabrics still bright and unfaded. The dyer tried to explain that madder root was in short supply at the moment, and woad could never be as bright as flowers. "I have walnuts," he said. "I can make the lady a cloth the colour of ripe acorn."

"She has too many brown clothes," Fleada told him. "Light, dark, chestnut, oak. She says they are all different shades of shit."

The trouble was that Aelfgifu, dissatisfied with the hues on offer, did not blame the dyer, the shortage of madder, or the nature of woad. She blamed Fleada. Not in so many words, but in her impatience, and sharpness of tongue at small failings that once passed unnoticed or were corrected with a smile.

When you are Queen of Denmark, Fleada thought, will you be content, with your every desire satisfied? Or will you be even harder to please?

As Aelfgifu's excitement at what lay before her floated above her anxieties, she became playful. She danced with Fleada, and they swung each other round. They rode out together with a wineskin each, and ate bread and cheese as they speculated on what kind of a man Knut might be, his age, the colour of his hair and the cut of his beard. Nothman's descriptions were obviously lies. Had he even met this Knut, this Lambert?

Did he have Nothmans' good looks, or perhaps Edmund's? Did he have their masculinity? Or was he as cold as Leofric, and as ugly? "Is he a big man?" Aelfgifu wondered, and the girls collapsed into giggles and drank more wine. Fleada was her friend again, and to point out how idle it was to guess the colour of a distant flower risked the slap of Aelfgifu's displeasure.

Aelfgifu, having drunk the greater part of the wine, went to her bed when they returned, leaving Fleada to take the ponies back to the stables. She was walking home when Thyra appeared beside her and fell into step. "How are you these days, Fleada?"

It was strange to be approached by one of Eadric's servants. She had no idea what Thyra did for him, only that she was good with numbers, and spoke Danish. She was a tall woman, strong of face and bone. Fleada had little to do with her, and was glad, for there was something frightening about the way her eyes watched everyone as if looking for something on which to pass judgment.

"I'm well, thank you." She hoped the cheese she'd eaten hid the wine on her breath.

"Your mistress is keeping you busy?"

"I don't mind-"

"She must be very excited about her future," Thyra went on. Plainly she had little interest in Fleada. "Apprehensive, perhaps. A little scared?"

"Excited, I'm sure." Aelfgifu hadn't voiced fear, nor shown signs of it. Nervousness, yes, but that was to be expected. It made her snippy sometimes, which had to be forgiven.

"She's about to be married," Thyra said. "To become a woman. Under a mighty warrior. A prospect to make any girl tremble."

"Is Knut a mighty warrior? Have you met him?"

"No," Thyra said. "I've heard. But Aelfgifu, she's less mature than she pretends, and I do wonder how she's coping."

"She's coping very well." Fleada wanted the conversation to end. Thyra must have been sent by Eadric, but if either of them thought that she was going to betray Aelfgifu's qualms, they didn't know her at all. Not that Aelfgifu had qualms. Not serious ones.

Thyra pulled her off the path that led towards Aelfgifu's rooms. "Does she have friends among the boys of Coventre or Lyccidfield? Has she had a sweetheart? You would know, wouldn't you."

"No!" Aelfgifu said. "I mean, yes, I'd know, but no, she hasn't."

"Not so much as a kiss behind a haystack? Asking you to disappear for a while?"

She wouldn't ask me to disappear, Fleada thought. She'd ask me to watch out for her. "Never." Edmund didn't count as a sweetheart, and anyway, Eadric himself had seen them.

"Listen, Fleada. This is important. Lord Eadric needs to know if she has been touched by a boy. Let me say it plain. By touched, I mean-"

"I know what you mean, and I swear, she hasn't. I'd know, and she'd not keep it secret from me."

"But you're loyal, aren't you. You'd keep it secret from me."

"Yes I would. But I don't have to." Was confirming Aelfgifu's virginity to Thyra as much a betrayal as denying it? She contented herself with keeping secret Nothman's attempted-

She pulled herself away, her stomach suddenly feeling like milk in a churn rolling down a hill. Nothman's advance, his attack, was not an attempt to get Aelfgifu's favour. He'd wanted to push the marriage to Knut sideways off a road and into a deep river.

He had been foiled, so it was none of Thyra's business, nor even Eadric's.

She hurried back to Aelfgifu, thoughts and fears tumbling over themselves with each step. Aelfgifu was another payment to King Sveyn, and thus was all Eadric's business. Nothman had tried to make her his. She was soon to be Sveyn's and Knut's, just as Eadgyth was King Aethelred's business with Eadric. And surely Queen Emma had been the Norman Duke's business with Aethelred.

Maids are but wares and merchandise.

She had not merely foiled Nothman, she had humiliated him. She doubted he was the forgiving type. Aelfgifu was all that stood between Fleada and his revenge.

She said nothing of her thoughts, fearing her mistress's pride and resentment if told she was goods to be traded for favour, though she surely must know this. Fearing too that telling Aelfgifu she was Fleada's shield from Nothman, was but a first step to losing her protection.

Instead, she reported the horses settled. Uninterested, Aelfgifu said "Tomorrow, we will go to the dyer. I cannot believe there is no madder in all Mercia, and I simply must have the brightest red cloak in all the land."

"If it's not available, it's not available, not at any price."

"Fleada, you're so sweet. He only says that to make me pay more. Well, I will pay more, but not much. He will find his madder when I tell him my Godfather wishes it. And if he doesn't, he'll find Lord Eadric is madder."

Lord Eadric, who gets what he wants. His daughter traded and wed. Dye for her cloak. The truth about her relations with boys. Fleada decided she didn't like Lord Eadric, not today.

"Did you see my joke, Fleada? It was good, don't you think?"

"He sent Thyra to me," Fleada said.

Aelfgifu forgot her bid for flattery. "Thyra? Why?"

"She asked me if you have ever been with a boy or a man. I mean, lain with, as in-"

"What a cow! What business is it of hers?"

"She wasn't asking for herself."

"What did you say?"

"I said no, you haven't. Not ever. Should I have said… what? Nothing?"

"I'd have told her to take a jump. You should have said it for me."

"She's a bit frightening."

"She's just a woman. Why Thyra, I wonder? Why not Eadgyth? Why not ask me to my face? Why go through you?" Aelfgifu paused, thinking. "Because you are not such a good liar as I am."

She made guilelessness sound like a character flaw, so

Fleada didn't know whether be proud or to hang her head in shame. "But there's nothing to lie about."

"She's still a cow," Aelfgifu said. "Was she wearing her brooch?"

This startling change of direction at least enabled Fleada to lift her head decisively as she asked "Her brooch?"

"The big one, with green-blue stones."

Fleada knew it. Gold, the size of her palm, with flowers garlanded around the most beautiful stone that was bigger than the moon. She had no name for the stones' colour, but elves would because their eyes must be the same. If Thyra had a more valuable possession then she had very wealthy parents, or she was being rewarded by Eadric well beyond her rank.

"Those stones match my eyes."

They didn't, not really. "So they do."

"She has no right to such a precious thing, and now she pries into my personal affairs."

Fleada didn't see how the two thoughts were connected. "No right? Why?"

"It's too valuable for a woman like her to own. It must be stolen."

"She wears it openly. She doesn't need to keep it hidden."

"I'm not saying she stole it, but someone did. Whoever gave it to her. Or, she did something wicked to earn it. Stuck her beak into other people's affairs, I bet."

"There's no way of knowing."

"I want it."

"I doubt she'd sell it, not even to you. Could you afford it? Unless Eadric bought it, to gift it."

"He won't do that. Not with what Thyra gives him."

What did Thyra give that Eadric might want? Oh. No. Surely not. "You know this? Or are you guessing?"

"I don't know for sure. But – oh, grow up, Fleada. You know it's true, you just don't open your eyes. What people want you to think of them, and what they actually are, are as different as swans and swine."

She remembered Nothman. "Oh," was all she could say.

Fleada thought that Aelfgifu's covetousness would pass with her wine-rich waters, but next day, she revealed her plan for stealing Thyra's brooch. "Obviously she can't be wearing it. So we have to watch for when she's using another. Then you take her a long way away, saying you have something to tell her about me and all the boys I've lain with."

"But you haven't. Have you?"

"No, and you're not to tell her that I have. But you can give her a list of every boy I've met since we were in Jorvik. You remember Taron?"

"Taron was just eight years old!" He'd been one of their playmates in Jorvik, the son of a Bernician thegn.

"Exactly. So nothing could have happened. All the way to Edmund Ironside."

"But there's nothing to tell."

"The point, Fleada, is to keep her occupied for long enough for me to get into her room and find the brooch."

"It's not a good idea." Fleada didn't like it, and didn't want to be involved. She didn't like the way Aelfgifu had become so greedy when soon, as Queen of Denmark, she will surely get all the trinkets she desires.

"If someone sees me, I can say I'm looking for her, to get advice about Knut. She knows the Danes. She speaks Danish."

"What the point? You won't be able to wear the brooch."

"Not here, no. But once I'm married…" Aelfgifu rotated her gold ring through several orbits of her finger, then said "No, you're right, it's not a good idea. If I'm seen going into her room, whatever my reason, and then her brooch goes missing… What if Eadric orders a search of my room and my boxes? And I can't give it to you to hide, because they'd find it even more easily among your few possessions."

How could Aelfgifu even consider asking her to hide a stolen brooch? If found, it would be the end of Fleada's world. She blew out her relief that Aelfgifu was having second thoughts.

"And also," Aelfgifu continued, "she's much more likely to come away with me than with you. So it has to be you who goes into her room."

"No!"

"It makes sense. If someone sees you, it's your belongings that will be searched, and nothing will be found because I'll have it, and they won't search my things."

"But I can't… I can't steal."

"It's not stealing if it's already stolen."

"But what if it isn't? And doesn't it just turn us into more thieves?"

"Not you Fleada. Because you won't be taking it. I will. You'll just be doing the work for me. Like combing my hair."

Aelfgifu had never before asked such work of her. This was not a task she wanted, or even imagined, but to refuse Aelfgifu might put in her a place she'd never been. She didn't know this place, but she was sure it was lonely, cold, and inhospitable; and Nothman lurked there.

"You don't want to, I can tell."

She had disappointed her mistress, and called forth ice in her voice.

"I'll tell you what. After we have it, there will be trouble like maggots in mutton. Then, I shall ask Thyra how she came by the brooch. If it sounds like she came by it honestly, we can return it. We'll let it be found somewhere. If her story is suspicious, then it doesn't rightfully belong to her, so it might as well belong to us."

Us?

Fleada was still trapped between the wintry landscape of

Aelfgifu's disfavour and the fear and guilt of thievery, but her feet were being danced remorselessly towards crime, and she had no power to lead them in another direction.

So it was that she and Aelfgifu watched Thyra to ensure she had not fastened her cloak with her brooch with the bright blue-green stones. Then Fleada followed at a distance, until Aelfgifu caught up with Thyra. The pair talked, and Aelfgifu led Thyra away without a backward glance.

She carried a basket of apples, a small gift of windfalls from the orchard and her pretext for calling on Thyra. Her heart thudded strong and slow as she came to Thyra's room, and sped up as she knocked. She knew there would be no answer, but wished for one so she could give the apples and run. As she opened the door and went inside her heart was pounding like a gleeman's rapping drum.

Thyra had a full feather mattress on an oak bedframe wide enough for two. Wool hangings were nailed to the walls, and the bed was covered by a linen spread embroidered with images of deer and rabbits, horses and some friendly-looking wyverns, framed by posies of flowers. A small table with a pewter candlestick and half-burned tallow candle stood beside the bed, and next to it was Thyra's chest of personal possessions.

Aelfgifu had told her to expect the chest to be locked, and had given her a slim skewer from the kitchen. "You must put it into the slot and fiddle with it to find the lever inside," she said, and then to answer Fleada's unasked question, she added "My father, my real father in Jorvik, used to punish me by taking the key to my chest for a week. It was easier than taking toys and stuff away. I worked out how to open it. You can practice. Hers will not be different."

Fleada hoped that she would fail to open this lock. She could pretend to have failed without even trying, but Aelfgifu had been right – she was a poor liar. The skewer rattled in the slot as her fingers trembled, but she felt the tongue of metal inside, and levered it one way then the other, and felt it give. The hasp dropped open. She lifted the lid and pulled aside linen undersmocks, knitted skirts, and a finely woven black wool overcloak that she wished she had the like of, to reveal a jewellery box three shaftments wide and two deep. It had no lock.

She wanted this over with.

The box held more wealth than Fleada had ever seen. More gold by far than Thyra displayed even at the grandest of feasts; more even than Aelfgifu had. Armbands, torcs and rings. Silver pendants on silver chains, bracelets, and brooches by the dozen. The floor of the box was carpeted knuckle deep with gold and silver coins. The brooch Aelfgifu coveted was not the most valuable object in the box, but it was surely the most beautiful. It was a jewel Thrya could not resist wearing, as if admitting to owning one precious thing while keeping her full hoard hidden from the world.

She did not understand. Surely this treasure should be locked more securely? Did Thyra think it safe, simply because no-one would suspect its existence? Or because no-one would dare steal from someone under Eadric's protection?

Fleada plucked the brooch from the box.

While her thudding heart cried out for her to replace it, shut the boxes and flee, she wrapped it in a cloth from her basket, and placed the bundle under the apples. She listened carefully at the door, hearing men's voices, muffled but nearby. Footsteps passed and faded, then all was quiet.

The most frightening part of all was opening the door without knowing what or who was outside. She feared being seen, but could not stay in the room. She pulled the door a sliver to look out, reminding herself of the excuses she'd make: Aelfgifu sent her to find Thyra; she saw someone lurking suspiciously; found the brooch dropped on a pathway, called to return it but didn't want to leave it unguarded. She would gabble and garble and be known as a liar.

The men had gone. No-one was outside. No-one was near. She skittered as slowly as she was able, but still too fast, to Aelfgifu's room.

When Aelfgifu returned, she examined the brooch like it was a living thing. She kissed it, and held it next to her face saying "Are these stones not the exact colour of my eyes?"

The blue that Aelfgifu always claimed for her eyes was in fact blended with green. The stones too had green, but were milkier. Fleada knew no flower like them, which made the colour all the more desirable, she supposed. "I always thought of elves as having eyes that colour," she said.

"Sweetest Fleada! That's my name! Gift of the Elves!" Aelfgifu kissed her, then the brooch, and slipped it under her pillow like it was a child's toy.

Fleada stayed quiet about Thyra's gold and silver, her ornaments and coins. She should not have this knowledge, did not want it. Aelfgifu might desire another dip into the hoard.

She lay awake all night, waiting for the door to open, for Eadric and Thyra to be stood at the end of Aelfgifu's bed, for Marton to hold a sword at her throat while Terning rummaged through Aelfgifu's boxes to find the brooch. Then what? Say to Eadric "Aelfgifu told me to steal it"? Or protect her mistress, and take sole responsibility herself? What would Aelfgifu say? Would she confess, or lie? She had to ask herself the question many times before allowing herself to accept the answer. Why have a handmaid if you're going to admit to crimes? Being Aelfgifu, she'd say something pretty. "Yes, I told her I loved Thyra's brooch. I never thought she'd be such a silly lamb and steal it for me."

At best, she'd get a flogging. At worst, she'd be birched to within a heartbeat of her life and sent back in shame to her family in Osbaldwick. No, at worst, she'd be hung.

Night was at its darkest when Fleada, crying silently, slipped her hand beneath the pillow supporting Aelfgifu's head. Her fingertips crawled like worms under a rock, touched warm metal, and slid on past, until she was able to bend them around the brooch. Slowly, gently, she eased it free until she could clasp it in both hands to her breast. She held herself rigid, more scared of Aelfgifu waking even than she'd been in Thyra's room.

She didn't know what she'd do when she got there, but she knew she had to go. With a shawl around her against the night air, she stumbled to Thyra's, and stood outside the door. Still not knowing what she'd say, she knocked tentatively. It was too faint a knock to awaken anyone sleeping inside.

She'd gone in once. She'd go in again. No. She'd open the door, push her arm in, place the brooch just inside the door, and retreat. If Thyra woke and saw her, she'd say she found it. She'd say she hadn't dared bring it openly because people might think she stole it. It was a weak story, true, but the point was, she was returning it, and the feeble lie might just save the skin of her back. All she had to do was open the door, slip the brooch inside, and close it again.

She'd face Aelfgifu in the morning, and if her mistress sent her back to Osbaldwick, she'd go with Jesus at her side.

She turned the latch carefully, and pushed the door open. She listened to Thyra's breathing, for any movement from the bed. All was silent. The air was still, cold, and dry. No-one slept here tonight. She crept inside, and closed the door. Now, return the brooch to its box, and the whole crime never happened. She crawled forward in the dark.

Shit! She almost said it out loud. She didn't have the skewer to pick the lock.

No matter. The brooch could go under the pillow. Thyra would think she'd gone mad, or blame the cofgodes and the imps.

Fleada groped her way to the bed.

A man's voice came from beyond the door, distant but speaking boldly as if he owned Coventre, because he did. "Ah, it had been too long," Eadric was saying. "And then we had not long enough."

"Shh." A woman's voice, and not his wife's.

"Pah," he said, and whatever came next was lost as Fleada scrambled to the only hiding place on offer, under the bed. She curled up as far from the door as she could, holding the brooch, wishing she'd had the presence of mind to shove it under the pillow before she slid under the bed. Was it too late?

It was. The door opened, and closed. Dim candlelight washed the floor, and two pairs of feet came to stand next to the bed, Eadric's either side of Thyra's. They were embracing. Please God, let Eadric be satisfied with their time elsewhere.

Thyra was on Fleada's side. "Now I need to sleep," she said softly. "You have exhausted me."

"I don't believe you, dokkse" he said. "The world knows that a woman in her prime will outfuck a man in his, and I'm not even the youth I once was."

"Spare me youths!"

"I don't know if you keep me young or drag me exhausted towards my grave. I confess, I don't care."

"You are like holly. You do not fade in winter, and your prick is sharp. Now I bid you goodnight. Or good morning, as it appears to be."

Eadric's feet turned, but did not step towards the door. His heels looked at Fleada like dark eyes, and the bed creaked as he sat on it. "One thing I want to ask you," he said. "Your views on young Leofric."

"Now?"

"Yes, now." Eadric was lord again, not lover. "He is intelligent. A thinker, and canny with it. He reveals little."

"True. I see him thinking, but there is no telling his thoughts."

"My concern is whether he's just a thinker, or whether he's more. Does he consider all the tunnels in the rabbit warren of events, so much so that he never chooses one? Still less gouge a new tunnel for himself."

"He is young still."

"When he matures? Will he be decisive? What's your intuition?"

Thyra was silent for a while, and Fleada held her breath, hoping she'd speak soon.

"At the moment he is careful. He walks under three shadows. His father's-"

"Ledwyn will soon be gone. I doubt he'll make two more winters."

"His brother's. Leofric knows he would make a better Ealdorman than Nothman, but he knows too that Nothman is the stronger warrior."

"An army of fighters will not beat an army led by a good commander. A good commander won't do battle with 'em."

"Then I'm sure Leofric would make the better commander. And he's also under your shadow. I think he watches you, and learns."

"Good."

"Why do you ask?"

"I have no heir. Brihtric? Well, my brother I hold in great esteem. I rank him alongside the greatest in the land, the equal of our noble King, no less."

Thyra spluttered laughter, and Eadric chuckled.

The brooch was forgotten as thoughts eddied in Fleada's head. If Eadric insulting his own brother was surprising, his lack of respect for King Aethelred was shocking. Was it treasonous?

"You are wondering if Leofric is the best candidate to be Ealdorman of Mercia when you are gone."

"Not when I'm gone, my dearest Thyra. When I myself am King."

Beyond doubt, this was treasonous. Fleada knew her peril was now tied to something far more dangerous than the brooch.

"My judgement," Thyra said, "is that when his father dies, Leofric will grow. But his brother is overbearing and – what is the word? – precipitate. Leofric will only reach his potential as a leader if he can free himself from his brother's shadow."

"Or be freed," Eadric said. "Thank you, my dove, my hawk who sees all. If you were a man, Leofric and all the Hwicce could go hang, and I'd make you the next Ealdor. But then I wouldn't be able to fuck you."

"It seems I'm fucked, then."

Eadric laughed, but Fleada thought that Thyra spoke more heavily than a joke required.

"So thoroughly fucked," she added, "that I need to sleep."

"We both do. It's a long journey to Lunden." He kissed her. "Thank you. For the fuck, and for the advice. You're a better wife than the one I had to marry."

"So you tell me." She kissed him back.

The bed creaked once more as he rose. His feet stepped to the door, and he left with no further word.

Thyra sighed, and paced around the room. Fleada waited for her to disrobe and get to her bed. It was very late, and Fleada hoped she'd sleep soon, and deeply, to let her crawl silently to the door leaving the brooch just under the bed, to escape before anyone is up and about.

Thyra sat on the mattress. From her movements, Fleada thought she loosened her hair but did not take off so much as a shawl. Thyra stood again, and paced the room. Please,

please, Fleada thought, please go to bed. You said yourself how tired you are.

Thyra blew out her candle, but remained seated on the edge of the bed. The moon's shadow through the window crawled over the floor.

Tap-tap. Tap-tap-tap. The door opened before Thyra said anything. She remained silent as someone entered. Sandalled feet came into view, and the rough and frayed hem of a dark robe. A priest.

"Father," she said by way of greeting."

"Thyra," the priest replied, and his voice was gentle, his accent comforting, at least to Fleada. For it would not have sounded out of place in Osbaldwick, her home village. He was surely born within walking distance of Jorvik. "Well," he said. "Anything?"

"What my bones told me was right. He wants Leofric as his heir for Mercia."

"My lord will be interested in that."

"But not shocked." Thyra said. "I hope he appreciates the confirmation."

"I'm sure it will please as well as tickle him."

An older man may have a younger voice, but Fleada considered it rare for a young man to have an old voice. Fleada guessed that the priest was middle-aged.

His comment seemed to puzzle Thyra. "Tickle him? Why?"

"I thought you knew. If you don't, I fear I shouldn't tell you."

"Father, you stopped protecting me when you placed me here years ago." Thyra's voice was a crushing millstone, then the stone was lifted. "Tell me, and I will give you more news, and your reward will be greater when you pass it on."

The priest did not to ponder. "Leofric has made his own contact. It seems to me that he is preparing for a time when Eadric is no longer his mentor, guardian and Ealdorman."

Thyra snorted a laugh that she might have learned from Eadric himself. "Hah! The rabbit does dig his own tunnel. I wish I'd known earlier. Not that I'd have told Eadric, but I like the tickle too."

"You have something else for me?"

"Two things," Thyra said. "One, Lady Eadgyth has been fucking one of your brothers."

"Is this your bones talking, or do you know for sure."

"My bones spoke. My ears heard. My eyes searched. He's a young priest from East Anglia by the name of Stigand. Do you know him?"

"No. But I can't say I don't envy him."

"Father, please keep your envy under your robe. I don't wish to know."

There was something about the way she spoke, at once respectful and familiar.

"Of greater weight is this: Eadric's wish to be King of England is no spring breeze. He is making plans. I don't know what they are, but…"

"When you find out…"

"Yes, when I find out… Now, best leave, because it will soon be light. You have a long ride ahead."

"I do. I'll probably still be there when… Will you be in the party?"

"Yes. So take care not to be seen with me."

The priest's sandalled feet took no step towards the door.

"Go!" Thyra ordered.

Still no step, just a shifting of his weight. "You know, it is both dandelion and honey seeing you like this."

"You placed me here."

"If I'd known how scarce and brief our times together…"

Thyra rose. "Father…" Her feet were either side of his. They were embracing. "One day we shall have a cottage together."

Were they lovers, Thyra and this old man? The priest stepped away from her. "Find a husband who will tolerate me, then."

Such a strange thing to say.

The priest left, and Thyra at last disrobed and got into the bed.

Fleada resolved to stay hidden until her breathing was deep and steady. While she waited she had an inkling that swelled into suspicion that sprouted into certainty. "Find a husband who will tolerate me." The priest was not just any Father. He was Thyra's father.

She tried to put together everything she'd heard. Eadric's ambition was a shock – she didn't believe it was possible for anyone who wasn't a Prince, anyone indeed who wasn't Edmund Ironside, to aspire to the throne. It was like aspiring to be God.

Then there were Eadric's and Eadgyth's adulteries. She remembered Stigand from the feast in Lunden. But who exactly was this priest carrying messages for Thyra, and who the lord to whom he rode? Prince Edmund? The King himself?

She squeezed the brooch tighter, thinking that Aelfgifu's self-serving suspicion was actually not so far wrong. The brooch and all Thyra's wealth were not stolen, but must be payments for a greater crime, treachery. That was the reason she couldn't flaunt it.

Aelfgifu could now keep the brooch, and tell Thyra not to speak of its loss, or Eadric would be told what she'd just heard.

No no. That was a game Fleada could only lose. Her instinct was to hoard this knowledge like Thrya hoarded her treasures, to speak it only when she needed. She must not even tell Aelfgifu, for all that the information might divert her wrath at Fleada for returning the brooch. There was no guessing how recklessly her mistress might play with the honed blade of these secrets.

She left the brooch under the bed.

Dawn ascended as Fleada wandered the crooked streets of Coventre. Low sunbeams shone on her between the wooden buildings, as warm as the relief that she'd not have to bear a thief's guilt, or fear of discovery. Those weights would have stayed on her, while Aelfgifu's anger at losing the brooch will pass. She'd surely not send her to Osbaldwick. Fleada felt too that her righteousness had been rewarded. Ah, it wasn't righteousness, it was merely a wrong redeemed. But still rewarded. It didn't matter how dangerous this secret, or what she did with it, just having the knowledge made her feel stronger. She went to the dyer and hammered her fist on his door.

When he came, rubbing his eyes, she interrupted his complaints at the noise and the early hour. "You have madder dye, I know you do. Or you can get it. My mistress will pay an eleventh finger on top of ten, but no more. And if you do not quickly have bright red cloth, Lord Eadric will hear, and I tell you this, he is fonder of Lady Aelfgifu than he will ever be of you."

She returned with head held high, armed with the dyer's promise of fresh crimson wool by the week's end, for a new red kirtle to divert Aelfgifu's ire.

6. The Jomsvikingr

(Eadric)

"He seems angry all of a sudden"

He rode with Thyra, Criba, and four dozen ceorls. The horses meant they couldn't go by way of Oxenford and the Tamys; but at least he could arrange good accommodations at Northamtun. Save Marton, none of the ceorls had travelled with him to Caestrfeld, for he had no need of tired men who wanted to tend to their hides, see their children, and fuck their wives or whoever they fucked.

The King hadn't needed to say why he wanted Eadric in the south. It wasn't to fight, so once more he needed sufficient men to command respect, yet not so many as to threaten. It was a narrow strait to navigate, but as intermediary between the English and the Danish Kings, he was getting used to it. He would again be precisely where he wished to be: at the very centre of events.

But events had never before been a massive invasion force, and the centre had never been occupied by anyone with the reputation of this legendary chieftain, this Jarl.

He went to Thyra's room, and after a brief but welcome use of her pleasingly warm sheith, revealed the true purpose of his visit. "Thorkell," he said. "Is he as tall as they say? Have you ever seen him?"

"I haven't seen him," she replied, looking up from her task of wiping the cream he had thoughtfully deposited onto her stomach. "But I know some who have, who say the descriptions are true. Outside Jomsborg, there is no doorway that he need not stoop to pass through. When he travels he takes his own bed. His wife must stand on a table to kiss him. Unless she's kissing his lem, when she does not need to bend." She threw the cloth to the floor and lay back on her pillow.

"And those people you know who've seen him, they've also watched his wife kiss his staff?"

"No. They've kissed it themselves."

Sometimes he wondered how reliable Thyra's tales were. "To be honest, I'm more concerned with how he kisses Sveyn's."

"I doubt he does."

"You know what I mean."

"I do. And as I say, I doubt he does. He's one of the few Danish lords that Sveyn respects, and the only one he fears. Or so people say. Sveyn owes Thorkell for taming the Wends."

"You speak as if I'm supposed to know who or what the bloody Wends are!"

"Bloody is the word. A barbaric people, not a single tribe. They came from dry and stony lands far to the south, and recently moved into the eastern parts of Sveyn's realm."

"If Sveyn fears Thorkell, why did he entrust Knut's military training to him? Why did Knut live at Jomsborg? He handed this man a perfect hostage."

"Yet Knut was safe. So his trust was repaid. Perhaps he wanted to give Knut the chance to make a friend of Thorkell. He will need allies in his life."

That made sense, Eadric thought. He decided that it was in his interest to make a friend of Thorkell too. He could always make an enemy of him later.

"Or perhaps he just wanted Knut to learn how to build a stronghold," Thyra concluded.

"And your views on Thorkell's arrival in Cantware? Is it at Sveyn's command, or with his knowledge?"

"I doubt Thorkell would come unbidden, and risk making

an enemy of his King. And so many ships… that took much preparation. Sveyn will have people in Jomsborg who would get word to him. They've probably agreed how to share the spoils."

Eadric put one arm around her shoulders, and with his free hand he squeezed her tit affectionately, thinking how astute his dokkse was. "Thorkell cowed those Wends, and Sveyn's reward is an invitation to bugger Cantware. He'll return to Jomsborg with silver enough to sink his ships."

They entered a febrile and frightened Lunden, whose streets were thinned of people. Eadric ensured his men were fed and sheltered, and sought out Wilmaer before meeting the King. He asked why Lunden was not in celebratory mood after the great victory at Tilberh?

"We are infested with rumour," the Reeve explained. "Queen Emma prepares to leave, and not to Wintancaestr but to Suthamton. Many people believe she is on her way to Normandy. If she wants to flee, why should anyone feel safe? They see Tilberh not as a victory, but as a portent of greater threats to come.

If he'd been King, he would not let her go. It didn't help that Edmund had departed west too, not in flight, but to muster a fyrd, which was barely more reassuring to Lundeners. They worshipped Edmund, and felt safer seeing their Prince here with a handful of men than watching him go elsewhere to muster thousands.

Not that the people matter.

Three days later Eadric was riding down the Watling Street with Thyra on one side and Marton on the other, in the midst of eighty ceorls. His own trusted men surrounded him; the King's ceorls formed the van and rearguards.

His mission had not surprised or shocked him. He'd known it was needed, and knew too that he was the man to undertake it. Not Brihtric, who had no wiles. Not Edmund, who would refuse. He was going to talk terms, to negotiate, and there was no-one better in the land to gain a reasonable settlement for the King. Thirty-six thousand he'd paid once, after Saint Brice's Day. But then, the Danish storm had been both wider and fiercer, while this time they had suffered an unexpected loss at the first confrontation. With the ten thousand so recently paid, Aethelred must be reckoning on having to extract from his coffers or his people another twenty. Thirty at most.

He'd been concerned at the King's reaction to Aelfgifu's betrothal to Knut. How strangely things turn out! Far from being worried, angered or insulted at the news, Aethelred was almost enthusiastic about it, saying that it wouldn't do any harm to his dealings with Thorkell. He seemed to see Aelfgifu as unimportant, and the marriage offer as a form of gafol, so Eadric basted the roast by describing how Thorkell was like an uncle to Knut, and Aethelred slapped his shoulder. He was glad Queen Emma wasn't around to cast her cold eye over the arrangement.

Eadric doubted that his new status with regard to Knut would do anything to soften Thorkell's mercenary ambitions, but still, the forthcoming negotiation held few worries for Eadric. So as he rode, he had time to reflect on the timing of Thorkell's invasion.

The failed attack was a diversion designed to ensure that the men not already on Brihtric's ships were drawn back to defend Lunden. Forty Danish longships were lost, but Thorkell had landed unopposed at Sanwic with two hundred ships, if the accounts travelling up Watling Street were not exaggerated. Two thousand and more Danes marched as they pleased from Sanwic's beaches, and Cantware was unable to resist. Village after village surrendered, thegn after thegn bowed before Thorkell and his commanders. The Danes took fewer lives than they might have, but more slaves, and all wealth was stripped. High Reeve Hlothar had reported that Cantenberh paid three thousand pounds from its fat treasury, Hrofcaestr five hundred, Meddestane a thousand. Asheford, Dofras, Cranbroka, all had emptied their coffers. Add the gafol that King Aethelred was resigned to paying once more…

When they spoke, the King had clearly thought that Thorkell's aim was to sweep up all the silver in the south. Eadric was not so sure. Undoubtedly Sveyn used Viking terror to suck on the rich milk of the Saxon tit. Whose silver paid the men who held Norway for him, and fattened the Jarls of Denmark? But what troubled Eadric was that Thorkell had come with his mighty fleet within a week of Sveyn receiving the niggardly gafol payment in Caestrfeld.

Whether he'd sailed from Denmark or Flandra, or all the way around Jutland from his Jomsborg havens was not the point. Two, three, or seven days' voyage, that could be done. But for Thorkell to muster all those ships, to get the men, their arms and their food on board, to plan the landings, the communications and chains of command for the spread of men across Cantware, and still leave Jomsborg defended – this was work of months. It had taken Brihtric weeks just to plan his fleet's move from Sanwic to Tilberh, and they were already gathered and crewed.

Which meant that it was as Thyra had guessed, that Thorkell had been ready to sail. The invasion was plotted and planned before Aethelred's insult to Sveyn.

Thus, it was about more than the gafol. It was about fatally weakening England. The question was not whether, but when Danes would fall on Lunden, and who would hold the axes: Thorkell's heathens marching north from

Cantware, or Sveyn's marching south from the Five Berhs?

Or both. Were they communicating by fast ships sailing from Sanwic to Seletun or Jorvik itself?

Eadric had little care for Cantware, nor for Lunden. He did worry that Thorkell could create a permananet base, for it was no part of Eadric's strategy that Sveyn have a strong Jarl in England. Pay him off and wave goodbye; on this Eadric and the King were agreed.

They were met at Cantware's gates by drunken Danish guards, whose leader said "You maggots had best be Eadric the famous Grasper and his followers, 'cause anyone else with swords, once they come through these gates, they won't be going back out." His English was good, too good to be one of Thorkell's men from Jomsberg. Sveyn's men were here too, then, sailed from the north. More planning in evidence.

The chief of guards called for "The Cristin", and within seconds a young priest appeared. Eadric was surprised to recognise Father Stigand, Ealdorman Ulfcytel's cleric from East Anglia, who had travelled to the Witan with him then suddenly disappeared.

"Is it him?" the guard asked.

Stigand said "It is," and announced "Eadric, Ealdorman of Mercia. Good day, lord."

The guards would not allow eighty men into Cantenberh, and Eadric had to proceed in a troop of three, with Marton and Thyra. Stigand walked alongside as if he was needed to guide them through the random layout of huts and halls to the cathedral. They could have found their own way, for the pyramidal roof topping the tower stood high over the town.

If Lundeners had been living as if about to be stripped and marched down an avenue of brutes who would beat them bloody with flails and clubs, the folk of Cantenberh were like survivors of that ordeal who'd been told they had to go back the same way. They cowered, and looked at Eadric not as a silver-laden saviour but as an omen of more pain to come.

"I had not expected to see you here," Eadric said to Stigand.

"Thorkell insisted that someone be at the gate who knows your face. He worried that the King might send a blademan in your stead. Apart from the Archbishop, it seems I was the only person in this city privileged to have met you before."

"And I am not a blademan?"

Stigand looked up at him. "You wield no knife. The rest is between yourself and God. What is between a King and his Ealdorman I am not privileged to know either, but it is inconceivable that Aethelred would give you such a task, or that you would accept."

No, but Marton has hands as strong as any man, even a giant from Jomsborg. And Thyra is as deft with a blade as any woman with a needle. These were not facts Stigand needed to know. Eadric suspected Stigand was less a servant of God than he was of Ulfcytel, and less a servant of Ulfcytel than of himself. Not that this mattered greatly. Eadric's mission involved neither blades nor hands, just tongues. "I meant that I did not expect to see you in Cantenberh," he said.

"Ealdorman Ulfcytel was pleased with what I brought to him from Mercia and Lunden," Stigand explained. "He wanted to learn what he might of affairs in the south-east, so he sent me here. It was in part a reward, for what priest would not pray for a chance to be in Cantenberh, to worship under the Archbishop?"

"And mingle with cardinals, and hope to come to the attention of said Archbishop. As you seem to have done with alacrity."

"You suggest I have got more advantage from the reward than my lord expected. I say being trapped in a cathedral overtaken by a thousand greedy, pitiless heathens is not a boon I would choose. Our friends from the north, even the unbaptised, live peacably amongst Christians. But most of these Jomsborgr hate the Church. What's worse, they act like they've never drunk ale before. Trapped I am, and they will not let me out. They know my face so I cannot even disguise myself as a ceorl or a beggar."

"It could be worse," said Eadric.

"How could it be worse?"

"You could be the Archbishop."

The Cathedral, the seat of the Pope's anointed representative in England, stood solid in Cantenberh's centre on elevated land above the river. The largest church in England glowed yellow in the evening sun, its sandstone walls like cliffs that would stand for centuries.

"If you follow me this way, we will come to the Archbishop's hall." Stigand led them around the south side, under walls that threw back the sun's warmth like God's benevolence. Eadric doubted the heathens would feel the symbolism. Fifty, sixty yards the building stretched, to the eastern chancel and the Archbishop's Great Hall. This was as wide as the cathedral, and near half the length, with its apex of a height with the cathedral nave. They entered a smaller assembly hall, still large enough to sit a hundred priests, its walls hung with tapestries and, above them, gold angels, silver crucifixes, and painted saints. Eadric wondered what treasure was on display within the church itself, and why this place had not been ransacked.

Stigand led them between rows of oak benches polished by a thousand holy arses, then through a heavy door into a smaller chamber, where he invited them to sit on cushioned chairs. There were eight set out, the three they sat on, which faced two pairs flanking a large oak throne crested by a carving of seraphim and cherubim, gilded in gold.

He left them and went through a further door that was guarded by two large monks. They wore habits, but Eadric had little doubt there were blades hidden in the folds. Before the door closed he glimpsed more monks beyond, in what Eadric assumed were the Archbishop's personal living quarters. He resolved to build like this in Coventre, or in Lyccidfield, or better, in both. To have a cathedral, a great hall, an assembly room, an audience chamber to receive his more important visitors, as well as personal rooms for eating and sleeping… this was civilised. A Roman Emperor would not have been ashamed.

They waited several minutes before the far door reopened. Stigand returned with Reeve Hlothar and a cleric, introduced as Cardinal Elfmar, head of Saint Augustine's Abbey that stood alongside the Cathedral. They were followed by Archbishop Aelfheah himself, stooping as he walked slowly towards his throne.

An unobservant man, or a heathen, would have placed Elfmar as the senior churchman, for Elfmar was dressed in finery with a richly embroidered chasuble glinting with gold thread, worn over a surplice as white as lye could bleach, with gold chains around his neck, heavy rings on his fingers, and soft kidskin boots on his feet.

Aelfheah, by contrast, was dressed as ever in his habit and sandals, and might have been mistaken for an old monastic retainer. The brass chain around his neck and the simple gold ring in the third finger of his right hand offered clues, but a man would have had to guess that the chain tucked inside the habit held the Archbishop's seal; and the gold band was the episcopal emerald ring turned on his finger so the jewel was palmed. Gold would be plenty for a greedy Dane, and Eadric thought that Aelfheah had better look out for that finger.

The Archbishop was old, but Eadric respected his abilities. The holy man was as good a schemer as any: he'd immediately seen the sense in their pact back at the last Witan. For years he had kept in check those with ambitions to succeed him, favouring no priest above another, sending any who had too much influence away from Cantenberh before they could build alliances to present credible opposition, then calling them back before they made too many friends in other sees.

All except for Elfmar, who had been his loyal cardinal ever since Aelfheah had saved his life in Wintancaestr, Aelfheah's previous see. He'd been Bishop there when Sveyn attacked in his anger after Saint Brice's Day, and the story was told that Aelfheah had personally offered his life that bloody day to save Elfmar. A Danish chieftain said he'd rather have Aelfheah's gold and silver than two worthless heads, and that was what he got. Having witnessed the carnage visited upon Wintancaestre, it was little wonder that Aelfheah had led the surrender of Cantenberh, and gathered the three thousand pounds of treasure with which to buy Danish mercy.

The Archbishop had age and a throne on his side, not to mention the Pope, but Eadric wanted there to be no doubt as to who was the power in this room. After kissing the ring, he declined to resume his seat and refrained from responding the Aelfheah's polite "It is good to see you again, Ealdorman Eadric, even in such trying circumstances. How are you?"

Instead, he wondered behind the chair and grasped the twin bosses carved as angels. "Have you met Thorkell?" he demanded. "What do you know about him? Have you had any message from him? Who received the payment Cantenberh made?

Instead of answering, Aelfheah held up his hand for silence.

"How many Danes landed at Sanwic?" Eadric added.

The Archbishop's eyes were closed, and his lips were held in a gentle smile that Eadric found intensely annoying. He dared not think what Thorkell might make of it.

Aelfheah opened his eyes. "I was offering a small prayer for Thorkell, that the Lord might grant him wisdom and mercy."

"The King's fortune will probably carry more weight. But I am not here to throw coins into the sky for him, I'm here to bargain, so I need to know who I deal with and what his strength is." He spoke angrily, as if his own money was at stake.

Reeve Hlothar cleared his throat. "Thorkell's numbers are not my Grace's concern," he said. "We are told there are four hundred in or around Cantenberh. The rest are spread across Cantware scire, and I hear they are working their way west. But we know little."

"Your Grace, if I may," said Stigand, and on Aelfheah's nod he turned to Eadric. "I have gathered what information I can. Thorkell sent one army along the south coast, and a larger one along the north. A third force departed here yesterday, and I can only assume it is to ravage the Weald." He gave Eadric a moment to digest this before continuing. "Some three hundred have taken people's homes here in Cantenberh, and one hundred are left in the camp at Littleburne, three miles east on the Abbey's vineyard. There will be no wine made next year. A large number remained with the ships at Sanwic. Thorkell may be mindful that the ships at Tilberh could be sent to attack there."

"My brother is not stupid enough to destroy the only means the Danes have of getting home. And I'd be surprised if Thorkell is stupid enough to think he is."

"I agree. Nevertheless, he has split his force into five, and if my summing is close, he came with near three thousand men, of which he lost a fifth or a sixth part at Tilberh."

Again, Stigand impressed Eadric. The Archbishop seemed concerned only with matters spiritual. Reeve Hlothar knew much about money but little about war. But this minor priest had drawn to himself the vital knowledge Eadric needed.

"So you have answered my last question. What about the others?" Eadric looked at Aelfheah and Hlothar. "You haven't met Thorkell, have you. Do you know where he is?"

"I should like to meet him," said Aelfheah. "It is said he speaks passable English. Which speaks of intelligence."

Eadric thought it spoke of long-laid plans.

"His location is unknown," said Hlothar.

"I would wager that he is in the Littleburne camp," said Stigand.

"A cleric who would gamble, Father Stigand?" This priest had a talent for being less than holy, yet placing himself close to Bishops and Ealdors. Including myself, Eadric thought. "Is there an intermediary?"

"A man named Vrangr," said Hlothar. "A Jarl under Thorkell.

"He styles himself 'The Crossbreaker'," added Elfmar. "I suspect he only adopted this the day he landed in a Christian land, but it strikes fear into people's hearts. And, I suppose, amuses his comrades."

"It was he who received our money, our silver, our jewels and gold, that we valued at three thousand pounds," said Hlothar.

"It is you who talks to this Vrangr?"

"I go, to represent the King," Hlothar said.

"And I, to represent the church," Stigand added.

"Then, Stigand, you shall go and tell him that Eadric of Mercia is now here to represent the King-"

"But I am-" Hlothar started.

Eadric spoke over him. "And I will see him at noon tomorrow. Your Grace, may we have use of your hall?"

Aelfheah granted his request with a nod.

"So tell me about this Vrangr."

"'The Crossbreaker' may be a recent name, but he does not like Christians," said Elfmar.

Stigand confirmed this. "I feared for my life every time he looked at me."

"Are you still here?" Eadric's voice cut Stigand's brash self-importance. "I thought I told you to take a message to this Vrangr Crossbreaker."

Stigand bowed, and left.

Elfmar cleared his throat, and resumed. "He crucified twelve good folk, even when we had promised money. Father Stigand said that he does not like us. No, he hates us, with the cruelty of a demon."

Cruel? Eadric saw the sense in Vrangr's action. The fear it won probably saved scores of his men's lives, and therefore saved many more Christians too.

"It was the cruelty of a warrior chief," Aelfheah admonished. "And he will burn for it. But his desire is gold. He is driven by greed. He only pretends to hate Christians."

"It seems he puts on a good show," Eadric said. "You may be over-charitable in your assessment."

"I'm not."

"Why do you say that?"

"Because when the moneys were paid for Cantenberh's safety, his overlord sent a message asking if he might pray with me. Thorkell is a Christian."

Stigand later returned with a counter-message. The King's representative was commanded by Thorkell himself to come to Littleburne two hours prior to noon. It was small surprise that Thorkell should set the place and the time, and surely he'd make them wait until noon and longer. It was exactly what Eadric would have done, but it was a childish game. King Sveyn himself didn't bother with it any more.

He considered who to have sitting with him. Wilmaer, of course, or there was no point bringing him from Lunden. Marton, because of his size, and Thyra with her insight into the Dane, though neither would speak. Thyra would be introduced as a Saxon, and would report any Danish whispers that Eadric could not understand. He had thought not to take any cleric, especially if Vrangr might be present, but if Thorkell was converted, a priest might be a good idea. Not Archbishop Aelfheah, who was too holy. Not Elfmar, because Eadric had no sense of his mind or what he might say if provoked. So Stigand it would have to be. The man was plainly as sharp as a crow, and unlikely to speak out of turn, and not high enough in the church to threaten either Vrangr the heathen or Thorkell the convert. Bloody Stigand, he had a knack for being useful.

The five who were to meet Thorkell rode to Littleburne at the head of two dozen Mercian husceorls. Eadric drew out what little else Stigand knew about Thorkell: that he became head of the Jomsborg warrior clan after his brother died when they fought alongside Sveyn in Norway. So he'd been close to Sveyn for many years. And young Knut had spent time learning the arts of war under Thorkell.

"Does he have children?"

"Two boys."

"No daughters?"

Stigand's face betrayed his ignorance, and his annoyance at himself for it. "I haven't heard of a daughter, but I can't be sure. Is it relevant?"

Eadric didn't answer, but left Stigand to sharpen up under his own stone.

The husceorls were left a quarter mile short of the

encampment with instructions not to be drawn into any fighting. Eadric did not fear for himself. Thorkell wanted gold and silver, so killing the man who offered it would be senseless, and would not please Sveyn. The King's Reeve was equally safe, as was Marton. Thyra was at risk if it was realised that she was Danish, so she would be Rowen for now. Eadric had to concede that Stigand was the bravest of the five, given Vrangr's self-generated reputation.

They were taken to a tent decked with furs and rugs, and told to leave their weapons outside. They were made to wait a full hour.

Eadric was prepared to be confronted by a big man, but when Thorkell arrived he had to conceal his surprise, for Thorkell was truly a giant. Marton stood tall as the proudest horse's eye, and Thorkell overtopped him by a good handspan, even after he removed his helm. He had the build of a horse too, and the movement. And come to that, the face.

His eyes surveyed them, and did not blink as they moved from one to the other. "Noble lord Eadric of Mercia," he said. His voice was strongly accented, a different accent to Sveyn's. "Welcome to my home." He gestured around the tent, and even to the encampment visible beyond the doorflap.

Eadric merely nodded, knowing better than to be drawn by this insult.

Thorkell introduced Vrangr, who stood with arms folded. If Thorkell was a horse, Vrangr was a boar, with a chest like an oak log and eyes so narrow it was hard to tell that they were open. A boar who spoke English, and growled "I am called Crossbreaker." The two others were Vindr, the skald who would recall for Thorkell the details of the talk and the settlement, and a young Jarl, Manne. None of the four bore arms, but three nameless Vikingr stood behind with hands resting lightly on their sword hilts and axes looped onto their belts.

Eadric introduced Wilmaer. "Reeve to King Aethelred, and closer to the treasury than I. Marton, my huscoerl. Rowen, who serves me as Vindr serves you. And Bother Stigand, who I believe has already befriended Vrangr."

The boar's eyes narrowed further. Perhaps he truly did hate Christians. English ones.

Thorkell smiled, showing his horse teeth. "Sveyn, King of the Danish and the Norse and the Sveor, known as Forkbeard, has told me much about you."

"None of it good, I hope," Eadric said, and Thorkell's smile turned to a laugh. "Perhaps you have seen him more recently than I? For I was welcomed to his home in the town of Caestrfeld in Northumbria – and it had thicker walls than this – just some three weeks ago."

"I have not been so privileged. Far away is my home, and Sveyn has not been there this year. But messengers are in constant travel across the West Sea."

"Then they will have told you the King's good news. Your King, I mean, not mine."

"There is rarely bad news from England. Which good news do you mean?"

"Why, his son's betrothal. Surely there is none better?"

Thorkell hesitated enough that he could not pretend he knew this. "Good news indeed. Though it seems strange to be told this by an Englishman. So who is to be my next queen?"

Stigand had been unable to say for sure that Thorkell had no daughter. If he did, and if he harboured ambitions for her to be Knut's wife, then Eadric had just thrown dice and risked an unnecessary mis-step. Thorkell's reaction did not seem to be one of disappointment so he pressed on. "My own Goddaughter," Eadric said. "Her name is Aelfgifu. She is very dear to me." He waited for Thorkell to digest the full import of this and see that this might make them, if not allies, at least no longer bloody foes. "I am sure Prince Knut is a worthy husband for a Christian girl."

Behind Thorkell, Vrangr gripped his belt as if his hand wanted an axe to grasp.

Thorkell nodded. "Knut was with me from the year of his chin's first wisp of hair until his beard was thick enough to tie like his father's."

"And I saw him take your Jesus water on his head," Vrangr growled. "For a name that isn't his."

Thorkell laughed without looking at him. "Vrangr thinks Sveyn betrayed his old gods by consenting. He thinks I betrayed them too. I tell him that the gods can look after themselves. And I pray at least one will watch over Knut and…"

"Aelfgifu."

"And Aelfgifu. Knut used to call me 'uncle'. And he is to marry your god-daughter. That makes us brothers, after a fashion, Eadric of Mercia." Thorkell shook his head in wonder at how things turn out.

The dice had fallen for Eadric. He threw again. "You could look at it that way. I have a real brother, of course. Brihtric. Who commanded the King's fleet on the Tamys. But let us not talk of that."

He was being provocative, but not a ripple passed Thorkell's face. "No, let us talk of it," he said. "My commander sailed into a trap, or so it seems from the accounts of those who returned. Sveyn told me of your craft and cunning, Eadric, but he didn't warn me about your brother's."

"It was not a subtle trap," Eadric said. But too subtle to have been Brihtric's idea, of that Eadric was sure. "Your commander must have been a fool, whoever he was."

"Was?" Vrangr's chin was set hard as a brick, making him even more boar-like.

"Was. I fear Brihtric was lured by wine and ale into the fleeting glory of placing one more head on a pole at Tilberh."

Vrangr's body began to tremble.

"I know, it was uncivilised. And worse, stupid."

"He was killed?" Vrangr was suppressing a roar, clearly outraged at such dishonourable conduct of war.

Eadric shrugged. "King Aethelred was not best pleased, and my brother might have to meet his ransom value from his own coffers. He'd probably count it worth the price."

"Your brother?" It was as if Vrangr was incapable of taking in anything not spelled out in plain words. Perhaps he was having trouble understanding English.

"Yes. He was killed by my brother's own hand. Not so cunning. Had I been there I would have urged the more sensible option of holding him for ransom."

Vrangr was now red-faced and sweating. "You are sure it was the leader of our ships?"

Eadric paused. "He did not deny it. He named himself. Kjell Ormsson. Was he your leader?"

Thorkell suddenly snapped "Vrangr! Leave!"

Vrangr stared like a bull about to charge, before turning to pound his way out under the tentflap he'd come in by. There came the sound of movement and metal, and for a moment Eadric thought he was going to re-enter sword in hand. He felt Marton tense behind him, and even Thorkell turned his head.

Feet stomped away.

"He seems angry all of a sudden," said Eadric.

Thorkell turned back to face him. "You just told Vrangr Ormsson that your brother executed his brother."

Eadric was silent for as long as he could be, before one word emerged. "Fuck."

7. Stamsford

(Walt)

"You going to do battle with that?'

Walt walked in rags. In the morning the sun had risen clear behind him, and in the evening, though the sunset was obscured, the rain in his face told him he was still going west. Just before dark it covered his noise as he went into a farmstead and stole an egg, then quietly milked a goat into his own mouth.

It might have been judged bold, but for his complete indifference as to whether he'd be caught or not. Having lost all he ever had, family, home and possessions, what difference would it make to lose a hand? Or to be hung on the judgement of some Ealdorman? He had wanted to kill Petwin and Gro, and now he wanted to kill Elfhelm. He'd get hanged like his father, but Walt would earn his hanging fair.

At least it would end the earache that, without Trud's potion, again filled the side of his head with pain.

He came to a village where an old couple took pity and gave him food. He waited to discover how these people wanted to use him, but they just sat him by their fire to dry, and told him their names, Drytt and Eana. They didn't pry when he said little about himself; instead, they spoke of their children: two daughters married to men from distant villages half a day's walk away; and a son, Smala, called to fight for their lord.

"Who is your lord?" Walt asked.

"Ealdorman Morkere," Drytt said with pride. "Who is yours?"

"Ealdorman Ulfcytel," Walt said.

"You should go back to East Anglia and offer your service, for his protection," Eana advised.

"He never protected shit," Walt said, and immediately heard his mother's scolding at his coarseness..

"Morkere protects us well," said Eana.

"He swears fealty to one King but pays tribute to another. Both get what they most want." Drytt explained. "We haven't seen a Dane in years, not an angry one, not since those that came and stole land. But they got dykes dug," he added, "So we're better off for them."

"We pay a heavy levy, but Smala keeps us safe." Eana smiled sadly. "I just don't know if he has a friend, or a girl, or if they treat him cruel or kind."

Drytt looked seriously at Walt with his clear grey eyes. "If you won't go to Ulfcytel, find Thegn Wilmund in Stamsford. He may take you, and feed you up."

"Ask for Smala of Wisbec."

That was what they wanted, a brother for Smala.

They showed him to a bed platform right inside their hut, and when he woke crying out of nightmare Eana hugged him, and Drytt told him not to mind waking them, and said that just because he's an orphan it don't mean he'll never have a home again, and when he does the bad dreams'll fade. Walt had never said he was an orphan; it must be written on his face.

In the morning they gave him an old leather jerkin and a blanket, a small loaf and half a fist of cheese. Fortified and protected better from tomorrow's wind and cold, he left Wisbec on the Stamsford road with a germ of purpose.

Their food saw him through one day. Chores and an ungrateful theft saw him through another, but on the fourth day when he came to Stamsford he was weak and hungry again. His cough was worse, the imps in his ear were hammering to get out, and he knew he needed good food, a fire, dry shelter and long rest.

At the gate he asked to see Thegn Wilmund.

One guard laughed. The other said "And whyfor's that?"

"I want to serve Ealdorman Morkere."

"What'll he want with a runt like you?"

The other said "It's the monastery you need, son."

But they let him in.

Stamsford was the biggest town Walt had ever seen. Behind the protective raised bank and the patched walls and fences that defended it against an uncertain enemy, were hundreds of little huts and houses separated by crooked lanes, with fenced plots crowded with pigs and chickens. It was a maze, and with no sun in the sky he lost all sense of direction. People walked with yokes and baskets and barrows, children ran like rodents, and hawkers backed themselves against walls. He pushed through to a teeming marketplace where food and cloth and trinket traders had their wares stacked high on trestles or low on groundmats.

And the church. Walt had never seen a stone church before. It was so big, and the height of three huts plus the square tower a fourth, that he thought at first that it must be the monastery, or contain it. He had no notion of what a monastery looked like, but when he went inside he knew this was not a place where monks slept, for it was like the chapel at Croming, only much larger. He saw no hall as he walked outside the church, nor did he see monks, so he guessed that the monastery was on the far side of the town, or outside it.

What he did find was the inner bailey, the fenced compound within the town's walls where the thegn and his husceorls would be. The gate had six guards, so it was obviously more important than Stamsford itself. He walked up and stood before them. The feeling in his stomach was the same as when he'd stolen the egg in the dark of night, and milked that goat: the void of indifference to any consequence. "I want to see Thegn Wilmund."

The guard uttered a "Hnh," and cuffed Walt's ear.

Walt staggered, but stood forth again.

"Why would he want to see you?" His accent had a lilt that reminded Walt of Bodil's father. He was at least part Dane.

"To let me serve Ealdorman Morkere."

The guard cuffed him again, and again Walt stood forth.

"He don't need you. No-one's going to need you, or even want you, so fuck off and don't waste my time."

Walt backed away, uncaring. He would abandon his new plan, and carry straight on with the old. He turned back to the guard. "Can I get to Jorvik from here?"

"You don't look like you can get to Jorvik from Jorvik." Sniggering, he turned to another guard. "You heard what I said? I said he can't get to Jorvik even from Jorvik."

"I heard. What's that noise? Is it me laughing? No, it ain't." The second guard was a Dane too. He addressed Walt and pointed. "Go that way. It's north. Go out the north gate. Walk north. Keep walking north. If you get lost ask for the north road. Walk north some more. If you come to Lunden you went the wrong way. If you don't come to Lunden, you'll come to Jorvik."

Both guards laughed.

Walt went to the gate the guard had pointed to, and left Stamsford. He forded a river, next to which was another church, even bigger than the one in the town. This sat among low wide halls, and was surrounded by neatly planted fields being worked by monks in grey habits. There were chicken runs, rabbit hutches, goat pens, and a muddy field of pigs, with pasture for sheep and cattle beyond. Monks here do not go hungry, Walt thought. He was hungry.

But he had come this far, and he didn't care, so he walked on. Anyway, what did he want with a monastery? How many Danes will a monk kill? How many Northumbrian Ealdormen?

It was late afternoon, and the clouds thinned to let the sun glow through. It was on his right. The west. He was walking south. The bastard Danish guards had made a fool of him.

He forded the river again, and this time walked around Stamsford rather than go through it. It was here, on higher ground west of the walls, that he saw an encampment of tents. Men moved busily between them, while others sat idly in the weak sun. To one side was a pen of horses, with scores of carts and wagons parked nearby. From a blacksmith's forge came the clang of hammer on steel. Smoke from many fires formed a haze that drifted slowly over trees and up the hill.

Walt began to skirt the encampment as well as the town, but the haze carried smells of cooking that made his stomach plead. The encampment had no fence nor guard, and it was easy to walk between the outlying tents. No-one shouted at him, no-one accosted him, so he made his way to the camp's heart where the smoke was dense, hurrying now, trying to look like someone with an errand. He heard bites of conversation, some in the melody of Danish, some in accented and hard to comprehend English. They must be from the north.

Men were clustered with boards and bowls, waiting to be served ladles of some kind of stew from a black iron pot, and claim a quarter loaf of bread each.

They weren't all men. Some were boys no older than he, and some were women. More boys, girls and women were on the other side of the trestle. He joined the gaggle and was slowly moved with the crowd to the front.

An old woman, whose once-fair hair was thinned and grey, spoke to him in Danish, and he shrugged his incomprehension. "Bowl. Where bowl?" she asked.

"Someone stole it," he said.

She spat her contempt. Whether it was his carelessness or at some unknown thief, he had no idea. She looked at him, and he must have lit some maternal ember in her soul, for she beckoned him to her side of the trestle. There was no easy way round, so he ducked down and crawled under. "There," she said, jerking her head sideways towards a tent with an open flap.

He went to it, and entered, to find inside a store of pots, jugs, ladles, spoons and spurtles, of cups made of wood and of clay, thick chopping boards, and even knives and whetstones. Did she mean he was to find himself a bowl? He looked, but the ones he saw were a sorry bunch of cracked earthenware or fractured wood. He took the best of them, a wooden dish clean but black from use, and split with a half-inch gap at the rim narrowing to nothing at the centre. He found a chipped cup too, and went back to the Danish woman.

She took the dish and laid a thick crust of bread the size of this hand across the split, then ladled some of the stew into it. The bread soaked up the gravy and stopped it leaking. He took the full bowl away, sat on grass between two tents, and first drank the gravy, then scooped the vegetables and the few morsels of meat into his mouth with his fingers. He was done in less than two minutes. With his hunger quelled, he ate the soggy bread more slowly, and took time to look around.

Four men swilled beer nearby, speaking loudly in Danish. They were old boys, they'd be older than his father if he was still alive. But they looked strong, like they'd survived a battle or two. He was fearfully close to his enemy.

One shouted something, but he could not understand so he ignored it. "You English?" another said, a burly man with a red beard and green eyes.

Walt's breath froze in his lungs, and he wanted to run. The only movement he could make was the slightest nod of his head.

"You coming with us? Or just helping here?"

Walt managed to shake his head. "I don't know."

"You with your father? Your brother?"

Walt was unable to respond to this man. He wasn't the Viking who had pissed on him, killed Jack and planted the dog's head onto his chest, who had knocked him unconscious and gone away to kill his father or brother or Benna, to steal Djorka. But he might as well have been.

The man nodded in the direction of Stamsford. "You best stay close to home. Won't last long where we're going." He translated for his friends and they laughed.

"I'm not from here."

"Where you from?"

Walt just asked where they were going.

"Could be anywhere. But there will be fighting, and spoils for the taking."

"Are you English?"

"I was born here. I think that makes me English." Redbeard translated again for his friends, one of whom punched his arm. He caught the words "English" and "Sveyn" in his words. Bodil's father was called Sveyn.

One of the men poured beer from a flagon into an empty mug, and offered it to Walt. He had to join their circle to take it. "They don't speak English," he said to Redbeard.

"Not these buggers, no. But their children do."

"Do you know Sveyn?"

The man roared with laughter, and his beard shook like a briar in the breeze. He translated again, and the other three laughed just as loudly. "Oh, we know Sveyn all right, he comes here, and we polish his crown every day."

Walt thought he must be talking of a different Sveyn.

One of them said something back. "Jorn says, he polishes our staves in return."

Jorn said something else.

"He wants to know if you're good at polishing, but don't mind Jorn, he's just hankering to get into Stamsford tonight, and into one of Stamsford's whores."

"Why does this Sveyn have a crown? Is he a king?"

Redbeard's laughter was open-mouthed with amazement. "Your thegn sent you as a levy, and you don't even know who your king is!"

Aethelred was his king, but Walt knew better than to say so. "Morkere is my king."

"No no no. Morkere is your Ealdor. You never heard anyone call him King Morkere! At least, I hope not, or he'd have two axes falling on his neck, one from Sveyn, t'other from Aelthelred."

"Which is king?"

"Well, that's a big question from a small mouth." Redbeard turned to Jorn and the others and spoke in Danish. This time they did not laugh. They looked serious. "Sveyn," they all said. Sveyn something.

"Sveyn Forkbeard is our king. Under him we don't get raided by the Norse, and he takes less tax than Aethelred, or so we're told. Though between you and me…" He leaned closer. "If Sveyn ever gets to rule everyone, he'll be raising taxes to make up for the gafol he'd not be getting from Aethelred. That's why we're heading south. To grab what we can while the grabbing's good."

"Doesn't that make us like the Norse?"

"Once Vikingr, always Vikingr!"

It was easy to join Sveyn's Vikingr army, Walt found. Easy to plunder the south. All he had to do was be there.

He went back to the woman who'd given him stew, and

helped her clear the trestle. Two youths walked down towards a stream, carrying a pair of iron pots each loaded with ladles and brushes. He relieved one of his load, who made no objection, and followed the other. They crouched next to the water to wash out the pots and clean the utensils, then brought them back to the kitchens, where a group of women were now at the trestles, chattering as they kneaded dough for the next day's bread.

Some logs were set out, clearly in need of chopping. He saw the axe and made a start until a brawny young man took it from him with a tut, and made faster work of the chore. But Walt hung around and helped stack the wood into two clay ovens. The man threw him a stale bun for his efforts.

Unable to find another way of making himself useful, he wandered through the camp listening for any conversation in English. He found a group of northerners sitting around a small fire, drinking and sharpening weapons, and he ran back to the ovens. With no-one watching, he stole one of the freshly split logs and returned with it, and asked if he could sit. For a log, they welcomed him. The evening had set in, and though it was not cold, a dew had settled. Walt was tired – he was always tired – but for once his belly was full and his feet were warm.

"You're not from Northumbria," one said to him. He was black-bearded, and his bare arms had the thickest mat of hair Walt had ever seen.

"No," he said. "But my family is. Was. Are you from Northumbera?"

"Aye," they all said.

This was good fortune. Perhaps they knew his people. There was the hairy armed man, one with a big nose, one with a scar where his eye should be, a fat one, and one with a crutch beside him. Walt turned his head so that his good ear was open to them. "Is it a big town?"

They laughed so hard they cried and fell on each other's shoulders. "It's huge," Hairyarms said. "Much bigger than that town there," He pointed in the direction of Stamsford. "Is that where you're from?"

Walt nodded, but was distracted by a sense that he'd misconceived something.

"He's the only one that is," Scarface said, and turning to Walt asked "Who's your thegn?"

"Thegn Wilmund."

"Well, go back to Thegn Wilmund and tell him to send men, not boys."

The lame one said "He won't send anyone, not 'less Sveyn tells him."

"It's enough the Five Berghs let us pass," Hairyarms replied. "We don't want to have to hack our way south before the real fight."

The other sniffed. "Their loss, not to be part of it."

"Where are we going?" Walt said.

"Who knows? Could be Lunden. Cantenberh. All the way to the sea…"

"Won't be Cantenberh. That Thorkell's got Cantenberh, he's Sveyn's man from home, that's the word."

"I fancy Wintancaestr myself. Lots of gold in Wintancaestr." Hairyarms tested his sword edge, and, satisfied, lay it across his knees and moved to put the stone into a bag.

Walt asked if he could borrow the stone, and when he was given it, he began to sharpen the slim knife bought from Trud. It felt like good steel under the stone.

"You going to do battle with that?"

"No-one's going to let him do battle!" laughed the man with crutch, as if he'd be allowed in any shieldwall. "He's here for the kitchens, aren't you son. For sewing up clothes and tents. For carrying water for the wounded, maybe? Or running messages. Which is it, boy?"

"All of them," Walt said. "Whatever's useful."

"Good lad," Hairyarms said.

"Are you English or Danish?"

"Well now, that's not a question that has much meaning where we're from. Might do down here, but back home, we're all mingle-mangled."

"I'm English," the fat one said. "Through and through. But my sister, she's married a Dane."

"No-one else'd have her."

"What do you mean? Everyone else had her!"

They laughed. Why did the fat one talk about his sister like that?

English or Danish? "Why doesn't it mean anything?" It meant a lot to Walt. "Didn't they invade you?"

"Ah, so long ago. But after Uhtred knelt to Sveyn without lifting a sword, it stopped being anything to argue about. See, the Danes, they're bastards at first, but once they stop robbing you-"

"You mean once there's nothing left to rob…"

"The point is, they stop robbing you, and then they make you their brothers."

"Uhtred is your Ealdorman?"

"Sveyn names him Jarl, but it's the same thing. Once he was Ealdorman Uhtred of Bamburgh, now he's Jarl of all Northumbria. Northumbria ain't a village, boy, it's an old kingdom, like Mercia, only bigger."

"So King Sveyn gave Uhtred all Northumbria?" Walt was careful to say it right this time.

"No, King Aethelred gave him all Northumbria, after Elfhelm got done in."

Elfhelm. Walt sat up with a start. "The Ealdorman? Of Jorvik?"

"Yes, that Elfhelm. The famous one."

"Famous for getting done in," Bignose added.

"Done in? You mean murdered?"

"Can't think he'd put a knife in his own eye."

The man who executed his father was dead. "Who murdered him? The Danes?"

"No, he was friendly with the Danes. Some drunken butcher, so go the stories. Afterwards, King Aethelred gave Jorvik to Uhtred, and made him Ealdorman of all Northumbria, north and south." Hairyarms paused to reflect on the ways of the powerful. "Didn't do Aethelred no good, mind, not once Sveyn Forkbeard came, and Uhtred went turncloak."

"So are you here all alone?" Bignose said. "No brother, no father?"

Walt shook his head. "I'm looking for Smala of Wisbec."

"Don't know no Smala," said Bignose.

"Don't know no Wisbec," said Hairyarms.

"Where you sleeping? You can come into our tent if you like." Bignose looked at the others, who nodded.

Hairyarms said "Find us another log or two, you can even share our beer."

Walt smiled.

He tested his knife with his thumb. Its fresh edge was keen now, sharp enough to cut heartwood, and the point would pierce leather. He handed the man back his stone, and stood. "I got somewhere."

If firewood was coin, he knew where to get spending money. He found his way back to Redbeard and his friends with another log, and they took it for their dwindling fire, and slapped his back, and poured him beer. They talked among themselves in Danish, but Walt didn't mind. He sat, keeping warm, and began to feel drowsy. "I han't got cover," he said to Redbeard. "No tent for me. You got space for a smallun?"

"Cheeky bugger. Yes, we'll fit you in. Get in there, you look knackered."

"I am, a bit," he said.

He crawled into the low tent of poles and a rope, guyed and staked out, and open at each end. He went to the far end, so his head almost emerged out the other side. He took his knife in his hand, and wrapped himself loosely in the blanket. He forced his eyes to stay open, watching the moon rise over the trees. Somewhere in that direction was Croming, or what was left of it, and his mother's soul, his brother's and his little sister's. Further away still, across a wide cold sea sailed by murderers, was Djorka.

The moon rose higher, and Redbeard and the three other Danes came into the tent, shuffling and groping for blankets by the light of a candle in a small pot. He thought they might uncover him. He didn't want to have to fight. He pretended to be deeply asleep while tensing himself to jump up and run if he had to, but there seemed to be enough spare blankets to share, and no conspiracy among the men to use him as those village boys had done back aways. The candle was snuffed, and they settled themselves with Danish salutations that he took for goodnights. One farted loudly but the breeze through the tent blew away the smell like yesterday's smoke.

Two men snored. Two others breathed deeply, sunk into their dreams. The moon arced higher. Slowly he snaked out from under his blanket, then he knelt with his feet outside the tent. His night vision was good, and enough moonlight flowed that he could make out one of the men's heads. From the bush on his chin it could only be Redbeard, who spoke English and was born here, but was going to fight for the King of the Danes, whom Walt's father had fought, so was surely an enemy.

He went closer, and saw where the nose was, and the forehead, and eyebrow. Walt took his sharpened blade and placed its point just above Redbeard's closed eye. He didn't want to think, because he'd decided what he was going to do the moment he realised he'd found an arm of the Danish fyrd. But he did pause for a second, to feel the flowering of the seedling hatred he'd been nurturing since he hid in that bush at Croming. Be revenged. Kill Danes.

The pause let in thoughts. Redbeard would cry out as the blade that would now pierce leather cut through the delicate eyelid. He would spasm as it sank deep and twisted, as the edge that would now cut raw meat stirred his brain.

The thoughts let in fear. Redbeard's fellows would grab Walt. They'd stab him there and then, or take him to their leader and he'd be tortured and killed in slow agonies.

His hands shook and his heart pounded. He was suddenly gasping and breathless. He'd been panicked before, but never so knowingly scared. He had the desire to take Redbeard's life, but not the courage or resolve. He knew how to hate, but not how to act on his hatred. He was yet a boy, not a man, and it shamed him.

He backed away slowly until he was clear of the tent. He picked up his belongings and ran between the tents and out of the encampment, up the hill and into the trees, turning for the direction he knew he wanted, running blindly and half deaf into the darkness of the north.

8. A Traitor's Daughter

(Godwin)

"Let me go you stinking bastard pigs."

Edward spurned the activities that had so engaged Alfred, leaving Godwin more time in Ecfrida's company. There were free from Emma's cold eye at any words passed, and free too, though Godwin wasn't sure why, from Edward's surveillance. Ecfrida bloomed, became skittish and playful, and made him feel a kind of tenderness, a protectiveness, and pleasure from her smiles that he'd never felt with Odylia or even, he realised, with Gret. So when she beckoned him to follow her out to the waggon, he went with a comfortable sense of curiosity. It grew when he found Cynethe was absent.

Ecfrida talked about her father the King. She loved him, but for so long she'd been his youngest daughter, and always last to be considered. Goda's arrival, far from changing that, had made it worse. Godwin heard her loneliness when she said that her girlhood was no more than a virginal wait for a husband to be chosen for her. Would it be an Ealdor's son from Wessex? Or a Norman, a Flandran, or an Eiran? She didn't want to be sent somewhere foreign, even if the alternative was marrying beneath her status.

"Would the King allow that?" Godwin asked. "What about a Mercian? Or an East Anglian?"

"My sisters are gone there already. Eadric's goddaughter surely will marry one of the sons of Ledwyn of Hwicce. The King might make me marry the other, but one is a brute and the other… well, he's like Queen Emma without her warm loving heart."

Godwin laughed. "And Eadric? Is he truly 'The Grasper'?"

"He is said to be a pig for his greed and a fox for his cunning."

Godwin wondered what animals Eadric's brother might be. Rat. Snake. Louse. He said nothing.

"And you, Godwin?" she asked. "Who will you marry?"

He shook his head. His father's treachery had made a pariah of him. Ecfrida seemed ignorant of his past, and he was not about to confess. "I am a poor ceorl. I'm not sure, I might even be a thuw now, if your brother wills it. No woman of any worth will look my way."

"Edmund would let you marry Odylia, surely."

Marry Odylia? The thought had never crossed his mind, and he said so. "I doubt it's crossed hers, either."

"You really don't know women, do you Godwin," she smiled.

With Deorleaf still gone, the remaining six ceorls began to behave like the louts they were. Godwin watched them ogle the willowy Cynethe as if she was Ostra herself, the Goddess of Spring. But she was untouchable, so they slid into the village and passed their days eating and drinking, spending time and money with the girls and women who, married or not, were attracted to these unbridled strangers with their cut coins. A Rye swain challenged Geareth, and lost a little blood and a lot of pride, for Geareth was a better fighter than his weighty frame implied. After that, nothing protected the maids of Rye except their own hands. Godwin suspected the local haystack count next year would grow by at least one.

Edward's disapproving glower was like his mother's, but his black looks were not directed at the ceorls, whose activities he was not aware of. He made it very clear to Theodric that he didn't want Godwin around him. In the morning, when he went with his friend Fulton to help Brother Sibbi, who, it seemed, Edward knew from younger years, Theo followed dutifully though there was little threat. Afternoon brought a minor panic when it was noticed that Edward had gone for a walk alone, with neither Fulton nor Theo, but the search never got beyond Rye village before Edward reappeared, carrying his boots and with mud on his feet. All he said was a curt "Paddling" in answer to questions as to where he'd been. A strange pastime, Godwin thought. If he'd been looking for mussels, he'd been singularly unsuccessful.

Godwin found himself idle, and spent his time tending to Ash and Linden, brushing them and letting them out to graze. The two Comtyn horses deserved their ease.

Odylia roamed the woods and fields searching for herbs to replace those she'd mixed into medicine for Alfred, "Because you don't know when more might be needed." Godwin was pleased, if a little surprised, that she took her responsibility as herblorist seriously enough to forage now she could no longer steal her ingredients. Perhaps she recognised the favour her expertise had won from Queen Emma.

Ecfrida again dismissed her handmaid, and invited Godwin to walk to the seashore with her. They sat on a pebble spit watching the waves, breathing the seaweed-sharp air, and talked of tides and seabirds and boats. "We came by boat to Meddestane," she said.

"I saw you."

"I quite enjoyed it. Alfred didn't. He was sick all the way."

"He has my sympathy. I get terrible sickness too."

"Have you had to sail much?"

The question led him close to a secret best not revealed. "No. And I hope it stays that way. Give me a horse every time."

"Do you have family?" she asked. "Where are they?"

"My father… He left. To fight the Danes." It was such a big lie he felt ashamed. His father might as well have fought for the Danes. "He could be anywhere."

"And your mother?"

He was driven to tell a truth, any truth, to this girl who confided in him. "They… they came to Comtyn, and they killed her." He let Ecfrida assume that 'they' meant the Vikingr. He found himself speaking of his sister, who'd had to run away when 'they' came. He hadn't seen her since, his little Rabbit. "She's the one I care most for in the world." He was suddenly overcome by a wave of loss for his family, his friends, his home "I should be protecting her. Edmund won't let me." The conker that suddenly grew in his throat gargled his voice.

Ecfrida pulled his head to her shoulder, and he could not prevent the sobbing. "You're serving Edmund, who fights the Danes. That is protecting her."

He nodded into her neck.

"But I know that's not the same as playing with her," she said. "I play with Goda. Nothing brings more joy than making a child happy, does it."

This did not help Godwin compose himself, so she turned her head as he coughed to clear his throat and wiped his eyes. She talked of her full brothers and sisters, most of whom had either died, or disappeared by marriage. Edmund these days was mostly with his husceorls fighting, or readying himself to do so, while Aelfrith lived her life in her grandmother's Abbey at Wherwell.

"Could you go to the Abbey?"

"I feel if I did, I'd never come out. I couldn't stand it."

"Your sister stands it."

"Mother died there birthing a tenth child when I was young. Aelfrith wasn't there. I was. Then Emma arrived, and Edward and Alfred came along, and I do love them, but they are boys. And Goda, she's in Lunden. But she's just seven. Nearly eight. The same age as your little Rabbit."

Godwin dared to squeeze the lonely girl's hand. She squeezed his back. "Godwin," she said. "I know who your father is."

He groaned.

"Edward told me. He wanted to- Well, never mind. I know you're ashamed. But it doesn't make any difference to me. You proved yourself by leaving your father. And Edmund trusts you."

She was kind. She was forgiving. He still wished it secret. "How did Edward know?"

"Odylia told him."

Why? Her father was as guilty as his own.

"Be careful with that girl, Godwin."

They went back to the hall for food, and found Odylia just returned from her foraging with a full bag of cuttings. As soon as Ecfrida had disappeared with Cynethe, she pulled him out of the hall and away from the village. When she wouldn't tell him why, he thought she was after a fuck in the woods, and though not greatly excited by the prospect, he allowed himself to be led towards Rameslege's outlying hides. They had cut through woodland to a muddy sea inlet that wound towards the low hills of the Weald. She made him hush and creep low, and follow her closer to the bank. They knelt in undergrowth, and she told him to look through the leaves across the inlet. There was nothing to be seen apart from the creek with mud exposed by the falling tide, and willows on the far bank. He pulled a questioning face.

"Wait," Odylia whispered. "He'll come any time."

She could only have been talking about one person.

They heard the rustle as Edward pushed aside the saplings and stood opposite them at the creek's edge. He had a small sword, which he used to cut and trim four-foot willow wands that he laid on the bank.

"What's he doing?" Godwin whispered. "They're too short for fishing."

"Just watch."

To Godwin's amazement, Edward was disrobing. His boots, his coat, his shirt and his leggings came off, then his undercloths. He stood nude, skinny and pale. His pintle dangled under its brown thatch. He held it cupped, and began to rub. Godwin wanted to leave, but if they moved, Edward would hear them, and Godwin could not guess the consequences of that. He wanted to close his eyes, but could not draw them away.

Edward's pintle now stood firm, surprisingly long, and thin. It had strange red marks horizontally across it.

Odylia suppressed a giggle. "Prefer yours," she whispered, somehow making the wrongness worse.

Edward picked up one of the willow wands. He began whipping his own stem and balls with it, and he showed himself no mercy as he added new red lines brighter than those already there.

Godwin uttered "Jesus," too loud, and Odylia punched him, but Edward did not hear over the crack of the switch and the sound of his own groans.

Godwin started counting. There were twenty-one more stripes all across the front before Edward stopped. But he didn't cease whipping himself. He bent to pick up the other strips, and held them in a bundle in one fist. He flogged his own back twenty-four times over one shoulder, then swapped hands and dealt another two dozen hard strokes over the other. Godwin knew the sound, so akin to the whup-smack he'd heard when his father had flogged him for some misdemeanour. Edward was administering real pain to himself. The boy was clearly mad.

Edward finished the lashing, dropped the switches, and

walked forwards onto the mud. He lay down and rolled about, covering himself with the grey slime, carefully keeping his head and hair clean. Then he stood and walked further, into the cold water in the middle of the creek. He washed himself, removing all the mud from his skin, revealing livid welts across his back and chest. They did not bleed, but the skin was slashed raw and would likely weep. He returned to the bank for hanks of grass to scrub himself with. Godwin winced. On raw wounds, that must hurt as much as the beating.

When Edward was dressed again and gone, Godwin turned uncomprehendingly to Odylia. "What the fuck?"

"He's in pain," she said.

"'Course he's in pain."

"Not that sort of pain," she said.

What pain then? "You mean, in his heart? His head?"

"Fucking torture, being devout," was all she said.

On the way back to Rye, he told her not to tell anyone.

"No. Right. Not now I've told you."

Her sneer made him wonder why she'd shown him Edward's self-mortification. She'd obviously come across him on her foraging, but why did she not keep the secret to herself? Was it too heavy a burden? Was she simply making mischief? Or did she have some plan to extract money or favour from Edward, which would demand Godwin's protection?

That evening, Edward saw Godwin and Ecfrida together, and instructed that he did want Godwin close by him next day after all. Cynethe clung to Ecfrida, and Odylia was in a strange mood, one moment attentive to him, the next surly. It seemed all three wanted to keep him from Ecfrida.

Odylia came to sleep with him at night, and put her hand to him. "Yes, definitely prefer yours.," she whispered.

That was why! It was pretty obvious. A girl would have known straight away. Odylia showed him Edward to give them something shared, to bring him closer to her. To pull him away from Ecfrida. He shook his head in the dark. She couldn't see, but she felt it, and withdrew her hand. For the first time in weeks Godwin thought of how it had been when he was fucking Gret, when having a girl was a simple thing. Then, as he fell asleep, he thought of Ecfrida.

Two days passed like holy days, with unspoken familial tensions but, for most of them, without God and Jesus.

Ordulf and Sibbi got on with their work, roaming the tracks, dykes and fields all morning and most of the afternoon, and compiling lists on parchment in the evening. By the third day after Emma's departure their survey was nearly complete, and Godwin had to follow as they toured Edward around all of the hides that were destined to go to Fécamp across the sea, which was, he learned, the reason Emma had come to Rameslege in the first place.

As they ate in the evening, Godwin noticed Theodric's silence, and a crease between his eyebrows. After the meal, Theo called the ceorls and the two monks together, because as Edward's personal guard he was in charge until Deorleaf's return. He explained what worried him. "The Queen planned to get to Meddestane in a day. Even if it took her two, Deorleaf and the others should have returned by now. So my guess is they couldn't find a boat, and have gone on overland, all of them. Or perhaps they will appear tomorrow. But I'm responsible for the Prince and Princess's safety, and I'm nervous about spending more time here with such a small guard. So we will leave tomorrow at first light. I hope we'll meet Deorleaf on the road. Godwin, tell Prince Edward and Fulton, and help them make ready. Odylia, the same for Ecfrida and Cynethe. The rest of you, check the horses and the waggons, and load everything not needed for tonight. If there's not enough room, leave clothes and trinkets behind."

Ordulf complained that he was not quite finished.

"Have you mapped the boundaries?" Theo demanded.

"Yes, but not everything within them," said Ordulf.

"Then either stay without us, or invent it. Your choice."

"We work for the Queen. You can't leave us here alone."

Theo sighed. "Godwin and Odylia can stay. They can help you finish, and escort you back to Lunden."

Ordulf was outraged. "They are children!"

"You can escort them, then," Theo snapped, and turned back to Godwin and Odylia. "Are you still here? Fetch Edward and Ecfrida, now."

Immediately after a rushed candlelit breakfast, the men hitched the carts and saddled their horses. Theo checked that everyone had capes and blankets, and told them to mount up swiftly. Edward refused until Theo acted on his demand that Odylia's mount be given to Fulton. When the time came to leave Rye with Ordulf and Sibbi, Odylia would have one of the garrons brought for cart-pulling.

Godwin went to Ecfrida, already mounted, who made no similar demand for Cynethe. "Linden is not Odylia's, she's mine."

Ecfrida could only shrug her helplessness. He went to Fulton as he prepared to climb onto the horse's back, and said quietly. "Look after her please. I want her returned." He made a stirrup of his hands to help Fulton up, and seeing him mounted so rigidly knew he was no horseman. "She'll see you right," he added.

Theo was able to lead his troop down the lane out of Rye before the sun showed itself above the sea-mist. Ecfrida waved at Godwin, and he wondered if he would ever see her again. "We won't catch them," he said to Odylia. "We might have horses, but the two monks don't."

"We'd better try," Odylia said. "Theo is worried, and he has six men. We're only two, and two monks. We should find the buggers and hurry them up. The sooner they finish, the sooner we can start."

Odylia's instinct for self-protection matched Theodric's order to assist the monks, but neither Ordulf nor Sibbi were to be seen. "You look in the marshes east," Godwin said. "I'll take Ash and look in the fields west. We'll give them until noon."

"Then," she said, "finished or not, break their measuring rods, snap their quills and spill their ink."

With the height Ash gave him, Godwin spotted Ordulf a furlong from the Weald lane, laying his rods end to end. He trotted Ash over and said "You have until noon, by Theodric's order."

"If you can hold a rod," Ordulf said, "I will finish in less time than that."

Ordulf showed him how to touch the rods end to end, and hold one still while Ordulf brought another past to kiss the first. "Lift it clear of the shrubs," Ordulf told him. "Alone, I have to lay them on the ground, and it's always the bushes and trees that lead to errors."

They made their way down the length of a field, and across its width, Ordulf making marks on his slate at every measure. "If your girl is helping Sibbi," he said, "he'll finish quickly too."

A skylark sang above as the sunny morning passed peacefully. Godwin asked Ordulf about the life of a monk, and was offered thoughts on the value of small but regular meals and a roof over his head every night for life, until God's call came. They were halfway across a second field when Godwin heard a rumble of hooves from a single horse approaching Rye at a gallop. What disaster had befallen Theo so soon? Was it Deorleaf or one of his men returned? Or some new visitor? Gallop must be met with gallop, so Godwin ran to Ash where he grazed and heeled him to the lane.

He recognised Freth, one of the troop who'd gone to Meddestane four days earlier. He hailed him. Freth reined in his horse and looked around for the source of the call. Seeing Godwin, he left the lane and cantered to him. Ash skittered backwards as the panting horse wheeled in circles at Freth's flailing hands and heels. "Danes!" he shouted. "Danes! Deorleaf said we have to get the Prince and Princess away to the west."

"They're already gone," Godwin said. "North, not west. Where are these Danes? How many? How far?"

Freth pointed vaguely inland. "They're ravaging Cantware. Deorleaf fought them. He must be dead now. Or captured. He sent me. People were fleeing Dofras and Cantenberh. They said Danes are everywhere."

"Where exactly? Are they on the road we took?"

"It was at Ceorring. Deorleaf is a Cantware man. After the Queen left us, he wanted to see his family and his farm. Just one extra night away-"

Godwin didn't want to hear more. "Curse Deorleaf for a fool, for failing his duty." But curses, unless from a witch or a bishop, were like foul breath. They'd make a man recoil, but not harm him. "Go back north. Find Theodric. Warn him."

"I'll run straight into the Danes. They saw me run."

"Then make sure you spot them before they see you again. Our duty is to protect Edward and Ecfrida. Especially as Deorleaf has failed to."

Freth, four years older than Godwin, circled his horse again, but this was not lack of control, this was reticence. "You can't order me."

"Theo put me in charge of Rye. You want to answer to him? Or tell Edmund Ironside you're too big a coward to protect his brother and sister?" Freth must know that I have Edmund's ear, Godwin thought. "Go! And you might redeem Deorleaf."

He had to find Odylia and get the two monks out of Rye. They might not even have the hours until noon. He galloped back to Ordulf. "Danes. Go to the hall, gather the least you need, and wait for me. Make a bag for Sibbi too."

"But-"

"Do it, or die." Godwin turned Ash and heeled him to the hides where Odylia and Sibbi worked. If he couldn't find them, how long should he search?

Half an hour later, and he knew he might be looking all day among the reeds, copses and creeks east of Rye. Worse, the rising tide might cut him off from the village. Odylia would order Sibbi back at noon, so he had best return and wait, ready to run or hide at the first sign of any approaching danger. He turned Ash down the path into Rye.

The four masts stood taller by far than those of the local fishing boats. The Danes had arrived already, come not by roadway but by sea.

Now the loyal idiot fought the wise coward: should he run to catch up with Theodric for whatever safety his men offered? Or should he find Odylia and Sibbi, to protect the monks as Theo ordered? No. Neither. Surely his first duty, order or no order, was to gallop north to add himself to the guard around the Prince and Princess. He should abandon the monks, and abandon Odylia too. Yet her presence here was all his doing. He recalled when she poured beer for him by the fire at Brimclif, then he remembered the premonition he'd had, that one day he could be called upon to choose who might live and who might die.

It was a confused scrap, which the guilty fool won. Godwin tied Ash in the midst of a stand of willows as close as he dared to the village, and crept onwards.

He entered the back of a barn, already emptied of animals, and quietly climbed the ladder to the loft. He expected to hear screams and yells, and to see flames flicker and rise. But as he looked between the planks down into the open square where the waggons had been, he saw that this raid was not mindless. Only three bodies lay on the ground, meaning Rye had swiftly succumbed. One was Vale, the Headman who had hosted Queen Emma and all her retinue so well. Godwin wondered if he died before or after surrendering.

The foreigners were a strange mix of men of fighting age, sons younger than himself, and their grandfathers. Twenty of them penned the disarmed villagers against the hall. A further dozen Danes surrounded Rye's pile of surrendered weapons now stacked in the middle of the square. Then Godwin saw that it was not the weapons they guarded, but a second, smaller pile, this one of valuables taken from people's arms and necks, their huts, their hall, and their church.

Danes raided for slaves as well as valuables, but these men seemed uninterested in separating the young, beautiful and strong from among the villagers. They were more concerned with Rye's stores of grain and dried fish, and its livestock. Pigs and cows were being herded into an enclosure, and more were being led straight towards the boats moored beyond the village. This was not theft by coastal raiders who would sail home on the next tide. These people meant to stay. They were an occupying army supplying itself.

The Danish leader was identifiable by his strut as he barked his orders, by the iron helmet he cradled, and the iron plates tied onto the breast and shoulders of his leather tunic. His hair was bound back, and his beard was trimmed spadelike. He was talking to an unarmed man, darker and younger, who then stood before the villagers. "We are the Jomsborg Vikingr," the dark man said in clear if accented English. "We serve Jarl Thorkell of Jomsborg, and you serve us. You are lucky. We shall only take half of your wealth. Half your animals. You're lucky that we have no room for more than six of your girls."

Wails rose as the girls realised what this meant, and there came a rumble of anger from Rye's fathers. To watch their daughters taken into slavery and whoredom was more than their pride could bear.

The Danes gripped their axehafts tighter, ready for the first who might try to run with his daughter to freedom. They wouldn't succeed, Godwin knew, and if they did, others would likely pay.

The crying and the cursing continued, and the ring of Danes closed on the crowd. They paused when the villagers' attention was caught by something happening along the track leading into Rye.

A familiar voice cried out. "Let me go you stinking bastard pigs." Odylia was being hauled by two big Danes who had her nearly off her feet. One of them had a cut on his arm, and held Odylia's dagger, which explained her bruised and bloodied face. She was lucky to be still alive. Two more Danes led a terrified Sibbi. By Bevis, how had they let themselves get caught?

The captors said something to the Danish leader, who in turn called to the English-speaker. Godwin had no idea of the words, but he didn't like the cold tone.

The leader issued another order. A big Dane with a bigger axe stepped forward.

"This is what you can expect if you resist us," the dark haired man announced, and before the villagers knew what was happening, before Sibbi himself knew, his captors shoved him to his knees and the big Viking swung his axeblade halfway through his neck. Rye gasped in shock at such cold and swift brutality. The Viking grinned at his leader as he extracted the axe from Sibbi's neck, and said one word that didn't need translating. "Cristin."

The leader merely looked at Odylia. She was pushed to her knees. The Viking lifted the bloody axe again behind his shoulders.

"I'm not Christian," Odylia told the world. Then she looked at the dark one who spoke English. "You buggers don't want me!" she yelled. "You want the Prince and Princess of England. I know where they are."

Godwin froze. So still was he, so shocked, that he felt he had to re-start his heartbeat by an effort of will, like lifting an anvil or a log.

The dark man translated, then at his leader's word the Viking lowered his axe. Odylia's neck would stay white.

Godwin had seen enough. He almost fell down the ladder from the loft. The noise was lost in the collective outburst of talk among the English and the Danes alike.

He returned to Ash. Brother Ordulf stood next to him.

"I have to go." He couldn't bring himself to explain why. "You must make your own way west. Find safety where you can. Or hide hereabouts – you know the land as well as the locals. The Danes will ransack the place and pass on, then you can return."

Ordulf nodded. "I thought the same." He unlooped the leather satchel from his shoulder, and thrust it at Godwin. "This is our work for the Queen. Everything, except the land Sibbi measured this morning. I shall go look for him."

"I fear Brother Sibbi measured less than six feet this morning. I'm sorry."

Ordulf's eyes closed, and his face turned upwards. The light of heaven only illuminated his pain. He muttered some words of Latin, then looked levelly at Godwin. "I will ensure he gets a proper burial. And your girl too. I'm sorry for your loss."

"Ha," Godwin spat. "There is no loss." She was indeed no Christian. Neither was Judas.

There was but one route north, and it was clogged by a herd of fifty more Danes, singing as they strode through Rameslege to join their cousins. Five of them rode horses. One of the horses was Freth's. The relief was that none were Linden.

Godwin watched the gaggle pass from where he hid among tall reeds, as Ash stood knee-deep in mud in the creek behind with his head safely below the swaying reed feathers. The good thing about these new arrivals was the hope that they'd delay the hunt for Edward and Ecfrida. But God help the women of Rye, he thought. He doubted that the Viking's promise to take only six of the girls would be held, not now. Had Odylia saved herself from that too? He didn't care.

As soon as they passed, he remounted Ash and galloped onwards, wondering if he was going to spend the rest of his life charging out of south coast villages. He took his own warning better than Freth had, and constantly watched for more Danes on the road, ready to leap ditch or hedge to run across country. He hoped that the few who might be mounted were poorer horsemen than he, or too important to chase one lone rider.

Climbing a hill, he saw a small group of people ahead, not on the road but crossing it, with carts and baskets, and their children leading livestock. Theo's party must have seen others fleeing Cantware for Soussex. Surely they know about the heathen army by now. Godwin pressed on through emptied villages, wondering how he might find them in all of Soussex.

A few miles on he disturbed a black blanket of crows, who flew up with a cackle and clatter from a body hacked beyond death, beyond reason, and beyond recognition. From the shreds of clothing, Godwin was sure it was Freth. He left him to the crows.

When he saw the lone rider pull to a halt half a mile ahead, he knew the man had seen him too. It was a fine horse he had, and the man sat easily in the saddle. A Dane? Alone? Godwin hoped not, as the pair closed warily.

"Hail!" the man shouted, confirming both his Englishness, and that he was no peasant. "I am looking for Deorleaf the Mown. Do you know him?"

"I knew him," Godwin called back. "But he is probably mown a little shorter now. Name yourself."

He was a handsome fellow, cloaked in thick wool, with a sword at his side and a bow on his back. He knew of Deorleaf – a good sign. His manner said he was not looking for a fight – a better one. "I am Heremond, sent by Prince Edmund Ironside. Who are you?"

"I am Godwin. I too was sent by Edmund. I was one of Deorleaf's group." He was close enough now to speak in normal tones.

"Then why are you not with him now, protecting the Queen?" Heremond barked like a man accustomed to being in command.

"She left us. Prince Alfred became ill. Deorleaf escorted them, and never returned. Theodric took charge and decided to go back to Lunden with Edward and Ecfrida."

"Theo. A good man. Good instincts." Heremond's face changed from lordly to suspicious. "You avoid my question. He needs every man he has. Even every boy. Why are you not with him?"

"He ordered me to stay, but that's not important now. Danes are-"

"I know. A horde has fallen on Cantware, and they mean to bloody their blades with every Christian they can find. That's why I'm here, while they are still off to the east."

Godwin felt he was being called a dolt. Heremond probably thought all ceorls were dolts.

"They aren't east," the dolt replied. "They've sailed round the coast. They came to Rye. And they know they missed the Prince and Princess by hours, and now surely smell ransom gold. I'm trying to find Theo's group before they do." As Heremond digested this, Godwin continued. "Look, if you've come this far without meeting them, they must have turned off the road south of here." And south of Freth's corpse too, he realised.

Heremond nodded.

"I passed a route to the west back a ways," Godwin said.

"You think they took it?"

"I think it's the place to look." He turned Ash around and urged him to a canter. He felt Heremond's eyes on his back, but didn't twist to look at him. More important to watch the road for Danes who might rise over every crest ahead.

They went to the waycross and took the road west, speaking no words until they passed a group of Saxons who had yoked a mule to a waggon loaded with the belongings of a whole village. It was too big for the beast, and the villagers had their shoulders to the waggon to help the mule pull it over the rough ground. "That was one of our waggons," Godwin said.

"Meaning Theo unhitched the horses to ride, for greater speed."

"Not much greater. They are garrons who'll pull a cart all day, but little more."

"If I were Theo," Heremond said, "I'd put the Prince and Princess on the two fastest horses, and take myself and my best man, and head for Lunden a swiftly as possible."

"And lose your troop?"

"Aye."

Heremond is no fool, Godwin thought. Nor is Theo. But Theo thinks he is ahead of the invasion. He doesn't suspect that there are now Danes actively looking for them.

9. The Two Christians

(Eadric)

"Which is the one they call the Arch Bishop?"

"Kjell was loved," Thorkell said. "Vrangr is feared. A thousand men and more are angered, and without a promise of silver into each of their purses, they will rampage across this scire and cover the land with blood in the name of both. Men will die screaming, women will die defiled, children will scream and be defiled too, enslaved, and taken to Jomsborg. And when we have feasted on Cantware and left its carcass so bare that crows will refuse to waste time pecking at scraps, we will turn on Lunden. Brihtric's ships cannot sail on land. So, Eadric. Blood, or silver? We shall see one of these, and we shall see it gush."

What parentage made Brihtric so stupid? Not the same as mine, Eadric thought. Instead of yielding a nice ransom, the bastard's victory on the Tamys had suddenly become very costly.

He was in little mood now to bargain hard. "The King will pay thirty thousand pounds of silver, and will not even deduct the amounts you have already received from within Cantware."

Thorkell shook his head. "When you have your one-tenth – that is what you take from your deliveries to Sveyn, is it not? – and three-fifths divided between him and myself, that does not leave enough for ninety score men."

So he had eighteen hundred men here. Stigand's guess had been close.

"Fifty thousand pounds," Thorkell said.

"My Lord!" Reeve Wilmaer gasped. This was far higher than the largest gafol payment yet.

Eadric held up his hand to quieten Wilmaer. "Forty. That is halfway between us. And I will grant you my one-tenth part. So it's worth forty-four to you."

"Forty-four it is," said Thorkell "Whence it comes and how, is not my concern."

"Agreed," said Eadric. He would tell Aethelred forty-eight, and give Wilmaer a choice between receiving a few hundred for his cooperation, or a visit from Marton.

"The King cannot-"

Eadric interrupted Wilmaer. "Half to you here, and half to King Sveyn by year end." Brihtric could be delivery boy for both, though for him to come within a scire of Vrangr would not be wise. "And you must promise to restrain Vrangr. He has the look of man who could do something foolish."

"Restrain Vrangr? And lose the respect of half my men?" Thorkell rose, and his head touched the tent's sagging roof. He started to raise the flap across the exit, but before he ducked low to leave, he turned back. "The tale of the Archbishop who went unarmed among those prisoners, baptised them, and sent them home, has been told and told again in my camps. Some think him touched by too much moonlight, some think he wants to be a Jarl in the Christian heaven. Some think he has no knowledge of men, and some think he may have Odin's wisdom. I myself am undecided, and I am baptised. But I tell you this, Eadric of Mercia. Unless your Archbishop can lead Vrangr to the Prince of Peace overnight, you must get Reeve Wilmaer to Lunden to begin counting coins. If my men do not see silver within days, they will see red."

Thorkell was right, of course. To save the people of Cantware, and probably Lunden, they had to get back to

Aethelred. Twenty-four thousand pounds must be swiftly exacted. People must be squeezed, coffers scraped, and mines scoured. They must depart immediately.

Once Aelfgifu was married to Knut and the alliance with Mercia cemented, perhaps it would be possible simply to agree a regular levy on folk, and dispense with the untidy business of swords and axes, arrows and boats. Silver, with no blood.

They returned to a Cantenberh loud with the singing and roars of unleashed drunken Danes. The English hid in their homes, but riding back to the Abbey escorted by six of Thorkell's men, Eadric saw families being pulled onto the streets, beaten, or worse, and their homes stripped. The Danes who'd taken over their city had already received three thousand pounds; this harrying should have ceased. The Jomsborg Vikingr were less disciplined than Danes from the north. Once a payment had beem made to Sveyn, or even promised, the bloodletting stopped, for a while. The sooner Thorkell took his silver, the better for these people, or so he hoped.

It was too late and too dangerous to leave tonight, so he warmed himself with Thyra under furs in the monk's cell he'd been offered. Marton was outside guarding the door, although the Abbey was probably safe for now. And if it wasn't, what could one man do? He shut his eyes but could not close his ears, and the raucousness outside pervaded his dreams.

He woke with someone's fetid beery breath in his nostrils, and a knife at his throat.

Behind, another man held a flickering torch. Two more carried axes whose blades reflected the flame. Beyond the doorway, four others showed four blades to Marton, who had but one.

"It's all right, Marton," Eadric called. "Do as they say."

Do as they say, because I will pay, I've always paid. Just take the blades away.

Marton lowered his sword, and Eadric did not even glance at his. One of the Danes pulled him out of bed, and the other threw his boots at him. They seemed to have no interest in Thyra, beyond watching that she wasn't about to come at them with a knife. He put the boots on, and whispered one word to her. "Stigand."

They shoved him to the door, then a hood was dropped over his head from behind, and all was black. His hands were bound behind him, and he had no choice but to stumble wherever he was pushed.

This is what happens when you have to leave eighty men beyond the city walls.

It surely was not Thorkell's will. It was not just dishonourable but pointless to mistreat the man from whom you have just extracted a promise of forty-four thousand pounds of silver. This invasion was mercenary for Thorkell, was it not? "You'll feel your chief's wrath for this," he said in Danish, and received a clout to the back of his skull that made him see suns and moons as he crashed to the floor, then stars as he was hauled to his feet and pushed into the chilly outside air. He would have fallen down some steps if he hadn't been held by the Danes. They walked over gravel, then uneven softer ground. They must be beyond the Abbey now, and into the city controlled by Vrangr the Crossbreaker, Vrangr the insubordinate, Vrangr the vengeful. Vrangr Ormsson.

Fuck Brihtric. Killing Kjell Ormsson had brought Mercia shame at the moment of its great triumph. The stupid bastard would pay and pay again, when he got home. If he got home.

His first instinct was that hostage taking was a game, and even Vrangr knew its rules. If the heathen wanted biblical revenge for his brother, eye for eye, tooth for tooth, life for life, then Eadric would never have left that bed alive. Fortunately Vrangr worshipped different gods, and it was blood-money he needed.

His second instinct was that if his brother Kjell had been executed in front of all Brihtric's men, Vrangr would want exactly the same public display of his vengeance.

They entered another building. It smelled of animals, and the floor was soft with mud and worse. The hood came off and he was thrown across the darkness. He fell, twisting, onto a body. It was all that kept his face from the soil. The door banged, a bar fell, and he struggled to his feet.

"Are you hurt?" A kindly voice. He was not alone, but, but… The voice was Archbishop Aelfheah's.

"My God," he said. "They came for you too."

"Us," said Aelfheah. "Elfmar, myself, and Reeve Hlothar, may God grant him eternal peace."

The body he'd landed on. Reeve Hlothar.

"He pleaded that Cantenberh had paid for safety. They cut his throat." Aelfheah's voice quavered, thought whether it trembled from anger or fear Eadric could not tell. "I believed Thorkell had a Christian heart. I did not think even heathens would stoop so low."

When captors will kill the hostage who will be counting out their ransom monies, the rules of the game are revised by madmen.

Elfmar's voice came heavily from the dark. "Your negotiations did not go well, Eadric Streona."

The dull insult did not pierce the shit that covered half of Eadric's body. "They went very well. We agreed a gafol price. All was set."

"Then why…?"

"Thorkell has lost control of Vrangr. And Vrangr has unleashed his men in Cantenberh. They seem to prefer his barbarity to Thorkell's deals."

"So it's not Thorkell's doing," said Aelfheah.

"It's more like mutiny." Eadric thought it likely that Thorkell's hold over his men was weaker for being baptised, but there was little to be gained by sharing the notion. "We have to hope that when the Danes sober up, they will see that silver offers more lasting satisfaction than slaughter. Have they bound your hands too?"

"Yes," said Aelfheah.

"So that we cannot pray," said Elfmar.

"Come behind me. I may be able to unpick your knots."

"In the dark? Behind your back?"

"Since it's behind my back, the dark makes no difference. One thing about sailors, they know that a knot must be as easy to untie as it is to tie."

He used his fingers to feel the contours of the rope binding Aelfheah's wrists, and pulled and worked at the knot until it loosened and the Archbishop's hands were free. But Aelfheah's fingers, weak and cold, could to nothing in the dark to loosen either Elfmar or Eadric in return.

The noise of rioting Danes quietened eventually, but dawn was a long time coming. Eadric shivered as the damp soaked through his cloak. Aelfheah offered his own cloak, but Eadric declined. The old man had greater need, for his sandals disappeared into the mud, as Eadric saw when pale light came through the gaps in the byre's timber walls. Elfmar, less austere for all that he was a Benedictine Abbott, had his leather shoes worn over wool hose. With the light come, Aelfheah could work at Eadric and Elfmar's ties to free their hands, then the two priests prayed together. Archbishop Aelfheah gave leave not to kneel this once, as they sought salvation for Hlothar now he was in God's hands, and His aid for themselves now they were in the heathens'. Eadric wondered what Archbishop Lupus would make of his gentle adversary's predicament.

By mid-morning, singing, laughter and roaring, and English screams across the city, told them that the Danes had woken and begun drinking again.

Morning progressed, and steam rose from the mud as the sun angled in through the slats. They stood in the narrow beams hoping to dry their damp cloaks a little, and felt hunger and thirst.

The bar outside was lifted, and eight bearded men with short swords in their hands and axes on their backs entered. They took little notice of the fallen ropes and less of the fallen Reeve, as they led the three outside into the sun. They were walked towards the centre of Cantenberh, with their guards standing aside so the invaders could pelt them with mud, stones, bones, and the occasional turd. The English kept to their houses, but some were brought out and forced to watch, while others peered from doorways and windows of their own volition. Some put their hands together and closed their eyes. All looked abject, bereft, and hopeless.

By the time they came to the square in front of the cathedral the English had withdrawn. Eadric, Aelfheah and Elfmar were surrounded by hundreds of Danes, jeering and calling insults, mostly in Danish and lost in the overall cacophony. Eadric could make out some. "Pig fuckers," "Cockless Christians," and "We'll use you for shitplanks" were among the wittiest.

Then they were face to slabface with Vrangr. He held a weighty axe in one hand alone, and the muscles of his bare arms swelled, hard as oak burls, as he waved it like a flag. He circled them, and Elfmar's face betrayed a terror that he was about to be beheaded from behind. Tensed muscles are no armour, Eadric wanted to tell him. Aelfheah's face was calm. Eadric tried to stand proud and noble, but covered in shit, it was hard to be sure he'd pulled it off.

Vrangr came back to stand in front of them. He planted his feet wide apart and raised his arms so he made an X, with the axe bridging fist to fist above his head. The Danish insults stopped, the clamour fell to whispers and mutterings.

Vrangr lowered the axe. He grabbed Eadric's beard and, as his men laughed, pulled him forward, forcing him to look down. With his other hand he swung his axe like a pendulum in front of his knees. He moved his hips as if swinging a mighty cock, and the Danes laughed louder.

Eadric wondered if he was building momentum to swing a full circle, change the arc from vertical to horizontal, and swing around his head to bite through Eadric's neck. Tensed muscles are no armour, and cause tense thought. He pulled his shoulder back and tried to relax them.

Then the swing slowed, and Vrangr shouted "This man's brother killed my brother Kjell. Not with honour in battle, but like a coward, when he was prisoner. This man's brother insulted Kjell. He insults my fathers. He insults me. He insults us all. This man's brother wanted to deny brave Kjell his place in Valhalla."

The Danes jeered and roared. "Coward," Eadric heard, and "Take his head."

"Kjell died bravely, and will not be denied," Eadric shouted in Danish. He hoped Kjell died a terrified and whimpering wreck.

Archbishop Aelfheah stepped forward. "Your brother will not go to Valhalla, but I will pray to Saint Peter that he be granted a place alongside the saints in heaven. Even at the very gates, it is not too late to repent of sin, accept Jesus our Saviour, and be cleansed in God's grace."

Vrangr was at first stunned by such boldness, then an anger came, and a growl rose from his throat. He swung the axe one-handed, swiftly up from still. It wasn't a full force blow, but must have taken immense strength. The blade's flat hit Aelfheah on the side of his head, and he collapsed like a half empty sack to the ground. Elfmar ran to him, took his senseless head in his lap, and looked accusingly up at Vrangr. He said nothing, but closed his eyes in prayer.

"Lord Vrangr," Eadric began. "We are surrounded by Christian fools. My brother is one. Here are two more, who insult you by praying for your brother." He could add Thorkell to the list, but that was pushing chance too far. Not that Vrangr was better than a heathen fool, because if he was about to throw away more gafol than had ever been paid, King Sveyn would not be happy, nor would his men. "My brother was wrong. Had I been there, Kjell Ormsson would have another chance to fight his way into Valhalla, and we would now be discussing a ransom, or a simple exchange."

Vrangr at least refrained from using his axe, but his fist fell hard and heavy enough onto Eadric's left ear that he lost sense and balance, and found himself on his back, seeing heavenly bodies again. Stars, or were those bright shining lights angels?

The sound of laughing Danes came through the ringing in his head. He tried to stand, slipped, and managed to rise. He put his hand to his throbbing left ear. Blood was coming from it, and running into his beard.

"A ransom, you say?" roared Vrangr. Then I say, five thousand silver pounds, for your life!" His men cheered.

Five thousand was a joke. That was half the size of the last gafol payment to Sveyn, and more than the whole of Cantenberh had paid. Vrangr was putting on a show to please his men. It was against Eadric's nature not to haggle, and he hoped it was against Vrangr's too. "Three," he said. "I am not a king." It could come out of his part of the deal with Thorkell. At the very worst he'd see no profit, but he'd have his life. "And your word that I'll not be rewarded the way Reeve Hlothar was."

Vrangr raised his axe.

Eadric didn't blink, but knew he should have agreed to five. "Kill me, and King Aethelred will pay nothing. Not to you, not to Thorkell, and not to King Sveyn. Your King will be angry, and who will he blame? Vrangr Ormsson."

"Vrangr Ormsson, who will be back in Jomsborg!" Vrangr roared.

"Back in Jomsborg with no silver. Not for you, nor for your men." He turned and shouted to the crowd, slowly, in Danish poor but simple, so each one of them understood. "I agreed with Thorkell a payment that will give each of you twenty pounds of silver!" It was an exaggeration, but they would not know. "You will be rich men!"

They cheered, the heathen fools.

Vrangr was not so stupid that he couldn't see that if he demanded too much from Eadric and got none, it was his own men who'd pay the price for his greed. "Four thousand," he said.

"Agreed." Eadric was suddenly weak and sweating as Vrangr clasped his forearm in his mighty grip. He seemed safe. But oh so tired.

Vrangr released him, and turned to his men, raising his axe in both hands once more. "That is the ransom for Eadric of Mercia. I will still have blood for my brother. Christian blood, for Kjell was killed in the name of their God."

The men roared again. With silver promised, blood was now more precious.

Vrangr swung his axe, and turned to look down at Elfmar, still kneeling over the unconscious Aelfheah. "Which is the one they call the Arch Bishop?"

Elfmar looked up at him. "I- I-" He could barely speak. He looked down at Aelfheah's head resting in his lap. "This… this is the Archbishop," he said, tears brimming from his eyes and running down his cheeks.

Eadric saw how easily Elfmar gave up the man who once saved his life. He'd have done the same, of course, but he made no claim to be a man of God.

Vrangr stood over Elfmar, looking down on the Benedictine's bald tonsure. He lifted a gold chain off his shoulders, and fingered the brass chain around Aelfheah's neck. He walked around them, and kicked Aelfheah's sandalled feet. He lifted Elfmar's chasuble, and saw his boots. He lifted Elfmar's hand, and inspected his display of ornate rings. He glanced at Aelfheah's, and saw but one band, and had no reason to turn the hand over.

"You lie. You have the stupid shaved skull that marks you as the chief."

"I am chief of the Abbey, not-"

"You have the shoes. That is but a poor old man with no family, nowhere to live, and no-one but you to serve. You are the Arch Bishop. Stand."

"No, no, I-"

Vrnagr pulled him to his feet. Aelfheah's head fell to the ground.

"I am not Archbishop! He is! I am the humble Abbot, Elfmar of Sherborne in Wessex."

"Your fingers wear gold."

"He is holy, he is the head of the church, the Pope's anointed-"

"Then why does he dress like a beggar?"

"He dresses like our Lord Jesus!"

Vrangr shook his head at the folly of worshipping a beggar. He turned to Eadric. "He claims the other is the Arch Bishop. Is it the truth, or does he just try to save his own life?"

Eadric despised Elfmar. Yes, he'd have done the same, and despised himself too. But if either the Abbot or the Archbishop must die… "He lies. He is Archbishop Aelfheah. The other is just a humble old monk."

"No!" Elfmar squealed in his rage and terror.

Eadric went to Aelfheah. He didn't want the old fool reviving, confessing, and making martyrs of all three of them. He held his right hand tight, and felt the emerald press into his own palm. He wondered if he might be able to slip it off. Why not? It would make the Archbishop safer, and provide some compensation for this mess.

Vrangr looked at the Danes who'd brought them from their prison, and they stepped forward and pushed Elfmar to his knees.

"Say your last words, Arch Bishop."

"I'm not the Archbishop!"

Vrangr spat at him. "Make your prayer to your weak God who takes weak men into his heaven filled with singing women, for that is where you go."

The Danes cheered, and Vrangr began swinging his axe before him, this time with both hands.

The cheering died. Silence spread across the square like a breeze ripples a pond. Vrangr's swing ceased.

Elfmar looked up in hope, to see Thorkell, striding into the square at the head of forescore men. Thorkell the Tall, who struck awe into those who confronted him.

All save Vrangr. "Do not interfere, Thorkell. I will have vengeance for my brother."

Thorkell did not answer at once, but let the hush spread across the square. When all would hear, he spoke softly but clearly. "Then have vengeance against the man who held the sword. Not against this innocent Christian, who just weeks ago saved one hundred of our cousins."

"He is the Arch Bishop, Thorkell. He took good men to serve his God Jesus. He preaches forgiveness like a woman, not revenge. Forgiveness! Service! These are words for the weak, not the strong. Which are we?" He addressed this to his men, who sounded their guttural war-cry and raised their axes. Vrangr shouted over them. "He must die so my brother's killers know the insult they dealt."

Then Thorkell saw it was Elfmar kneeling, and saw Eadric with Aelfheah, who was just regaining consciousness. He came, and knelt, and took the true Archbishop's naked hand. "Your Grace, I pray for forgiveness for this."

Eadric sighed.

Vrangr was amazed. "That is the Arch Bishop?"

Thorkell rose, and looked down on Vrangr, whose head came up to his chest. But Vrangr didn't retreat, and still had both hands on his axe.

"That is the Archbishop, and he has my bond of safety. I agreed a price with Ealdorman Eadric, and you will not break Jomsborg's honour."

"You promised the Arch Bishop's safety?"

"I promised the safety of all of Cantware."

Vrangr paused. The square was silent. Vrangr roared "I will have revenge for my brother!" and the men around him, his men not Thorkell's, erupted in cheers and howls. "This is not a Cantware man," he shouted, looking down at the kneeling Elfmar. "He himself said he is from Wessex." He lifted his axe.

Thorkell stepped between Vrangr and Elfmar.

The crowd bayed, wanting blood.

Vrangr looked up at Thorkell, his lord, and at the eighty men behind him. He lowered his axe, and the crowd's roars ebbed into a dissatisfied mutter. "If not blood, then money," he said. "For us all!"

"There is money for us all."

"More. Kjell was not in your bargaining. We demand blood money for Kjell!" he shouted this to the crowd, and they began to chant "Gelt, gelt, gelt."

Eadric knew Thorkell must acquiesce to this. To do otherwise was to risk fighting between his men and Vrangr's. He lifted Elfmar and told him "Go to the Abbey. Better, to Lunden."

Elfmar ran. Eadric suspected he'd not stop until he was back to Sherborne.

Thorkell came to the dazed Aelfheah, who was trying to take in what was happening. He looked at Eadric. "Three thousand?"

Eadric nodded. The King would find three thousand pounds for the life of the church's leader.

Aelfheah struggled to his feet. "No," he said weakly. "No, I do not accept this. The Archbishop will not be ransomed."

He was still reeling from Vrangr's blow. Eadric turned to Vrangr. "He has not regained his senses."

"I have, I have," Aelfheah said, standing straight now. "I will not be part of any heathen's blood money bargaining."

"He pisses on us," Vrangr shouted. "We offer mercy, and he pisses on us. So be it." He raised his axe.

The crowd roared. Thorkell stood tall to face Vrangr, but madness was in the air, and Danes closed in on Aelfheah behind him. A chunk of rock was thrown, a squared rock, with a dressed face. It must have been hews from the walls of the Archbishop's own cathedral. A second rock hit Aelfheah full on his spine, and he grunted, and fell to his knees. That was when he saw his ring was gone, but by then it didn't matter.

Thorkell cried "Stop!" but the baying Danes were deaf to him. More stones hit Aelfheah. Eadric backed away as they surrounded the most holy man in England, lifting the thrown rocks to bring them down again onto his shoulders, his legs, his feet. Eadric clearly heard the crunch of crushed bones.

Aelfheah tried to stay on his knees, and he chanted his own evensong until another rock dented his skull. He fell, and still they continued, and Eadric was glad he could no longer see the Archbishop. All he could see was blood-covered cathedral stones being lifted, and crash down, to be lifted again.

Clutching the emerald ring tightly, Eadric crawled backwards away from the murder, expecting at any moment to feel a rock crack his own backbone or split his own skull. If he must die, let the blackness be instant. He heard Thorkell ordering his men to gather, but he couldn't work out why, for it was too late to save Aelfheah. Eadric followed the sound, hoping that the blood-crazed Danes would see him for the bringer of silver that he was.

He managed to stand. Thorkell, with his height, was prominent. He was taking his men towards the cathedral, trying to defend it, because Vrangr's men had found flaming torches. Half of them closed in on the cathedral. The other half went into the houses around the square, and pulled out the Cantenberh people, the people who had paid three thousand pounds of silver for safety. They were skewered by sword and decapitated by battleaxe. Folk ran screaming from burning houses, preferring death by steel than by flame.

Eadric got to Thorkell, who saw him, and pulled him behind the front line. "I am shamed," was all he said. Then Eadric found himself between Marton and Stigand. So Thyra had found him, and Stigand had found Thorkell.

Vrangr's men outnumbered Thorkell's, and seeing they would not fight, they just flowed between and around them. They entered the cathedral with torches which they laid under pews and on the stripped bare altar. Others dragged Christians to the doors and threw them inside. Then all left the cathedral, barred its doors, and stood back until smoke funnelled through the broken windows.

"Follow me," cried Thorkell. "Jomsborgrs who know loyalty, follow me!", and he led his men out of the square. "I renounce this barbarity," he said to Eadric. "This is not what we came to England for."

10. Soussex

(Edward)

"You buggers don't know what you've got here, do you."

Edward knew Heremond, because it was on Heremond's recommendation that Theodric had been appointed as his personal guard. It was a good appointment too, and with the trust built up there was every expectation that Theo would one day take charge of Edward's personal husceorls.

So to hear him calling them from behind as they rode by the skirts of the Wealden forest, and to see him bringing his panting and sweating horse to a halt alongside Theo, was worrying, but not unwelcome. Heremond explained that he had been sent by Edmund to warn them of the Danish attack on Cantware. They knew of this already from the throngs of fleeing villagers.

Then Godwin hurriedly told his story. Edward was doubly shocked, and rage burned his face. Odylia's betrayal was unbelievable... and yet, utterly predictable. Theo would die to protect him, but Odylia? Never. He turned his face to stone.

Sibbi's death caught him in a place he didn't know existed between his heart and his stomach. He'd known Sibbi from the age of eight, when they had learned Latin and numbers, and studied the scriptures together, until Sibbi had left for the monastery two years ago. Never had anyone so close been taken from him so violently. Straightaway he wanted to be sitting with Fulton, safe by the millpond, finding comfort in talk and his steady presence. He was glad that Fulton seemed more at ease now on the horse – he would lean forward and pat its neck and call it by its name, Linden. He'd been right to take it from Odylia. He'd make Fulton a gift of it once they got home.

Heremond's advice was for himself and Theo to take Edward and Ecfrida rapidly to Lunden. Theo overruled it. "We don't know where those Danes are," he said. "And they certainly don't know where we are. But we might run into others, and if we do, we'll need seven armed men, not two."

Heremond started to argue, but Edward spoke over him. "I agree with Theo. There is no new cause for panic. We should stay together."

If either man was surprised, they hid it well. If either suspected that Edward would not consent to leaving Fulton behind, they hid this too.

Heremond and Theo rode at the front with the big Haystackman, the lanky old one, and the fat one they called Plum; Ecfrida rode with Cynethe, who looked constantly in danger of losing her seat as she bounced on her old garron's barrel back. Godwin rode behind them, with the other two ceorls making up the rearguard. Edward had picked up their names, Ecgulf and Tidwyn, but wasn't sure which was which. They were ordered to keep a rotating rearward watch. One stopped to look back down the path to see if anyone followed. As the main group was about to disappear ahead, he galloped after them, and when he caught up, the other took the standing lookout. The three at the front did the same. Edward thought about the ploy. It would not help against an ambush, as attackers would stay hidden. But it would warn of a chance encounter, the more likely danger.

And so they progressed, westbound along woodland tracks, as fast as Cynethe's reluctant mount allowed. Theo ordered greater pace, but soon all the horses needed rest, especially Heremond's, tired by its long journey through Cantware.

High ground and thinner trees allowed them to see smoke rising, away to the south. Heremond observed that the Danes had found places to land other than Sanwic and Rye. "Haestings?" he wondered.

Edward recalled what the old monk who'd schooled him had told him. "The Haestingas are Jutish folk of old," he said. "I think there was an understanding. They never get raided."

"This is an invasion, not a raid," Heremond snapped, rather too curtly.

"I think we're too far from the coast," Theo said. "But then, so is that smoke. We should leave the road, and make our way under cover of woodland."

Heremond agreed.

Edward also agreed. He thought it unlikely that any Danes bent on finding himself and Ecfrida for ransom could still be on their trail, but there might be others coming inland in search of plunder and supplies. "Yes, we should," he said. He wanted to show support for Heremond, then feared that the older fighter just saw it as a reminder than he, Edward, was the Prince here, and was now even more annoyed at him.

They struck out for the densely treed high ground of the southern Weald. Even old woods have their tracks made by foresters, colliers and swineherds, by archers and by the deer they hunted. The troop was drawn to those tracks, but the paths they followed so easily on horses whose hooves they could not entirely hush, were just as useful to others.

A dozen men leapt out of hollows on either side, as a dozen more charged from behind shrubs. All were ruthlessly silent, not screaming and yelling, nor roaring foreign cursewords. They frightened Edward all the more for that. Three hacked down Ecgulf at the rear before he could even draw sword. Theodric drew his, and shouted "Don't fight! Run!" and crippled two Danes at his right before four at his left axed his horse's gaskins. The beast collapsed to its haunches, and Theodric had no height or balance, and axeblades and spearpoints sank deep into his thighs, his belly, his shoulder, his neck. Six more used the same tactic to fell Heremond. They had identified the two strongest among the English and swiftly despatched them. Edward felt naked.

He, Fulton, Ecfrida and Cynethe were protected from the first onslaught, but half of the attackers saw the two girls, and stopped to point at them, still maintaining their grim silence. Edward and Fulton heeled their horses to break through the encircling men. They got clear unscathed, but Fulton's mount took an axe blow from one side that broke her shinbone, and a sword on the other that sliced deep into her shoulder. She stumbled on a few yards then collapsed, throwing Fulton from her back. She rolled on the ground screaming, then stilled, never to rise.

Edward knew Fulton was no longer with him, and, clear of the melee, he turned. Two Danes were closing in on Fulton, one with a sword, the other with an axe poised behind his shoulder. Fulton pulled himself to his feet and drew a small seax. His eyes darted from sword to axe, readying himself against whichever blade swung first. The pair watched each other for the signal to attack simultaneously.

Godwin had Ash between Ecfrida and two more Danes, giving her time to charge her horse away as he slashed his sword like an eagle's wing to keep the attackers back. When he saw them raise their axes, their eyes not on him but on the horse's hind legs, he dug in his heels. Ash sprang forward, and the axes missed.

He was clear, but a throwing axe spun through the air to bury itself in Ecfrida's horse's rump. It wheeled and reared, screaming in pain, and Ecfrida was thrown. Godwin caught up to Edward, and turned too.

Beyond Ecfrida, Cynethe with her bright gold hair had drawn eight men like wolves. One swung the flat of his axe to knock from her hand a knife she'd drawn, then others grabbed her feet, her legs, her waist. Ignoring her swipes and punches, they pulled her backwards off the garron to the ground. Hands clawed at her clothes, and the more of her white skin was exposed the faster the fingers ripped.

The Plum, the Haystack, old Ingwald and Tidwyn were surrounded by the main part of the pack, who still kept a grim silence, probably thinking how to kill the riders without wounding any more of the valuable horses.

Ecfrida picked herself up from the ground. Three of the men around Cynethe saw her, and abandoned one prey for another.

Fulton stepped back from the two who confronted him, only to feel the point of a longsword prod his back. The one behind could have killed him with a stroke, but preferred to join the other two and savour Fulton's fear. His face was that of a boy who knew he was about to die.

"Do something," Edward told Godwin. It was more a plea than a command.

Godwin might turn and flee on his big strong horse. Edward was sure he wouldn't. He might go to Fulton, or help the terrified Ecfrida who was retreating from the Danes with their awful leers, or stay where he was to protect Edward. Most likely he'd save none of them, and die; certainly he couldn't save them all.

Cynethe was screaming.

They were all going to die, unransomed.

Godwin stepped his horse forward and stood tall in his stirrups. He yelled out: "You buggers don't know what you've got here, do you?"

Perhaps it was his voice, speaking boldly and not pleading for mercy, that gave the attackers pause. Edward was stunned. Godwin was going to betray them. He had turned into Odylia.

"Don't any of you fuckers speak English?"

All was suddenly still. One looked at the others, and stepped out of the ring surrounding the ceorls. "I do." Edward was disgusted to hear a Soussex accent – a local in the pay of the Danes. A mercenary.

"You have Edward and Ecfrida," Godwin said. "The King's son and daughter. Prince and Princess, carrying a mighty ransom. You don't want to be killing them."

Edward realised: Godwin wasn't betraying them, he was saving them. And, yes, surely hoping they didn't want to be killing him now, either.

The man looked around at his employers. "'Course we know. But which is who?" he demanded.

Edward spoke without thinking. "Him," he said, pointing at Fulton. "He's the Prince." He pointed at Ecfrida. "And she's the Princess."

The three around Ecfrida smiled and pointed their swords at her. Four left Cynethe and moved towards Fulton, their faces glowing from exertion and the sweet smell of gold. Fulton was stunned into momentary silence. One second he was about to die, now he was alive again, and a Prince. But if Princes are ransomed, and handboys killed… He looked up at his liege, and croaked a word. No-one heard. Only Edward saw the shape of his name on Fulton's lips.

Ecfrida understood what Edward had done. She pointed at Cynethe. "That is my sister Princess Goda who you assault."

Grown men hung their heads. They understood the enormity of raping a princess. It must not happen. Cannot happen. It certainly wasn't their privilege. One said "Sorry my Lady."

The silent attack. Assailants bearing short axes and pikes, not battleaxes and shields. Godwin spoke Edward's thought. "You're all fucking English!"

English, but not Saxon. These were Haestinga Jutes, Edward was sure.

The spokesman said "They came upon us, all of a rush. Find us Edward and Ecfrida, they said, and your homes will be spared."

"Traitors!" Fulton yelled.

The man turned on him. "And what did your father ever do to protect his people? Time he was gone!"

In the seconds of silence and uncertainty, Godwin charged forward. The men confronting Ecfrida had their backs to him, and as they turned he drove his sword deep into the neck of one, pulled the blade free and hacked at another, who tried to use his axe handle to defend himself. Godwin's blade slid down the shaft and severed four fingers, and the man retreated with a howl; he'd chop no more than kindling now.

Plaemond, Geareth, Ingwald and Tidwyn turned outwards and tried to battle their way free of the men who held them at bay, still unwilling to cut the horses' legs from under them.

Godwin turned back. The leader stood in front of Ecfrida. He rode at him, flailing his sword wildly to force the man away. "Climb up," he shouted, and she scrabbled at his waist and thigh, and managed to get one leg over his horse's hindquarters and cling on. His sweeping sword kept the man from swinging, but as soon as Godwin turned to get away he'd be able to slash at the hind legs. More of them closed in, and now one was behind, one before, and three more with bloodstained axe blades were coming to their aid. Ecfrida struggled to hang on, then pulled herself up behind him.

Edward charged without thinking. His sword sliced the bare neck of an Englishman too slow to turn at the hooves drumming the soft ground. Edward galloped on, screaming, to the three who surrounded Fulton, diverting Godwin's assailants, giving him time to kick his horse clear. "Stop!" Godwin yelled.

It wasn't his word that stopped Edward, but Fulton's "No!! Save yourself!" And the look in Fulton's eyes. It was many things, but it was no longer fear. Edward had no name for what he saw there, but he knew he would never forget it.

"They won't hurt the Prince," Godwin shouted, keeping up the pretence, and Edward pulled the reins, and wheeled around, looking all the time into Fulton's face, before heeling back towards Godwin and Ecfrida.

The leader looked from Edward on his elegant piebald palfrey, to Linden's corpse: the fine steed and the workhorse. "You're no prince," he sneered. Fulton turned to run and was felled by a swinging pikehead that shattered his ankle. His arms splayed out in front of him, his seax still in his grip until an axe fell to detach his hand from his arm. Only then did he scream.

Edward would never remember hearing it. He would only remember one of the men turn Fulton onto his back, and Fulton's naked throat, his soft white skin and his Adam's apple trembling, and the blade that sliced deep into it. Fulton's scream was a red fountain of spewing blood.

Plum Plaemond, Geareth, Ingwald and Tidwyn were dying on their horses, forced to defend themselves on one side and suffering slashes to their thighs on the other. Ingwald tired first, and with deep cuts in both legs he simply toppled from his saddle to meet three waiting pikes that speared him like a fish. Pleamond lost his sword, and was hauled down, and his face was split with an axe, plumlike to the end. Tidwyn followed when his sword-arm was slashed. Geareth the Haystack was doughty, until the attackers lost patience and felled his horse. Human and equine screams mingled until both died.

Edward sped ahead of Godwin and Ecfrida, then realised he must slow a little or he'd leave them behind. "Keep changing direction," Godwin shouted, and Edward obeyed.

Ecfrida sceamed "We can't leave Cynethe!"

But they had to. And she wasn't Cynethe, she was Goda, a princess, and too valuable to harm.

They galloped a mile, then two, before Godwin called him to slow to a canter. "They have horses now," he said as he drew level. "Charging ours to exhaustion won't outrun them, not for long."

They let the horses recover their wind, and kept looking for hunters coming from behind.

"A child could follow our hoofprints," Edward said. "We should leave the horses, and go deep into the forest on foot."

"We're faster on horseback," Godwin said.

"Faster than walking," Edward argued. "Not faster than them. Not like this." He was looking at Ecfrida seated behind Godwin with her arms tight around his chest.

"Edward's right," she said. "They'll outrun us, with two on your horse."

The young ceorl was insistent. "We keep ahead till dark, then they won't be able to track us. We don't have time to argue."

You're right, Edward thought. So stop arguing.

"I understand," Ecfrida said to Godwin. "You don't want to abandon Ash after losing Linden, do you."

Godwin growled "It's a hard nut to swallow unshelled."

She moved one hand from around his waist and rested it on his shoulder, a gesture of – what? Sympathy? Familiarity?

You and I have just lost our closest friends, Edward thought. We, brother and sister, should be supporting each other now, not-

"You walk if you think that's best," Godwin said to him. "Ecfrida can take your pony. Better for all of us."

Why oh why could he not just assert himself and give an order? How was he being insulted and commanded so? And who by? By the traitor's son, that's who. "Come morning they'll have all the traitors in Soussex onto us," Edward said.

"That's if your father left any." Hah! That made Godwin flinch.

But Edward was defeated by the idea of surviving alone in the forest, and he knew Godwin would have his way. For now. The ceorl would pay for this contumation later.

Then to Edward's surprise, Godwin halted Ash, raised his leg over his neck, and slipped to the ground. "Fuck," he said, shaking his head and patting Ash's neck. "I'm the one who has to walk. You two ride fast till nightfall. Walk slow at night. Follow a stream so you leave no trail. You know the north star? The mossy side of trees?"

Ecfrida leaned down and touched Godwin's shoulder again. "What about you?"

He ignored her question. "Find a village. A headman or thegn. You have silver? Use it. Now go. I'll be all right."

Ecfrida nodded, and took Ash's saddle and reins. "Thank you."

Edward said nothing.

They turned away at a trot, a canter, a gallop.

"And look after my bloody horse," he shouted after them.

Edward turned, to see Godwin running into the forest undergrowth.

"Pray for him," Ecfrida said, next time they slowed.

"He'll be alright."

"Pray for him," she repeated. "Without him, we'd be hostages. Like Cynethe."

What would happen to Cynethe when, inevitably, it was discovered that she was not Princess Goda? She might pay for her pretence… but she was a beauty in any land, so she might at least survive. She'd be given to the Danes in the hope of saving some Haestingas' homes. Edward pitied the girl. He pitied Ecfrida for her loss.

"We might be dead," his sister added.

Like Fulton.

11. Reunions

(Emma)

"I may be able to help."

Poor Goda was distraught. Hendi had died of the pox despite the cross Goda had put above her friend's bed, the scented garlands she'd hung around it, and the incantation she sang over and over.

"The snake comes through the door, the snake bites
Jesus comes through the door, Jesus smites
The snake into nine parts breaks
To each part Jesus speaks:
Fennel, nettle, mugwort
Wormwood, betony, fleawort
Lambscress, crabtree, thyme."

The leech had taught Goda this spell, but the leech was as useless as his fennel, nettle and mugwort. At the end he had but three words: "The Lord's will."

After Hendi's burial, Emma wanted to hold Goda's hand for longer. But a more pressing matter demanded her attention. "The will of God must be endured," was all she offered her daughter.

The will of Kings and Princes, however, may be steered; so it was Alfred she guided to the hall. She wanted to hold his free hand, but he'd not let her. She had to restrain him, to stop him swinging ahead and making a childish entrance to show off his crutch. "You are here to listen, you are here to learn. One day you will be advising a king, and you'll be taking counsel yourself. You need to understand what's at play."

Alfred was more than keen to be present at his first war council. He clearly found this so much more exciting than the Witan. No, the argument she was rehearsing was in case Aethelred took a notion that he was still too young. She was glad Edmund had returned to Lunden with reinforcements from Wessex; he would support Alfred's presence. "But say nothing, Alfred. If you have questions, whisper them to me."

They entered the small hall where the King, Edmund, Brihtric, and Ealdormen Aelfric and Athelmar were seated around a large table. Aethelred was his fretful self. "We couldn't have known, we couldn't have known," he wailed, his hands waving like a widow's at a funeral.

Emma attacked the room as soon as the door closed behind her. "Why wasn't I told?" she shouted. It was an exaggerated display, but it was good to intimidate these men from the start. "I need to be here. I have a right, because I was almost caught up in your battle. I am your ambassador from Normandy, and Normandy is your only ally. And my son and your daughter are God knows where."

Messengers had been sent out, but they hadn't returned, nor had their pigeons. There was no way of knowing if any had avoided the Jomsvikingr's mayhem in Cantware and managed to get close to Rye.

Edmund tried reassurance. "Deorleaf will look after them. He's a good man, and he has a good squad."

She turned her fury on him, and now it was genuine. "Half of them were obese, and the other half children!"

"Edward and Ecfrida haven't been captured," Aethelred said. "If they had been, we'd know the ransom demand within a day."

"Not if Thorkell wants to make us sweat first," she said. The King might be right, but she saw little point in agreeing with him. "Edward and Ecfrida could be killed, or worse, without a Dane even realising who they are. How many of the invaders speak English?"

"Of course you should have been told, dear," Aethelred said, trying to calm her. "Edmund," he snapped, "Why wasn't the Queen told?"

Edmund just held his hands wide.

Emma sat down at the big table, with Alfred looking small beside her. No-one would question his presence now. "So what could we not have known, exactly?"

Edmund reiterated for her. "We couldn't have known Thorkell was coming, nor the size of his fleet. We chose to shield Lunden from Sveyn, rather than protect Cantware. I admit that at the time I thought it a mistake, for we can defend Lunden at Lunden. We needed to defend Cantware at Sanwic. But our boats couldn't have stopped a fleet the size of Thorkell's, and we don't have men enough on land. So having them at Tilberh turned out well."

"How many boats did he sail?"

"Some two hundred. If he'd chosen to come up the Tamys with all of them, he'd surely have broken through at Tilberh."

"But he only sent a smaller part," said Brihtric. "Which means he's not here to take Lunden."

"He's here to squeeze more silver out of our treasuries and our mines," Aethelred said. "That's the Vikingr way now. Once it was respectable raiding, now it's their trade, and they're as canny as an Abramite. When your brother returns we'll know what he's agreed for me to pay."

Emma had to admit that Eadric showed a big pair of cullions going to meet this Thorkell, this great warrior of unknown temperament. Onion-sized. Unless another King, the one Thorkell served, had guaranteed Eadric's safety. She would never know.

"What's an Abramite?" Alfred whispered.

She hushed him, mouthing "Later."

"We are gathering reports of how far he's come through Cantware," said Brihtric. "Is he into Soussex? How close are his forces to Lunden?"

"Soussex?" Emma said sharply. If they were into Soussex, they could have marched through Rye, or sailed past it. Edward would be trapped there, or worse. She hoped Deorleaf had the sense to hide him, to disguise him. And to reveal him, if it came to capture. A prince is safer than a peasant.

"So far," Edmund said, "they seem to have gone to the main towns along the north to Hrofcaestr, and settlements between the Downs and the Weald, like Meddestane."

Emma shuddered. It could so easily be herself and Alfred being held for ransom.

"The question is how far west does he wish to venture?" Edmund continued. "How far along the south coast? And which towns do we defend?"

"If any," said Brihtric. "If we must pay silver anyway, why weaken ourselves?"

"You mean we shouldn't defend Lunden?" snapped Aethelred.

"Or Wintancaestr? Suthamtun?" added Aelfric.

Brihtric quailed. "No no, of course not."

"It seems to me there's another question," Emma said.

The men looked at her, but none invited her to enlarge. When Edmund spoke, he said "There is. Possibly it's an even bigger one. What are Sveyn's own forces doing? Is that your question?"

Emma nodded. "Our thegns and abbots across the Five Berhs and the North, what are they reporting?"

"It's confusing," said Edmund. "Some report nothing. Others report a muster, and gatherings of levies at various towns."

"Sveyn is always gathering a force somewhere," said

Brihtric. "He is so strong in Lindesege now that its towns are safe from attack even by Norsemen. His attention will shift to East Anglia." Then he added, almost as an afterthought "And he threatens Mercia."

If that were true, Emma thought, Mercia would have been first on your list.

Edmund ignored hm. "A levy came to Ledecaestr, and gathered more men. But there was no report from Snotengeham. Surely a force from the north would have passed through Snotengeham? I question the loyalty of some thegns and ealdors."

"When Uhtred betrayed us and turned to Sveyn," Brihtric said, "it made many of them nervous."

"Uhtred must pay," muttered Aethelred. "As Elfhelm paid."

"Sveyn will not be resisted by putting fear into this or that thegn." Edmund was clearly frustrated. Any plan that did not involve a strategic war on Sveyn frustrated him.

Old Athelmar spoke up, his voice as thin as his hair. "We must plan for the worst. What if Thorkell's fleet and the thousands of Danes are more than just another harrying to extort silver? What if Thorkell is come to attack Lunden from the south, while Sveyn sends armies to attack from the north? Or if he plans the same strategy for Wessex, with Thorkell coming west from Cantware, and Sveyn descending on us by the Icknield Way?"

"We can't defend everywhere!" Aethelred wailed.

"We can't defend anywhere," said Edmund. "But we will, soon."

"So when you have your fyrd assembled, Edmund," Emma said, "where will you march them? Go north, and Lunden is exposed. Stay here, and Wessex is open. Turn on Thorkell in Cantware, and Sveyn can choose to attack where he wishes, Lunden or Wessex."

Edmund was reduced to shouting. "How come Sveyn steers the cart? Does he have more men in his realm? Does he have more swords, or horses?"

"Probably," said Brihtric.

"And why? Because you and your slimy brother have for years obstructed any kind of warring on him, and sent silver that pays Sveyn's armies when it should have been spent on ours."

Brihtric demurred. "Advice was always from the whole Witan."

"Why did you learn to speak Danish?" Edmund yelled, rising and throwing his chair back to the floor.

Alfred looked up, shocked. He didn't like seeing his big bother's loss of temper.

Emma thought Edmund was going to stomp out of the room, but he merely circled the table. "And why has your brother given away his slutgirl to Sveyn's son?"

She recalled the child she'd talked to at the feast, the orphan girl, soon to be wed to Prince Knut. Slutgirl? Had Edmund wanted her?

"Why is Edmund angry?" Alfred whispered as Aethelred tried to calm Edmund down.

"Because he sees the land he wants to be king of disappearing," Emma whispered back, and wished she hadn't, for Alfred was a prince too.

Aelfric was saying that the girl will give her husband currency in Northumbria, where they remember her father."

"Armed men are bigger coins," Edmund growled.

"It's of little concern," Aethelred said. "She's not even his daughter. I'm surprised Sveyn didn't swat Eadric's arse and send him back where he came from."

"We have a truce with Sveyn over Mercia at least," Brihtric said.

Edmund returned to his place at the table, but he didn't

pick up the chair. He leaned forward on two braced arms, his face as close to Brihtric's as the table allowed. His words came low, and grim. "A truce we need to break."

The next days were riven with rumours flying like bats. A Danish army was assembling at Stamsford, it was said, and was growing larger as troops joined from parts north. Where would Sveyn have it turn? Speculation spread from house to house, from street to street. He was going to fall on Lunden, so leave if you can. He will harry Wessex, so there is nowhere safe to go. Thorkell will sail his whole fleet up the Tamys, and won't be beaten twice. He will sail it around the south for Wihtware, the island that Sveyn had occupied so many times it was more Danish than Denmark, and Suthamtun and Wintancaestr will be sacked yet again. He will sail to Eassex and join his force with Sveyn's into one mighty irresistible wave that will swamp Lunden and roll across the land all the way to Defenas.

Tension tightened like a twisted windlass rope, and Lunden seethed with fear. Markets were emptied of goods as people hoarded for siege. Arguments became riots. Theft from neighbours had no consequence, or was a lesser risk than having nothing with which to buy mercy from a Dane who has broken your door down. Murdered bodies were found on the streets, and women feared to leave their homes. Somehow now was the time to settle scores and steal whatever was forbidden. Priests quoted Archbishop Wulfstan's missives that Judgement Day was upon the world, and the prospect meant that now more than ever sin must be resisted. But the end of days did not constrain men, it made mortal wickedness trivial.

Edmund swore to Aethelred that his fyrd would match

Sveyn's, but neither talked of matching Thorkell as well. Emma did, though. She went further, saying to Edmund "We need three fyrds. One for Lunden, one to confront Thorkell, and a third to face Sveyn." She poured him a cup of wine.

It was the night before he was to leave again for Wintancaestr. They had repaired to her room, having both kissed Goda and Alfred goodnight, having both looked helplessly at Edward's empty bed.

Edmund shook his head in despondent fashion, but there was a fire in his eyes that he failed to damp down. Perhaps he too had a plan. "Thorkell's forces have divided into four, it seems. I think that if I fielded an army to face him, be it large or small, he would simply flow around us like a stream around a boulder. It may be that Sveyn would do the same. It's certainly what I would do."

"And what do you conclude?"

Her son by marriage was reticent to confide in her, which further notched up her respect for him. But Emma had no strategem that would be undermined for being shared, not with Edmund. "I shall tell you what I conclude," she said, to make it easy for him. "Your fyrd should forget about Thorkell and Sveyn altogether, and strike into the Five Berhs. Sveyn considers those lands his."

"My father differs."

"You and I know which king Sigeferth and Morkere really serve, for all their protestations of loyalty to us. Now is the time to make them stand by what they say, and assert our overlordship."

"My father will not have us harry our own folk."

"Did I say harry the Five Berhs? No, just make an example of the biggest traitor. I suspect it's Snotengeham's Thegn."

"Why not Sigeferth or Morkere themselves?" He was not suggesting it. He wanted to know her mind.

"Not yet. They are more useful alive, once they are truly ours. Threaten Lindesege."

"You think I care about Lindesege?"

"I think you'd be a fool to. But I think Sveyn does. It would help, of course, if we knew Sveyn's mind better."

Edmund snorted. "We are dependent on Eadric for that. The King uses him as envoy. We don't know what he learns, we only know what he chooses to tell us."

"And now he has managed to put his girl close to Sveyn's affairs, and at the heart of Knut's. You can be sure he will draw from her all he can."

"It may not be much. Sveyn and Knut surely have sense enough not to tell her secrets."

"But they won't take out her eyes or cut off her ears. What we need is our own source." Emma suspected she had needled a sore there.

Edmund's terse reply confirmed it. "I'm sure Sveyn has a sparrow in my camp. I'm buggered if I can get one into his."

"I may be able to help."

"How?" he demanded.

"I can't tell you," she said. "Leave it with me."

"Mother, your aid will be well received." Edmund took her hand and kissed her ring.

He had never called her mother before.

Edmund left next day to resume the muster in Wessex, and for a few hours Lunden was sunk in a black depression as if the Prince himself was the bastion against Danish doom, not the King and his enlarged fyrd.

But come afternoon, two events calmed Lunden's mood like honeywater for a thirsting man, like a golden heirloom from a forgotten uncle.

First, Higfrith, Thegn of Tenrige, a Hundred in Suthrige where it met Cantware, rode into Lunden with twoscore men protecting a boy and a girl. As soon as word came from Suthringework that Edward and Ecfrida were safely home, Emma and Aethelred took Alfred and Goda to welcome them. Aethelred's ceorls cleared a space at the north end of the bridge, and Alfred shouldered his way between Higfrith's men to limped to Edward. One of them lifted Alfred onto the piebald's rump behind his brother, and Alfred balanced on one leg with one hand gripping Edward's shoulder and the other waving his crutch like a returning hero. It was Alfred's first display of affection for Edward for months, as far as Emma could recall.

Alfred swung the crutch above Edward's head and launched it over the side of the bridge into the Tamys.

The crowd roared and cheered. Emma smiled at her little man. She wanted to run across to her sons. She looked down at Goda beside her. "You go. Someone will lift you behind 'Frida."

Goda's lips stayed downturned, and she shook her head. After Hendi's death, the poor girl had scant interest in allowing joy back into her life.

Emma recognised Ecfrida's mount. It was the boy Godwin's horse. Ah well, if he and Deorleaf and the rest had died in Rye so that the Prince and Princess were saved, theirs were worthy deaths. The ceorls' families should be rewarded.

They waited as the horses approached. Alfred was joyfully prattling to Edward, no doubt telling him about the battle he'd witnessed, the boats, the fires, and the beheading. Edward hushed him and dismounted for Emma to hug all breath from him. Aethelred was even more demonstrative, lifting Ecfrida to his chest and spinning her until she pressed to be put down.

He promised Higfrith rich reward, but later, when they sat

Edward and Ecfrida down to hear their tale, it was clear that Aethelred had been overly generous. The Thegn had done nothing other than feed and shelter them, and escort them home. Emma suspected that he was happy to be in Lunden, rather than Tenrige awaiting a visit from Thorkell.

Deorleaf's family would feel her wrath, if they were still alive, for he had let her down by not returning straight to Rye. As for the rodent Odylia, nothing would save her from ultimate retribution should she survive the Danes.

"It was Godwin who saved us," said Ecfrida. "He was, he was… I can't describe it. He didn't just fight men bigger than him, it wasn't just that he was courageous. He was clever. And when he saw that the best way to save us was to give me his horse, he did it with no hesitation."

"He let Fulton die," said Edward sadly.

"I know." Ecfrida took his hand. "I told you, Edward. His duty was to help me." She turned to Aethelred and Emma. "He couldn't do both."

Fulton dead? Poor Edward. He loved that boy almost like family. Now they'd have to find a new friend for him, like they would for Goda.

"Fulton was so brave," said Edward, tears brimming his eyelids. "He… He…" But he could say no more, and ran to his room.

Emma wanted to go after him, but Edward had chosen not to cry into her skirt. To follow would insult him. When Alfred moved away, she told him to take Goda.

"Where is Cynethe?" Aethelred asked.

Emma wanted to slap him. Ecfrida would tell in her own time, in her own way. For now, the tears flooding her eyes spoke clearly enough. Emma gripped his arm. "Don't ask the girl that."

He growled.

"Edward was brave too." Ecfrida said. "You should be

proud of him. He charged, to save Fulton."

"Bloody idiot," Aethelred said, pleased at the diversion from Cynethe's fate.

"It gave Godwin time to get me out. Where is Edmund? He should know what Godwin did. Godwin should be rewarded, and generously."

"If he's alive he will be," Aethelred said. "And if he's dead, his family will."

Emma realised that the King didn't know who Godwin was. Why would he? Godwin's first reward was that she had no intention of telling him.

"His mother and father are both dead," Ecfrida said. "He has a sister, that's all."

She wondered what happened to Brothers Ordulf and Sibbi. She hoped they found refuge somewhere, and weren't so foolish as to stay in their habits. Had Ordulf kept the records of his survey, which was after all the reason for the damned trip to Rameslege? They were probably lost, monks and records together.

So passed the morning and most of the afternoon. Then in the evening came an event still more important to Lunden. First there was panic, for the initial report was of hundreds of axebearers marching up the Cantware Road, headed by Goliath himself. Then Reeve Wilmaer himself came riding ahead to say that Ealdorman Eadric was returned with such good news that Lunden must celebrate.

Eadric rode in. Alongside him, on a rare thick-necked and broad shouldered Flandran Percheron that reminded Emma of home, rode Magog reborn, the greatest giant Lunden had ever seen. All knew his name.

Behind Eadric rode Father Stigand, and behind him came twoscore Danes. The crowd had turned out to witness events, lured by the rumour that the giant had renounced his king, but they kept a wary hush. Lundeners knew that the devil hid in rumours, knowledge that didn't stop Lundeners spreading them.

Emma ensured she was present at Eadric's meeting with the King and his Ealdormen, although the price was not being able to spend time with Edward. She left him opening his bible, but surely reading psalms was slim consolation compared to a mother's love?

The war council reconvened, this time with Eadric and Thorkell. Aethelred once more saw no reason for Stigand's presence, and Eadric agreed he was an upstart. "I agree with you both," Emma said. "I do not like the man. He is arrogant, presumptuous, and venal, I'm sure. He has a leer that, believe me, turns the stomach of all women he regards."

Stigand bore the insult with no more than a double blink and a raised eyebrow, before leaving.

That should do it, Emma thought, hoping that he had sense enough not to be slighted and flee with his tail beween his legs back to Norwic.

The King welcomed Thorkell with due respect, but was unsure what to make of his arrival, even after Eadric explained the circumstances of Thorkell's defection from his own Jomsborgrs. Emma's first thought had been whether this could be a ploy to discover the English plans and defences. But no leader sends himself as a sparrow. He sends a trusted captain. Then was Thorkell Sveyn's trusted captain?

Something was not being said, she was sure. This Vrangr, why did he suddenly decide that Aelfheah, who had already surrendered three thousand pounds, had to die? It made no sense.

Aethelred seemed most affected by the death of the venerable Archbishop. "Truly a martyr. There was never a time I did not know him." The Wessex Ealdormen nodded grimly, for Aelfheah had been Bishop of their towns, Bath, then Wintancaestr.

Eadric plainly wished to move the discussion forward. "Thorkell brings two hundred and forty fighting men, now camped south of Suthringworke. In addition, forty-five of his ships are sailing to Tilberh with a letter of safety from me. You, Brihtric, must send a similar letter overland. We don't want to welcome them as we did Kjell Ormsson."

Brihtric nodded, looking down, avoiding anyone's eye. It was unlike Brihtric to show anything resembling contrition. With Edmund departed, he would surely want to remind the King that he was the victor on the Tamys.

Thorkell spoke with a resonant voice all the more impressive for its low volume, although Emma could imagine it booming out over a battle. "Each of my boats has fifteen oarsmen fighters, or thereabouts. If you can provide as many again, they will sail faster and fight better."

Forty-five boats, near a quarter of the Danish fleet, had come over to their side. He had brought close to nine hundred men, enough to turn a tide. "Has Edmund been told?" she wanted to know.

Wilmaer bowed his head "I sent messengers to Wintancaestr."

"I make one condition." Thorkell's voice was low so they had to strain to hear. "My men will follow where I lead, except in this: they will not fight in Cantware against their brothers from Jomsborg."

"Peace in Cantware, this we have to buy," said Eadric.

"I was waiting for that bad news," Aethelred growled.

"And that is only for Cantware." Eadric wore a grimace that cut his face like scars, and Emma knew the price was high.

"Forty-eight."

"Forty-eight? Forty-eight what? Eggs? Apples?" But Aethelred knew.

"Thousand pounds. Of silver."

Aethelred's shoulders sloped. He was not even angry.

"Why?"

"Because the Vikingr of Jomsborg are monsters," Thorkell told him. "And Vrangr is the worst monster of us all. It is not so bad. Three parts in ten will be for me and my men here. That buys you a big stock of contentment."

"I will vouch for Thorkell the Tall," Eadric said.

"I'm sure you will," Emma said. "Who vouches for you, Eadric Streona?"

Eadric snarled at his Queen. It was brief, but she saw it.

Emma had to swallow the gall of Arsindis's disapproval when she sent her to the Abbey to find Father Stigand. She wished she had no need to tell her to ensure Stigand came secretly to her. Emma had no intention of inviting him to stay, but equally, she had no intention of explaining herself. Arsindis would see soon enough, when she dismissed him.

It was three hours later that Arsindis showed Stigand in.

Emma immediately told him to remain standing. He plainly hadn't expected formality. He took a wide stance and stood tall. His fngers were interlocked down below his waistcord. He was the image of a strong yet humble priest.

She waited until Arsindis had shut the door on them. "Eadgyth," she said sharply. "My daughter in law. Ealdorman Eadric's wife."

He hadn't expected this either, and stood there blinking.

"You fucked her."

"I- I-" he started, and it was too late to deny it. His hands parted. "It was before I met you, my lady."

Ha! The fool thinks he is here to face my jealousy! She was right about his arrogance. "You realise what would happen to you if Eadric found out?"

He had no answer.

"There might be a remote monastery you could hide in, but I doubt it."

Stigand tried to gather himself. "You wouldn't do that."

"I have no regard for Eadric, and Eadgyth is a whore who deserves to be shamed."

"But-"

"You're thinking I'm more vulnerable to shame than she? I have someone who heard you boast of your conquest." She gave him a few seconds to work out who she meant. "And you can't imagine that he would ever reveal what he witnessed later."

Stigand was defeated, but she had more. "My handmaid will say how you pressed your unwanted attentions upon me, and my husband will believe her."

His shoulders had slumped, his spine was no longer stiff. "He can do nothing other."

He was intelligent. That's why she liked him. In fact, that was why she trusted him. "You're right," she said. "Until then, he will have no seeds of doubt about me, because he knows how much I despise your venal manner."

"But you love my venal manner!"

She had to laugh. There he was, held in her palm, at her mercy, yet still able to find the wicked charm that was his only weapon. Well, almost his only weapon. "All right, Stigand. Sit down. I don't want you in a monastery fearing that the next travelling guest is Eadric's blademan. I have a job for you. It's one that you may even find has a pleasing benefit."

"I can only agree, be it to swim in shit."

"Don't be bitter, Stigand. Just take your predicament as a lesson in caution."

He became more humble, or pretended to. "And what is this task you set me?"

"Before you return to Ulfcytel, and before Eadric returns to Mercia, you are to go to Coventre or wherever Eadgyth is.

You must convince her that you are Edmund's servant, and tell her what he wishes her to do. It's not dangerous, but if she demurs, tell her that her dalliance with you is no longer secret. She will understand. Then you may dally away."

When she had told him, and ensured he understood fully the message and the need for secrecy, she bade him depart.

"I am still your… your servant," he said, with that half smile, that half tilt of the head.

"And so you are," she snapped. "And so you may be again. But not tonight. Learn caution, Stigand, and tame that arrogance. Too little of one and too much of the other will kill you." Then, loud enough to ensure Arsindis outside could hear, she ordered "Now leave me!"

Next day she made a point of eating with her husband. First she played the military tactician, then she played the caring mother. "Sveyn's plans are unpredictable," she said. "He's at most five days from London as we speak, and Thorkell's men are still split. And who really knows Thorkell's ambitions? How far can we trust him? What if," she whispered low, "what if this is just a cunning ruse to get eight hundred men into Eassex unhindered, to join with Sveyn?"

"Don't be an idiot," Aethelred snapped. "He could more easily have simply sailed there in force from Sanwic."

It was sometimes useful to be thought an idiot, especially by Aethelred. Better than being thought clever and devious. "You are right. To be honest, it's not my fear, but Edward's. The poor boy has had a terrible shock. After his ordeal he needs somewhere safe and calm. He grieves for Fulton, and for Theodric. He is more sensitive than Alfred."

"Born in the wrong order, those two."

"And Goda is still unhappy. She misses Hendi so. She needs to be in the safest place possible."

Aethelred understood her, and was easily persuaded. "Take 'Frida too," was all he said.

12. Thegn

(Godwin)

"If ever you need my help."

It had been hard work persuading the fat guard to get the husceorl in charge to come to the inner gate, but at least his pressing had revealed that Queen Emma was here in Wintancaestr. Godwin had feared he'd need to go to Lunden, or Escancaestr far to the west, or even to Normandy. The guard had stomped off into a hut, then after a moment looked back in the hope that Godwin might have disappeared, then walked into the dark. Godwin pulled his cloak about his shoulders in readiness for a long wait, wishing he could have stayed in Comtyn.

He'd been exhausted when he'd stumbled along the path between patchwork fields of wheat a mile from home. He heard his name called as folk abandoned their work to trail him into the village. All familiar faces: Whitstege, with her baby tied to her back, limping Nin, Adred the Stick, and little harelip Merewyn whose teeth bit her bottom lip when she smiled. Women and old men and children were all that Comtyn had left, and they reached for the hand of the boy who had saved them. Merewyn ran off towards the village.

Work to rebuild the houses was going slowly. One, which had lost little more than its roof, was being re-thatched that day. Two others, whose upwind gables and a section of roof were unburned, were half finished with new frames fixed to old, yellow wood against sawn back but still charred stumps. Strips of willow for wattle walls were piled up, enough for only two or three huts. Knee-high heaps of soil and stone for cob infill lay scattered around the village. They wouldn't go far.

Godwin knew the problem: not enough people to cut trees, saw planks, dig a limepit, or to wield hammers and adzes, not when the old and the young needed feeding, the cows milking and the crops tending. No coins for timber or labour.

His own house, that of his father and mother, was still a mound of fallen stone and charred fingers of timber pointing up from the ground. The mead hall that might have sheltered the homeless was the same.

With word come from Merewyn, a small crowd led by Brother Snell was already gathered to meet him. Saewin ran and jumped onto him and would not let go, so she was squeezed in the embraces from Gret, then Eagbert, then Selferth. Brother Snell and all the others reached through to clasp his arm and slap his back.

When Godwin was finally given space to breathe, Cudbert could finally offer his hand. "I feared we'd not see you again."

"You nearly didn't. Tell me, what… what damage did Brihtric do that day?" He couldn't bring himself to directly ask the hardest question.

But Cudbert answered it. "From Comtyn, only your mother and Cenwig were killed. We worked out that Cenwig was spotted on his way back, so he'd got all the way to Bosham. A grandfather there would not leave his home, but everyone else ran, just in time. Thanks to you. There was burning and looting, but they missed Bosham and Walderton's grain stores, and we saved most of the livestock. Homeless folk got sheltered in chapels. It will be a hard winter, but we'll cope. As you see, we are rebuilding."

"I'm sorry we didn't do any work on your house," Sel said.

"Don't be a dump, Sel. My house is the last priority."

"Everyone will have shelter for the winter," Brother Snell said.

Godwin looked around the village. "Not at this rate."

Snell ignored him. "Come, to the chapel."

"To pray?"

"To hear your story," Snell said. "To offer thanks. And I have something for you."

First, Saewin took Godwin to their mother's grave. "I planted flowers," she said. The grave was high with toadflax, hawkbit, yarrow and daisies. "I collected them."

"That's good. That's nice." They stood, and he felt her hand grasp his. "I'm sorry, Rabbit. I had to go. I had no choice."

"I know," she said.

"I have to go away again soon, but I'll be back straight away."

"When?"

"A couple of days."

He could change his name, and stay in Comtyn forever, farming, rebuilding, marrying. Everyone would think Godwin perished in Soussex. There'd be no-one left bearing the stain of Wulfnoth's treachery. Ah, but folk talk, and one day he'd be called to a muster with Sel and Eg and Cudbert, and someone would spot him. Besides, he wanted Ash back.

Snell went to an oak chest in his hut beside the chapel, opened it, and lifted out a bundle wrapped with cloth. "I managed to get it off your mother before the Danes could. I think she'd forgive the indignity."

The bundle was so heavy it could only be metal. Snell peeled back the cloth, to reveal the shiny rings of chainmail.

"I feared to tell you at the time. Brihtic's men were all around, and if one heard, he'd likely take it, even out of the chapel. I had it repaired. It still won't stop a bodkin, but it will turn a sword or glaive." He lifted it, and passed Saehild's hauberk to Godwin.

His mother might have let him turn his back on his father. She'd never have allowed him to renounce himself.

"Now come," Snell said. "The people are waiting."

Comtynians stood shoulder to shoulder, yet the chapel overflowed, and people stood outside straining to hear Godwin recount his adventures. He spoke simply and factually, trying not to show pride. He did not even pass a judgement on Odylia, although he heard his audience's hiss when he described her betrayal. Some had family down by Bosham, and knew her. Eg, Sel and Cudbert certainly did, and Godwin felt their scrutiny as he talked. Were they thinking as he was, that if not for Godwin's action at Brimclif, Odylia wouldn't have been in that perilous situation in Rye? He passed hurriedly on, to speak of the events in the Wealden forest, wondering if rescuing Ecfrida somehow redeemed him for condemning Odylia.

Godwin had no need for pride. Comtyn overflowed with it. That a son of Comtyn had been taken to serve Prince Edmund Ironside himself was wonder enough. That he'd been in Queen Emma's guard in Cantware, and had fowled and fished with the young Princes, was status unheard of. To have saved the lives of Edward and Ecfrida was scarcely believable.

As the sky turned pink, before he could take the meal Cudbert offered, he was pulled into the woods outside the village by Gret. "You've come back to marry me," she said as she took him into her. "You know you has."

"Nearly didn't get back at all," he grunted.

"I've known it," she whispered, "since mother suckled us, one tit each."

Gret was warm and soft, and their pleasure together as comfortable as falling asleep in a warm bed. Was he so close to the evening of his life already, to be thinking that having a family and growing old with her was no bad prospect? He felt that it was barely morning for him.

He was invited to sleep in Cudbert's hut on the platform next to Sel. Sel wouldn't leave him quite enough space but he didn't thresh like Eg who offered the alternative.

Next day he asked for two shovels, and took Cudbert to look at the ruins of his house. They kicked through the debris. "Me and Sel searched the ashes, looking for anything valuable," Cudbert said, "But the place was looted by Brihtric's men."

Godwin took bearings. Here was the doorway, its frame a charred remnant, and a hole where the threshold stone had been. Thereabouts, a window. And over there, definitely, had been the fireplace. The stones were all gone, taken for new doorsteps and hearths. He didn't mind. He paced from all three, and marked a square in the ground with the shovel. "Here. Dig."

The hole was small, lined with planking, and had a base of large stones. Godwin and Cudbert squatted next to it. The planks were beginning to rot, but the box that stood on the stones had been tarred. It had no lock, but still they needed knives to prise off the lid. Inside was an oiled hemp bag, heavy with gold and silver coins.

"I'm amazed your father didn't take this," Cudbert said.

"He didn't know. Mother had this dug when he was away, and swore me to secrecy."

"She didn't trust him either," Cudbert said drily.

"Either?"

Cudbert remained squatting looking into the empty hole. "You can owe a man loyalty without trusting him. You do your duty by him, but it ain't out of love."

Godwin stood. "You did your duty. You kept your promise to my father and my mother. I release you from it."

"Thing is, Godwin, I reckon they'd 'a wanted me looking after you all the more if they wasn't around."

"I'm not a child."

"Nor's the king, and he still has husceorls."

Godwin gave Cudbert two gold coins from the bag.

"Ain't for money, Godwin."

"Maybe, but you need it, you and Sel. Give another to Cenwig's family. The rest is for rebuilding." Godwin took two coins for himself, and gave the heavy bag to Cudbert.

"Two silvers?" Cudbert said. "Where you going? You just got here."

"Wintancaestr. To find out where Queen Emma is. I have something that's hers."

When the fat guard bought a lean old husceorl to the inner gate, Godwin explained again who he wanted to see and why. The husceorl snorted contemptuously and reached for Ordulf's leather bag. "I'll take that to her. Be on your way."

Godwin snatched it back and kept his feet planted. "Tell her Godwin is here."

The guard's sneer slid into a twisted smile, and he grunted like a disappointed hog. Godwin was allowed to enter. It seemed his name was recognised.

The husceorl had kept him out of sight as he ingratiated himself, or tried to, with the Queen. Rather than simply announce his name, he forced Godwin to walk through the doorway for the effect of his appearance.

Emma nearly spilled the wine she was pouring. She put down the pitcher, and stood. The man sitting with his back to the door turned. Godwin was both surprised and pleased to see Edmund. Things might return to normality.

But surely it was not normal for a Queen and a Prince to stand on seeing a ceorl such as himself?

They said his name simultaneously. Emma commanded the husceorl to fetch Edward, Alfred, Goda and Ecfrida, and Edmund said "It's good to see you safe. Come and sit, and drink wine with us. Would you like a cake?"

He went to the seat Edmund offered. As he passed, Edmund threw his arm around Godwin's shoulders and pulled him tight to his side. His free hand slapped Godwin's chest hard enough to leave bruises. "You're a hero, Godwin, a fucking hero. I knew it. I knew it the first time I saw you. I thought, this boy is worth having. He'll do us proud." He turned to the Queen. "He's done more than that, don't you think?"

The Queen poured wine into a glass beaker. Godwin had only ever drunk out of wood, clay or horn. "We are in your debt, young man," she said.

The door opened, and Alfred shouted "Godwin!" and limped as fast as he could across the room to hug him. He only stood away when he saw his mother's glare.

"How is your leg?" Godwin asked.

"It still hurts a bit, but there's this huuuge scar-" he drew his finger from knee to hip "from here to here." He looked up at Godwin proudly, beaming as if he'd just been given a shiny new sword or a horse, forgetting that Godwin had seen the cut, and it wasn't half that length.

Ecfrida followed Alfred more slowly, came to Godwin and embraced him. "I'm so glad you're safe," she said. "I have your horse. I've looked after him."

He felt his cheeks flare, and couldn't look at her as he said "Thank you my lady."

She took a step backwards, glancing nervously at the

Queen. They'd made friends in Rye, but that was after Emma left.

Edward stayed near the door, his lips moving without parting as if dismissing anything he might start to say. He was holding a girl's hand. Eight years old, Godwin guessed, dark of hair and eye. She stared as if there was no joy in the world, and Godwin was not the person to bring some. Edward fell back on formality. "I thank you for your… for your… help. You will be rewarded." He let go of the girl and stepped forward with his hand held before him, for Godwin to kiss his ring. Godwin had to comply, and hold back his smile that this was a protocol Edward had never initiated in Rye. He wondered where Edward went to flagellate himself these days.

Godwin straightened, and removed the leather bag from his shoulder. "This is Brother Ordulf's work. I should have given it to Prince Edward, but things were too fraught." He handed it to Emma. "I fear Brother Sibbi was killed. Beheaded, for no reason. Well, to insult Our Lord, and to terrify the villagers. I hope Ordulf made his way home on foot."

"We shall pray for Sibbi's soul and for Odulf's safety," Edward said.

Emma clapped her hands. "We shall! And we shall organise a feast in your honour, Godwin! We shall have gleemen and tumblers, and for one night at least there will be no talk of Sveyn or Thorkell, or fyrds or fleets." She turned to Edmund. "You don't have to leave immediately, do you?"

"Not for a day or two," he smiled. "But we should talk of fleets. Have you had word of the victory at Tilberh?"

"No news came to Comtyn. The only talk is the invasion of Cantware. Everyone lives in fear."

"I was there," Alfred said. "I saw it! A hundred Danish ships-"

"Fewer than fifty, Alfred," Edmund said.

"And we trapped them on the river," Alfred continued, "And there were fire arrows, and ships burned, and more smoke than anyone ever saw, and the Danes were drowned or killed or captured, and the leader, he was beheaded by Brihtric of Mercia-"

A chill swept over Godwin like a cold wave. His face began to curl, which Alfred saw. Confused, he stopped his excited description of the battle.

"That'll do, Alfred," Edmund said.

"I was just-"

"Enough, Alfred. Enough." Emma supported Edmund.

"Yes, Godwin," Edmund said. "Brihtric. Your friend and mine. He claims credit for the victory when I'm not around. I know who deserves the credit. We'd not have sprung the trap without your lesson of how to use wind and tide and fire."

Godwin bowed his head and said nothing. Most of what he'd told Edmund about fighting at sea had come from Odylia, another person of whom there would be no talk.

Emma whispered to Edmund, and he murmured something back to her. She looked at Godwin, then at her children. "Now, there is something we want to say to Godwin in private. So if you will leave us, please…"

Alfred swung himself back to the door, stopping only to turn and say "Can we do bowfishing again?" then leaving before Godwin could answer because, as Prince, he knew the answer was yes.

Ecfrida took Goda, and departed more reluctantly, smiling as she bade her farewell. Edward hesitated, and Godwin could not read the reason on his face.

"Edward, this is something that it would be unfair to Godwin to share with you. Now, please…"

He held his mother's gaze for just a moment, then turned and left.

Emma looked again at Godwin. "You saved my son, and that earns undying gratitude. The King has said you must be rewarded. You, and your family. Ecfrida tells me you have a sister. How old is she?"

This unexpected question surprised Godwin. "Eight years."

"Is she sweet?"

"Sweet? As a ripe blackberry, I suppose. With those annoying seeds that get stuck between your teeth. But then, I'm her brother, I see her differently. She has many friends, that I do know."

"She has friends. Good. My daughter Goda has lost her friend, and needs a new one. Your village, it is near here? You must go there, and bring your sister."

He had no choice but to agree. "As you wish."

Edmund spoke. "We won't take her from home if she doesn't want. What is her name?"

"Saewin."

"Well, Saewin herself can decide if she wishes to stay with Goda as her companion and handmaid."

"But you should advise her," Emma said, "that there will be nowhere safer, in this land or any other, than beside my daughter."

No doubt Cynethe had felt the same about her position alongside Ecfrida.

"And she will be well fed, well clothed, and will receive gifts and trinkets, and as she grows, she will meet young men of wealth and standing."

She was telling him that to refuse Sae's services would be not only insulting, but mad. His reward was Rabbit's safety. "Thank you, my lady."

"I know who your father is."

Godwin's eyes closed, but when he opened them, he felt strangely relaxed. The weight he carried like a boulder was not removed, but was at least revealed.

"For myself, I want you to know that in my eyes you are redeemed of your father's crime. You shall have money from my treasury as well as from the King's. If ever you need my help, you have only to ask."

The Queen's protection! She was bestowing a rare honour and privilege. Godwin bowed, and again said nothing.

Emma offered a reassurance. "If your sister comes to us, it won't be known who she is. Edward and Ecfrida may be curious and may even guess. If they do, I shall bind them to silence."

She seemed to have finished, so he bent his head to kiss her hand. "Thank you, my lady." He saw that she expected him to show gratitude, not just speak it, so he smiled, and knew she saw through it.

"Edmund?" she said.

What now?

"Sit down, Godwin," Edmund said.

Godwin was pleased to sit, and to give his attention to this man who was so much more straightforward than Emma, or indeed, like any man, than any woman.

"Your father was stripped of his thegnship," Edmund said.

"Rightly so," Godwin confirmed.

"In the name of Aethelred, King of England, I grant it back to you. Your Ealdormen of Wessex will agree-"

"As will the King," Emma said decisively.

"I will sign the charter-"

"As will I," Emma said.

"To confirm to all that you, Godwin, are from this day Thegn of Comtyn and Bosham and the lands in between, with all the duties and privileges of the position."

"Thank you, Lord," Godwin said, keeping his eyes respectfully lowered.

"You can have a little time to tell your people," Edmund said. "Then I want you and that big lout I saw, and as many good aged boys as remain along that valley, to come to my fyrd. I give you until Saint Dunstan's Day."

Godwin raised his head. "You spoke of reward. Comtyn needs trees felled, a quarry for flint, a new lime pit. Bosham needs them too. And hired men if we can find any, and mules, and a new smithy for tools."

Edmund threw back his head and laughed. "That's my boy!"

Emma's smile was not such a gale, but a wafting May breeze. "It shall be," she said.

13. *"More Danica"*

(Fleada)

"The Danes have customs that we must meet."

When Aelfgifu complained about the hard journey ahead, Eadric told her that she should count her blessings. Gegnesberh was where Alfred the Great had married Ealhswith, and it lay even further from Wessex than from Mercia.

"So why did he marry her?" she demanded.

"Her father was chief of the Gegni."

Aelfgifu was still petulant. "If the Saxon King travelled all that way for her, why can't the Danish Prince travel for me?"

"He did. He sailed from Denmark, so quiet yourself."

The two-day journey to Tamwerth was worse than the one to Lunden. In a time of high gafol, thuws were put to work in fields and workshops, not repairing potholed ways. Aelfgifu of course had her palfrey, and she demanded that Fleada be allowed to ride the pony she'd used on their outing with Godgifu, but Eadric said it was too valuable. Fleada was offered a mule with no saddle. Fleada opted to walk.

At Tamwerth they could at last step onto barges. She could recline on a cushion beside Aelfgifu, and watch Mercia flow by. Eadric was in the boat ahead with Eadgyth, while others of the retinue sailed behind. Thyra sat among them, wearing her best brooch. Aelfgifu had not been harsh when Fleada confessed to having secretly returned it. She told her not to cry, and said "I forgive you," for which Fleada was grateful even as she wondered why she had to feel guilty twice over.

No-one sat within earshot of them save the oarsmen, allowing them hushed confidences. "Nothman is coming," Aelfgifu told Fleada. "My father told me this morning." She had taken to calling Eadric "father" recently. "His beard must have grown back," she giggled.

Fleada could not join with her amusement. She feared Nothman.

"He's behind us on the river somewhere, with Leofric and a score of Hwiccan followers. Uhtred of Northumbria will be there, and Malcoluim King of the Scots, and they were not long since at war! Even King Aethelred sent a letter. Eadgyth carries it."

Fleada confessed that only as she learned of all the great and noble guests who would attend did she fully realise how important this wedding was.

"I'm to marry the next King of Denmark," Aelfgifu said. "What could be more important?"

Fearing she'd insulted her mistress, Fleada stumbled to explain herself. "I meant for England," she said.

Aelfgifu hugged her. "Isn't it exciting!"

Yes, Fleada thought. For you.

The Tam became the Trehynt, as wide as the Sabrin, flowing strongly with no fords and no worrying scrapes on the riverbed. The lands were gentle and towns sparse, but there were hamlets, and jetties built out into the stream with small boats moored. Folk waded in the river with nets. Fleada knew they were out of Mercia and into Sigeferth's lands now, or was it Morkere's? The Five Berhs, in any case.

They rested for two days at Snotengeham, and Eadric roisted with the two Ealdormen, who hosted them generously before joining the entourage.

The Trehynt swept them eastwards, then north into the flatlands of Lindesege. They stopped again at a place called Torksey, where people talked and shouted unrecognisable words in tones more rolling and melodious than the flatter sounds of Mercia. They had come to the borderlands of a foreign country.

A camp was to be set up, where the travellers would stay for two nights before the last leg of their journey to Gegnesberh. Two women waited at the mooring, mother and daughter, brought by the Headman. He spoke clear English, and introduced the older woman as Jyordis and the younger as Lota. "Jyordis is the volfa and the gyoja," he said, but offered no translation. Aelfgifu looked at Thyra, knowing she spoke Danish.

"Jyordis will be in charge of preparing you properly," Thyra said.

Fleada heard her own wail: "That's my job!" For this occasion, more than ever.

To her relief, Aelfgifu took her hand. "I will not entrust myself to some foreign hag with no sense of beauty or colour.'

Eadric stepped in front of Thyra. "You will do it together. The Danes have customs that we must meet."

Jyordis spoke incomprehensible words, and held out her hand to Aelfgifu.

"She wants you to go with her," Thyra said.

"Thank you for telling me." Aelfgifu's voice was as haughty as her walk. "I shall need my things."

Fleada asked two oarsmen to bring Aelfgifu's boxes and chests, and was surprised that they did so without a look or a question. Do they think I'm her sister?

She ran after Aelfgifu, Jyordis and Lota to a solid timber house backing onto the limpid waters of a small tributary to the Trehynt. Jyordis would not let the oarsmen past the threshold, so Fleada had to struggle to drag the chests inside on her own. The main room had a claypit hearth at its centre, and a curtained doorway leading to a smaller sleeping room at the back. This was furnished only with a broad sleeping platform and a thick feather mattress. Here Fleada was to make up a bed.

The girls were woken next morning by Lota. She motioned for Fleada to dress Aelfgifu, and mimed putting everything on: Aelfgifu's shoes, her stole, her jewels, and something for her head. So Fleada dressed Aelfgifu as she would be tomorrow, and fixed her brooches, put necklaces over her head, and ensured her rings were matched. Lota had kindling and a sack of charcoal, and set about lighting the fire. Fleada thought it unnecessary on this sunny morning, unless they were to cook. She saw no pots..

Eadric and Eadgyth came. Jyordis let Eadgyth enter, but stood in the doorway against the man. "I have a special gift," he called. Jyordis ushered them out to him.

He stood with a casket of polished oak, its lid carved with a simple knot device. "Explain to your new husband and his folk that the knot is a symbol of a bond between two people, and between two peoples."

It was no such thing, Fleada knew. The knot was the symbol of Stafford, Eadric's home scire. It was a secret mark of continued ownership.

He opened the box for Aelfgifu to see inside. There lay a gold circlet for her hair, resting on a bed of blue fabric the like of which Fleada had never seen. It rippled as water, and had a sheen of silver. Aelfgifu gave the circlet to Eadgyth to hold, and took the liquidlike material from the casket. It was a magical scarf of pale blue, made with threads thinner than any spider ever span. Smooth and light, it flowed like a stream bubbling over rocks as she lifted it, and when she held it up to catch the breeze it floated like a high summer cloud. It was so fine that even when Eadric laid it over Aelfgifu's head, and put the gold circlet over it to keep it in place, her face was still visible, as through mist.

"This is Byzantian silk, my dear," Eadric said, "And there is nothing else like it in all England."

Jyordis had come out of the hut, and she looked at the display in admiration. She came to Aelfgifu and lifted the crownlet to adjust the veil so it was clear of her face, then she put the gold ring back. Aelfgifu replaced the veil as it had been, over her face. Then she lifted it with both hands, and mimed a kiss for Jyordis. "See?"

Jyordis said "No, no," and stopped Aelfgifu. That's when she saw the gold cross on its chain around Aelgifu's neck. "No. No." she said again, and tried to lift the necklace over her head.

Fleada realised, and Aelfgifu's horrified face showed she realised too. Jyordis was a priestess preparing Aelfgifu for a pagan ritual, not a Christian marriage.

Aelfgifu pushed her away and turned angrily to Eadric. "You said Knut is a Christian," she screamed. "You said he was Lambert."

"No Lambert," said Jyordis.

"He is," Eadric said. "But Sveyn is not."

"I'm not marrying Sveyn!"

"Well, in a way, you are. You are marrying the Danish people, and you must do it after their fashion."

"I demand a Christian wedding!"

"The church has a word for it. More Danica, the Danish custom. The Pope will respect this marriage."

"Cristin. No," said Jyordis firmly.

"She has a right to a proper wedding," Eadgyth said.

"And she shall have one," Eadric said. "A true Christian marriage, Aelfgifu, as soon as we can get you, Knut, a church and a priest assembled."

"It has to be tomorrow," Aelfgifu insisted. "Before tomorrow night!"

"Yes yes. There are Christians in Gegnesberh."

Such was Eadric's desire to make this match that he had

considered nothing that might obstruct Sveyn's will.

Jyordis gestured that Aelfgifu was to replace the silk veil and gold circlet in their box, then she pulled Aelfgifu, Eadgyth and Fleada back inside the hut and shut the door fast. The room was now lit by four candles in clay holders on the floor. The fire was well established, with glowing charcoal giving off little smoke. Lota had a small bellows to heat it further, and the hut soon became an oven. Jyordis used blacksmith's tongs to transfer hot stones from the fire into a clay bowl, then ladled water from another pot over the stones. They hissed, and steam billowed. Jyordis went to Aelfgifu and unpinned her brooches; Lota went to Eadgyth with the same intent, but Eadgyth pushed her away. Fleada didn't know what she was supposed to do as Jyordis's trespassing hands removed Aelfgifu's clothes until she stood resolutely naked. No, Aelfgifu was more than resolute, she was proud.

Loosening her own smock, Jyordis barked something in Danish that was clearly an instruction to Fleada and Eadgyth to do the same. Lota was already as naked as Aelfgifu, so Fleada shrugged and dutifully stripped.

Jyordis's fat and sagging breasts were painted brown with three interlocking triangles on one, and interlocking moon crescents on the other. Her shoulders and back had an image of a giant tree, with leaves under the sky and roots under the ground. The lines were crudely drawn, and Fleada saw they were raised: these were not paint, nor tattoos of charcoal ink, but scars from hot brands.

She took her wobbling breasts and bottom to Eadgyth and started to unfasten her clothes. Eadgyth resisted. "No. No," Jyordis said, and continued.

Eadgyth looked from lumpy Jyordis to the three naked girls, sighed, shuddered, and disrobed too. Fleada was amazed that a woman so old – she must have near thirty years – could still look so magnificent. Her body had been spared childbirth.

Fleada wondered why that was, and what it meant that Eadric turned to Thyra, while Eadgyth turned to that visiting priest.

Lota took all their clothes into the bed-room, and returned to sit on a stool beside the fire.

In what was now a steam hut, Jyordis sat on another stool, and gestured for Aelfgifu, Eadgyth and Fleada also to take places around the hearth. She picked up a bundle of long willow twigs, fresh and still in leaf, and beat her back with it. She passed the bundle to Aelfgifu for her to do the same, which she did, with more gusto than Fleada thought necessary. Lota followed, then Fleada, then Eadgyth brushed her back with the leaves. Jyordis rotated the hot stones between the fire and the clay bowl, and poured more water, then began speaking to Aelfgifu, who looked blank. So Jyordis turned to Eadgyth. Her words were no clearer, but there was no mistaking the gestures she made, pumping two fingers of one hand through a circle of thumb and forefinger of the other.

"It seems I am to impart what you should expect in the marriage bed," Eadgyth said.

Aelfgifu repeated Jyordis's gesture, laughing. "Spare yourself."

Jyordis looked horrified, and Fleada realised why. To Jyordis, she had just confessed to not being a virgin. Fleada whispered her thought.

"No no," Aelfgifu said. She moved her hands down between her legs, then placed them flat over her pubis. "No no. Never." She shook her head, and Jyordis was satisfied.

Fleada remembered Nothman, that night in Coventre. Was Aelfgifu remembering too?

The fat crone now gestured from her forehead outwards, spreading her arms and splaying her fingers, and the same from her heart, outwards and back in, and she spread her legs and repeated the instruction from her woman's secret folds.

Eadgyth looked away, while Fleada wished for more steam

in the room.

Jyordis spoke more, and turned expectantly to Eadgyth.

"I think she wants you to share your wisdom too," Aelfgifu said to her. "As a woman."

Eadgyth folded her arms and crossed her legs, not to hide herself, Fleada thought, but because she had forgotten she was naked, red, and sweating. She looked at Aelfgifu, and then into the fire. "Be content with one thing, and you'll have more than me," she said. "Children. I'll not know the pain of childbirth, and I'll not know motherhood."

It was as if that was all she had to say, but she returned her gaze to Aelfgifu. "Be content with two more things, and you'll have as much as me. Civility. Demand your husband be as civil to you as to any man he respects. And discretion. That he does not make a fool of you, and on no account will you make a fool of him." She stood, and seemed to Fleada more beautiful naked than she ever looked clothed. "And above all, never forget that you are English." She looked at Fleada. "Either of you."

Eadgyth walked into the sleeping room for her clothes, leaving Fleada wondering what this meant. Thyra had told that priest of Eadgyth's adultery with Stigand. She had been discreet as far as her husband was concerned, for Eadric seemed unaware of it. Thyra had penetrated the discretion, but seemingly was not inclined to inform him, meaning Eadric couldn't fully trust either his wife or his dokkse. Did Eadgyth know about Thyra, and demand only discretion from Eadric?

By the time they heard the back door open then close again, Fleada had decided she was learning more than she wished about the house of Eadric of Mercia.

Now that Eadgyth had fulfilled her matriarchal duties, Jyordis beamed at Aelfgifu. She took more stones from the fire, poured on more water, and picked up the willow. She stood behind the girls, and beat them, and herself, until all four were red, sweating, and stinging. Fleada was happy to be sharing this ritual, for all her doubts as to whether it was too big an honour for a mere handmaid. Jyordis must consider her not Aelfgifu's servant, but her friend, or possibly, since Eadgyth stood in as a mother, her sister. Fear that once this ritual was done her status would fall to nothing crushed Fleada's brief flicker of pride.

Jyordis took their hands and led them through the back room and outside. She ran them down the slope to plunge screaming through rushes and lily pads into the cold water of the little river. She had placed cloths on the bank so they could cover themselves as they came out cleansed.

That night, Aelfgifu talked in bed of this Knut. But knowing nothing of him beyond his age, five years older than Aelfgifu's fifteen, it was hopeful speculation. "He will be strong," Aelfgifu said. "His father is strong, and will have married a strong woman."

"I'm sure he'll be strong."

"But will he have a forked beard?" Aelfgifu giggled.

"If he does, you should be worried. A man who copies his father will only do so weakly."

"It's not his beard that worries me," Aelfgifu said.

"I know, I know."

"Do you think that too will be forked?"

"Oh no! Like a serpent's tongue!"

"What will they call him, the bards, in his life or after?"

"Knut the Handsome," Fleada suggested. "Knut the Strong!"

"I hope he's Knut the Bold. Knut the Rampant! Knut the Ravisher!"

"Not Knut the Gentle? For one night at least."

"No, my sweet. You are Fleada the delicate, and I love you, but I want a man among men for my husband."

The sadness that Fleada had been suppressing these last

days suddenly overcame her. She found herself crying, and once started she could not stop.

"What is it? What is it? Don't cry for me." Aelfgifu held her tight and let Fleada's tears wet her linen shift.

"Will you… When you are married…" But Fleada could not bring herself to ask.

She didn't need to. "Of course I will. Knut will be away, he'll travel with his father, he'll do battle in England or in Denmark. You'll still be with me."

Fleada sniffed.

"And I shall have children, and you will help look after them. Poor Fleada! I should have said."

On the eve of her wedding that, for the first and only time, Aelfgifu consoled her handmaid with her tongue. Then Fleada reciprocated, and the girls slept soundly in each others' arms.

Next morning Fleada and Lota walked through Torksey calling at each house to collect posies made by the village children, and together they dressed the boat that Aelfgifu would take to Gegnesberh. The flowers that would adorn Aelfgifu's bodice and veil Lota put in a lidded pot of water for freshness, to be pinned and tied only at the very last minute, once they were back on land.

For the final leg they shared Eadric and Eadgyth's boat. The sun shone, which everyone agreed augured well for health, prosperity and happiness. The people of Torksey waved them off, and threw flowers and leaves as Aelfgifu stepped aboard. Folk followed them along the riverbank for a mile, led by drummers and pipers, then were left behind as the fleet sailed down the broad brown Trehynt between willow and reed.

They saw a kingfisher, which Eadgyth promised meant

peace and joy, because the kingfisher was the second bird to leave Noah's ark when the rains had ceased, which was how it caught its sunrise-red breast. When they spotted otters snaking to their riverbank holts as the boats neared, Eadgyth said they too meant family. Fleada wondered if she might just be making this up.

Aelfgifu saw long-legged birds standing in shallow water on the inside of a bend, and said "Look, storks!"

Storks definitely meant children, but Fleada thought these were herons, and from the awkward expression on Eadgyth's face she thought so too. If she knew a heron's meaning, she kept it to herself. Then she looked up brightly and said "It's Friday. The marriage is on Freya's day, and she blesses families."

"I'd prefer Mother Mary," Aelfgifu said.

They came towards Gegnesberh, where the river was lined with many scores of tents. "Sveyn has called people from all around," Eadric said.

Fleada observed that there were few women and no young children around this encampment. Nor were there many old men. Most were young and strong, with hair and beards braided and tied, and axes on their backs. Shields rested in piles like giant turtles, and clusters of spears stood like spruce trees. This was not a festive gathering, this was an army. Fleada was glad not to be a southerner.

Sveyn's men and women awaited them at a landing stage, from where they were led to a meadow already filling with Danish warriors whose rowdiness told that they'd breakfasted on beer.

Eadric instructed his servant Criba to ensure there was space at the front for the Mercians. More boats arrived, and Fleada recognised the Hwiccan brothers, travelling in separate vessels.

Whether blessed by Freya or by Mary, a wedding is a

wedding. It is the bride's day, and Aelfgifu was excited to see the bower under which she would be wed. Nearby, a goat and a sow were tethered. Aelfgifu pointed them out to Jyordis, who passed her fingers under her throat. "Oh," gasped Aelfgifu, "They are to be sacrificed! How barbaric." Her flushed cheeks betrayed her excitement.

Jyordis put two fingers beside her forehead to indicate the goat. "Thor," she said. And then she oinked, and said "Freya."

Aelfgifu went "Baaa," and said "Jesus," laughing at her joke. But Jyordis didn't laugh. She nodded, and called an instruction to Lota.

Fleada leaned close to Aelfgifu and whispered "I think you just ordered that a lamb be found for sacrifice."

"As long as we get to eat it!" Aelfgifu seemed to have abandoned any scruples at this mixing of holy and heathen.

Lota fastened Aelfgifu's flowers, as Fleada put the silk veil over her face and placed the crownlet on her head to hold it, to Jyordis's continuing disapproval. Then it was time to stand under the bower.

Across the field behind her came a bevy of men, led by the forkbeard father, and the son, who walked with firm strides to stand like a mighty pine alongside his silver birch of a bride.

He was the handsomest man Fleada had ever seen, more pleasing than the priest, more than Edmund, and definitely preferable to Nothman.

Aelfgifu had to keep facing forward. Fleada wished she could whisper into her ear "I believe your husband will be bold. He has yellow hair and beard, and both are trimmed, not like his father at all. He stands tall, and broad of shoulder and of face. His forehead is high and his cheeks chiselled from stone, yet his blue eyes are intelligent, observing all, and ready to laugh, I'm sure. You have your man among men." But she could only think it.

A greybeard who had been standing beside Jyordis stepped

forward and spoke in English. "Greetings all, and welcome. Welcome, Prince Knut, to English soil. Welcome King Malcoluim of the Scots. Welcome Eadric Ealdorman of Mercia, and Eadgyth daughter of King Aethelred of England. Welcome Uhtred of Northumbria, and Nothman and Leofric of Hwicce. And of course, welcome Aelfgifu, who graces us with her beauty. Welcome, men of Mercia and of Northumbria, welcome to Gegnesberh and the realm of King Sweyn of Denmark!"

He repeated his words in Danish, then went on "I am Kustaa, Gothi, who hears the gods. I am with Jyordis, Gyoja, who hears the gods." He looked at Sveyn. "Has the medgif been paid? The dowry?"

Sveyn said "Ja. Yes, it has."

"Has the mundr been paid? The brideprice?" He looked at Eadric, who said "It has. Ja." He bowed to Sveyn. "My lord is generous."

Kustaa said words to Sveyn, who took a jewelled sword and sheath from a man behind him. He drew the sword, and gave it to Knut. This was no battle sword, Fleada could see. It was too slender, too light and too polished, and the jewelled pommel made it far too valuable. Knut held it level, balanced in his palm, and his father placed a gold finger ring on its point, and hung a coiled gold armring over the hilt. Knut let the point tilt upwards.

"Follow Knut," Kustaa told Aelfgifu.

Eadric took a short silver dirk from a tooled leather sheath and gave it to Aelfgifu. She held it as Knut did, for Eadric to place a gold ring on its point and an armring on its hilt, as Sveyn had. Her hand shook, and her eyes looked not at the dirk but at Kunt's steady and smiling face. Fleada prayed that she would keep the blade pointing upwards for she knew beyond any doubt that to let the ring fall off would curse the marriage. Then she stopped, for such a prayer was surely blasphemous.

Knut offered his blade to her. She held hers to him likewise. Knut took his ring off the point of the sword, and held it out to let her insert her finger. She did the same with her ring. He took the arm ring off the sword and pushed it up her arm to the shoulder, and squeezed it to tighten the coil. Aelfgifu took the bigger armring off the dirk's handle. It was an open circle that she struggled to get past his thick bicep, and when she did she could not tighten it. He squeezed her hand and the armring as one. Fleada saw her wince at the pressure, but knew that Aelfgifu had loved touching Knut, and the way they had together closed the metal around his arm. Then Kustaa indicated that they stand side by side, and he placed Aelfgifu's right hand in Knut's left, and tied their wrists together with a long cord. It was wool, in strands of daffodil yellow, plum purple, grass green and rust red, all cleverly woven to create a pattern of colours down its length.

The symbolism was obvious. Each family's protection passed down, and each family's wealth and commitment. Two people and two families were tied together. Fleada found it touching, as she had the women's purification ritual yesterday. So much more meaningful, these actions, than the words of a Christian wedding and just the rings exchanged. She gritted her teeth against another blasphemous thought.

The ceremony was not over. Kustaa the shaman held the goat, Jyordis held the sow, and Lota a sheep brought from somewhere. Before the animals had time for fear, their throats were slit and they died with barely a squeal. Kustaa caught their blood in a bowl, and Jyordis dipped a small branch into it. Applewood, Fleada thought, from the small waxy leaves. Jyordis flicked drops of blood over the couple. Knut merely blinked, but Aelfgifu squealed and tried to protect her lovely veil, but failed. At least it kept the blood off her face. Jyordis was not happy. This was why she'd wanted the veil lifted.

Fleada stepped close to Aelfgifu and whispered "Give me the veil, I shall wash it." Aelfgifu lifted her crownlet to allow Fleada to take the silk, and stood stoically while Jyordis flicked blood at her. Danes clapped, happy that their Queen-to-be had received the sacrament of their gods. Perhaps they thought the passing of the veil to a sister was a Christian tradition.

"Is that it?" Aelfgifu asked of no-one in particular. "Are we married now?"

"Not yet," Kustaa told her. He seized the dead goat by its horns and lifted the carcass high. What now, Fleada thought?

A horde of Danish youths charged at them, screaming and yelling as if into battle. They carried neither weapon nor shield, yet the wall of muscle and bone was quite terrifying. They punched and kicked at each other as they raced to claim the goat, the sow and the sheep. They fought to tear the carcasses from each other's hands, and soon were red with blood. Not all was from the animals. With the fastest and strongest carrying the dead beasts, they charged for Gegnesberh.

"The winners have the honour of cooking the animals for you. The losers will be the serving boys!" Kustaa clearly thought it huge fun, as the last of the lads, bruised and bloodied, got to their feet and trailed the winners, resigned to their menial duties.

Aelfgifu and Knut followed the gang, and Fleada followed Aelfgifu. Eadric stepped past her to walk alongside the new bride. "You are welcomed into the Mercian family," he said to Knut, who merely nodded. To Aelfgifu he said "You did us proud, my girl."

She did not even nod.

"I am mindful that you are no longer my ward," Eadric continued. "But you are still my goddaughter. My Reeve

Terning has found a priest, who – by your leave, Lord," he said to Knut, "will bless you with a proper Christian wedding as soon as we have a quiet moment."

"Fits," Knut grunted.

In fact two priests stood behind him, next to Reeve Terning. One was old and balding, with hair greyer than his habit, and the beginnings of an aging stoop. The other was not so much younger, but he stood tall and strong, and his hair and beard were equal parts chalk and charcoal.

Caught between her old world and her new, Aelfgifu looked up at Knut. Was Lambert a true Christian name, Fleada wondered?

"This is Father Anderby," Terning said.

The older of the two priests placed his palms together and bowed to Knut and Aelfgifu. "It will be an honour, my Lord, my Lady, to sanctify your union in the sight of God. But not yet. Only when the Danish way of marriage is finished. To conduct a church wedding in the middle of it would be a blasphemy."

"Against which God?" Eadric said.

Knut guffawed, but Father Anderby did not find the comment funny. "Against the Lord our maker! A blasphemy!" He turned to his colleague for support. "Would it not be?"

"Blasphemy indeed," the middle-aged priest said. "Of the highest order."

Suppressing a gasp, Fleada barely registered the hint of irony in his tone. It was his accent that startled her, homely and so familiar. She'd heard that voice before, when she lay under Thyra's bed. Surely this priest was the co-conspirator that night? Hadn't he even said something about still being somewhere when Thyra arrived? She wanted to hear him speak again, but Anderby was leading him away.

"Knut should thank you, girl."

Someone was walking beside and just behind her. She

couldn't see his face, but she knew the voice too well.

"If not for you, that girl would be mine. I'd be Eadric's heir, if I'm not already."

She shivered, though the sun was warm.

"One day, girl, I'm going to fuck you or kill you."

Her legs kept walking, but her shoulders seized as if tensed muscle could turn a sharp blade. People were all around. She hoped she was safe.

"Or both. Be careful when you walk alone at night."

No. She'd be in Gegnesberh, or Jorvik, or even Denmark. With Aelfgifu. Wouldn't she? She should tell him to fuck off. If she hadn't been so taken aback at hearing that priest's voice, she'd have done so already. She turned, but Nothman was gone, melted into the crowd.

When they came to Gegnesberh's mead hall, Knut stepped ahead and stood tall in the doorway, barring it to all, holding the decorated sword that would doubtless one day be passed to his son.

Aelfgifu's son. Whom she, Fleada the handmaid, would look after, infant and child, if Aelfgifu kept her promise. She was destined to help raise a King. Would that keep her safe?

Jyordis pushed Aelfgifu to Knut. He picked her up to carry her through the door, where he put her down, and did something inside that Fleada couldn't make out from where she stood in daylight. Only when she entered did she see Knut's sword and Aelfgifu's dagger plunged into a post, high above people's heads.

The Danes continued to give Fleada higher status than she deserved, with a place at the high table and only Eadgyth and Eadric between herself and Aelfgifu. Once she was seated, Knut stood and placed a wooden mallet onto Aelfgifu's lap. Fleada could only guess whether this meant Thor guarded her chastity, or if it gave strength to her children, or something else. Aelfgifu was equally ignorant but clearly loved it.

Boys and girls came with jugs of mead to fill every mug in the hall, which were emptied and refilled. Eadgyth leaned close to Fleada. "All the bees in England must have laboured a year for this volume of mead," she said. "Aelfgifu and Knut must drink mead for twenty-eight days, so they will be happy for the first month of marriage. The Danes call it their month of honey."

These were more words than Eadgyth had said to Fleada in years. Had their nakedness yesterday somehow made them friends?

Sveyn stood, and gave toasts to Odin, to Thor, and to Freya. Knut stood too, and held his horn high. "And to Jesus," he called, and the Danes answered with a roar of "Jesus!", as if Our Lord Saviour was welcome in their pantheon.

Sveyn raised his arms until hush settled over the feasters. He declaimed in Danish, for the sake of his newly arrived countrymen. Knut stood up next to him to translate into English, although at first there was no need because Sveyn was reciting a long list of names, welcoming the noble and notable guests to the wedding feast, each of whom stood to claps and cheers when named. Here was King Malcoluim, the Scots King, who barely lifted his lean frame before sitting again to stroke his sharply trimmed beard as he surveyed the hall. Next to him was one Siguror the Stout, Jarl of Orkney, then his wife Olith, the Scots King's daughter.

And opposite him, Uhtred, her own Ealdorman from Jorvik, who appeared a lonely figure in spite of the Northumbrian thegns accompanying him. She'd first heard his name years ago, when men from her village had left to help lift the siege of Dunholm after Malcoluim invaded Bernicia. Malcoluim was hounded back to Scotland, and the Northumbrians returned richer. They joined Uhtred again when he tried to extend his realm, but this time many did not return at all. Had Uhtred and Malcoluim agreed a border, or did Sveyn's power ensure their enmity was forgotten for this day at least?

Here was Knut's younger brother Harald, and jarls who had sailed with him from Denmark, whose names were lost on Fleada. Near the front of the hall were Leofric and Nothman, both of whom she knew better than she wished to. She looked for Godgifu of Coventre, but could not see her. Her father, a mere thegn, did not rank highly enough. At the same table sat two more brothers, Sigeferth and Morkere whose lands they had passed through on their long journey down the Trehynt river, whom she had seen briefly in Snotengeham. They were with four youths, sons or nephews perhaps, who mumbled and joked between themselves but resisted the efforts of their elders to converse with them.

Also with them sat a young woman of beauty rivalling even Aelfgifu's. She leaned towards Sigeferth, and at times he placed his hand over hers; so Fleada surmised she was his wife, despite the age difference. Wife or no, she had the men around her entranced. They listened to her words and laughed at her jests. What glamour did she have, to make men do this? Even the dour Leofric smiled happily in her palm, laughing and making jokes of his own.

Sveyn ended his list, and began his address.

"My people," Knut translated, which caused a ruffle of concern among the Mercians and the Hwiccans. "We come to witness and celebrate this great event, the marriage of my son – I think that's me," at which the English speakers laughed, "– to the beautiful and brave daughter of Jorvik and Mercia, Aelfgifu. That's you," Knut said, and put his hand on her shoulder. "And you surely are," he said in a tone meant for her, but loud enough that the English would hear, and cheer. She blushed.

Sveyn continued.

"It seals a friendship between me, that is, my father," said Knut, "And my friend, his friend, Eadric of Mercia. We all know Eadric." Cheers went up from the English and the Danes alike.

"They cheer for the silver," Eadgyth whispered to Fleada, "Not for Eadric." Perhaps she'd drunk too much mead.

Fleada heard the name Ledwyn of the Hwicce, at which Nothman and Leofric stood and raised their mugs in his name. They sat down, and Nothman turned to give Fleada the coldest of stares.

Eadgyth leaned close to Fleada. "I fear Nothman resents you sitting at this high table."

You have no idea what Nothman resents, Fleada thought.

"He has grounds," Eadgyth said. "You are being highly honoured, Fleada. Far more than your true station."

"I know," Fleada answered modestly.

Knut continued translating. "My father wants to remember all those who could not be here, who are keeping our homeland safe." Knut lowered his voice. "This could take some time," he commented for the English, who again laughed, to Sveyn's renewed puzzlement. The talk was punctuated by cheers from men whose home town was named.

Eadgyth then leaned sideways again. "You must earn this."

Fleada was confused. Earn it? How?

"Knut will stay in England now, which means Aelfgifu will be right at the heart of things. You must encourage her to take an interest, and you must talk with her about everything. We need you to discover all you can about Sveyn's plans. Do you understand?"

Fleada nodded.

"Use your wiles, and do not be suspected. Someone will

come, and you will pass on to him everything you have learned. Everything. Do not decide what's important and what's trivial, for you cannot know."

I'm just a handmaid, Fleada thought. I cannot know how trivial it is that you laid with that Father Stigand, that Thyra conspires with another priest who has come here to Gegnesberh, that Leofric wants Mercia and has made his own contacts with the Danes. Your husband wants nothing less than to be King of England. You'd be Queen. How trivial is that? Do you even know? I cannot tell you this. You yourself just advised discretion so I am suspected of nothing.

"Tell no-one that I'm asking this. Not Aelfgifu, and not my husband."

Then who does Eadgyth speak for? Her father King Aethelred, or her brother Edmund Ironside? "Why me? Why not Aelfgifu herself?"

"If she is seen with someone from the south, she will be suspected."

And if I'm suspected, it doesn't matter.

"You can avoid being seem, and you can make up a reason if you are spied with a stranger. Say he is your uncle, or your betrothed."

As if her uncle would be a southerner. "Who will it be?"

"I have no idea. You will know, though. He will name me. You'll be rewarded. Your family will be rewarded."

She remembered the box of treasures that Thyra's work against Eadric had earned. She was not Thyra. But she was curious. "That priest, the one who stood with Father Anderby. Who is he?"

"I believe his name is Usmaer. Why do you ask?"

Fleada looked down at her lap. She shouldn't have asked. She shouldn't appear curious, not even to Eadgyth. She wanted this conversation to end. "I- I like priests," she whispered. "They make me feel…" She trailed off, not know what to say, because priests made her feel nothing at all.

But they affected Eadgyth, didn't they, the younger ones. One did, certainly, if Thyra's bones, eyes and ears were reliable. Fleada suspected they were.

A cough forced its way from Eadgyth's throat like a frog jumping from a pond. She turned away, picked up her cup of mead, and drank long.

Sveyn came to the end of his list of those not present, and held the silence. Knut had nothing to translate. The room sensed Sveyn had something of import to say. When he spoke, his voice was low. "There are three names you have not heard pass my lips," Knut intoned, matching his gravitas. "The first of these… is Kjell Ormsson of Jomsborg. You all know of his dishonourable execution. Blood money had been paid and the matter is settled.

"The second name is Vrangr Ormsson. I would have wished he could be here, for he has taken Cantware for me. And so I name him Chief Jarl of Jomsborg!"

A cheer rose from the Danes, and some shouted the name of Jarl Vrangr, but it was not a full-throated cheer. They were uncertain of the full meaning of what they were hearing.

Sveyn continued, and his voice went graver still, and again Knut maintained his tone in the translating. "The old Jarl I will not name. The old Jarl's name will never again pass my lips, nor will I hear it. He has committed the blackest of treasons. He has deserted his King, and taken untold men to another King. He has deserted his Gods, and taken untold men to another God. I have no quarrel with his God, and I do not prohibit any man to worship him, or to worship his son, or his wife."

Knut crossed himself quickly. "My father means Mary, mother of the Lord." He resumed translating for Sveyn. "My son shows the truth of this. Praising a new God does not mean turning your back on your people. But one man, a man I trusted, has done this, and I now banish him from Denmark! He is forbidden to return! If he does, the man who brings me his head will be rewarded. He always was too tall."

Now the Danes laughed and cheered, and began to chant Sveyn's name.

Knut held up his hands for silence. "Be not joyful," he said, and they paid attention, for now their Prince spoke his own words. "I am sad, for Thorkell the Tall…" There was a momentary gasp at this deliberate flouting of his father's word. "…has been like a second father to me. I cannot find words for the grief I feel that he has made himself our enemy."

Sveyn glared at him, and for just an instant it seemed that he would rise in anger. But even the King would not fight with his son, not in this place, not on this day.

Knut was a prize, for sure. His eyes were full of laughter, and after the formalities he made jokes in Danish that had all around him laughing, then explained the jokes to Aelfgifu that she might join the merriment. He was attentive, and gentle. She grew flushed on the food, the drink and the attention. When the time came for the unmarried girls and boys to chase them with whoops and screeches to their bedding place, she went willingly, her demand for a priest to marry them that day forgotten. Perhaps her husband's toast to Jesus sufficed, Fleada thought. Or the sheep. The grey old priest, Father Anderby, was nowhere to be seen. Nor was Usmaer.

Eadric leaned sideways as if to speak to Eadgyth, and it took a few seconds for Fleada to realise he was addressing her. "It seems you will be sent away for most of the coming honey-month."

It took her a moment to realise what he was saying. Sent

away? No! This was the very time Aelfgifu most needed her! The shock must have shown on her face.

"You must understand, Fleada. He is a man, he needs to fully own his wife. He needs to get to know her. He needs to be her confessor, and she his abettor. Neither can happen as long as you are there. He knows what girls are like."

"He doesn't want Aelfgifu talking about the size of his boat's dragonhead," Eadgyth said.

Eadric laughed. "I saw him naked in the steam hut. I can say he'd be well satisfied with that news spreading."

She did not want to think about Knut's prow.

"Don't worry, Fleada. He will allow you back. Otherwise, Aelfgifu will make his life a misery, if I know her at all." Eadric rose. "I believe it is now our duty to keep vigil outside Knut's hall, or wherever he has taken her." He strode away in the direction of the shouting and carousing.

Fleada was unsure whether it was her place to join the vigil. But she knew she wanted to, and believed Aelfgifu would want her to, so she rose. Eadgyth rose too, and together they left the hall's increasingly drunken mayhem, and headed for the equally boisterous carousing outside a small hut lit with candlelamps and flaming torches on stakes. As they walked, Eadgyth said to Fleada "I'm sure you would rather stay here. I do understand. But it is a chance for you to go to your family. You haven't seen them in, how many years?"

"Six."

"A long time. They are in Jorvik, no?"

"A village nearby, yes."

"What's its name?"

"Osbaldwick. My father is Headman." She had been too young to know her father's feelings when she was required to go into Elfhelm's hall to be a playmate for his daughter. But she knew his pride well enough that she was the one chosen as handmaid, to accompany Aelfgifu in Mercia when Eadric offered to take care of her after she was orphaned.

Eadgyth nodded, and repeated the name Osbaldwick.

They approached Knut's bedding hut. All around it folk celebrated. The gleemen had come, and the old danced with the young. Girls hugged; boys chased and wrestled. Conversations had to be shouted, and little sense was spoken. Ale was spilled, but more was drunk.

"Don't forget what I said," Eadgyth whispered, "Gather what information you can. But tell no-one, not even Lord Eadric. You are English, Fleada, and you serve the English King first of all."

Fleada recalled how magnificent Eadgyth had looked when, in that steam hut, she had stood naked and told her never to forget that she was English. How could she?

Eadgyth continued. "Your family in Osbaldwick, they too are Aethelred's subjects. His true and loyal subjects. Am I right?"

The image of naked Eadgyth vanished as Fleada's stomach lurched, and she knew herself to be a fool and a plaything. Now she was Thyra in the darkness, now she was Usmaer the sparrowing priest. Now she had made her family hostage to her successful pursuit of Sveyn's secrets.

The rowdy night became very cold.

Historical note, places, and words

Warning: this note contains spoilers, so I recommend not reading it until you've finished the story.

I am a novelist, not a historian, and this is a novel, not a history.

The tale is told to sustain narrative flow, to heighten drama, and to create distinctive characters; and I'm not above blurring the line between attested history, legend, valid speculation, and pure invention.

Purists may complain, but I follow a tradition of playing with facts and taking advantage of the many blank pages in the historical record. I hesitate to place myself alongside literary gods, but Homer built myth and legend into his story of the fall of Troy. Shakespeare played with known history. Malory built on a legend of Arthur that may or may not have had a living seed. Don't get me started on the Bible.

Invention happens still, as with different presentations of the ages of the two Boleyn sisters. And Hollywood's mythmaking, shortcuts and calumnies are biblical in extent.

This saga is hung onto known events of the eleventh century up to 1066. Key events surely happened, described in short sentences in the Anglo-Saxon Chronicles and elsewhere. Like the gospels, different authors chose to retell different parts of the story, and told them slightly differently. The Chronicles give no analysis, and only commonplace speculations about cause and effect. Unlike the gospels, there are no quotes, and little moralising.

Another major historical source is the Encomium Emmae, written about and for Queen Emma by a Flemish monk. In its favour, it was composed within her lifetime; but it is a hagiography that can hardly be considered objective.

Other elements of the history have been exaggerated by chroniclers writing decades or even centuries later, giving modern historians endless ambiguities and contradictions over which to argue; and giving novelists acres of blank canvas on which if not to paint, at least to write in colour.

These events almost certainly happened: the marriage settlement with Emma following Aethelred's failed invasion of Cotentin; the St Brice's Day massacre; a dispute – we know not what – between Wulfnoth and Brihtric; the theft of Aethelred's boats and the loss of more boats in a storm; the numerous and escalating gafol payments (subsequently known as Danegeld); and Aelfgifu's marriage to Knut.

Most of these occurred over the years between 1009 and 1013, but I have compressed the timescale greatly to sustain the novel's flow. Some historical figures have been excised for simplicity. So, sorry Aethelstan, Edmund's older brother, who actually died within this period, but does not appear to have played a dynamic part in the history.

The major nobles, bishops and leaders existed. Stigand too is a real figure, but the adventures of his early years here are speculation, reverse engineered from some historians' conjectures about his later ones.

Some names have been changed to reduce but sadly not eliminate "Russian Novel Syndrome", whereby too many long and unfamiliar names make it hard to keep track of who is whom. This is especially problematic with aristocratic ladies whose names mostly start Ead- (meaning wealth) or Ael- (meaning elf – Aelfgifu means "gift from the elves"). The elves left at least three notable gifts in the era, but I've had to give them different names. Sometimes it is convenient to Latinise them, but there are still too many Ediths, Ealdgyths, Eadgyths, Eadgifus and the like. Changing one or another to Aelswyth only helps a little. Leofwyne of Hwicce and Morcar of the Five Berhs have become Ledwyn and Morkere to distinguish them from characters who will appear later. I hope the family lists will help.

Of their natures and personalities, we have very little to go on. Aethelred is known as the Unready, from unraed, meaning ill-advised (not unprepared, although he was that too). I've not gone against the common view that he was a ditherer. Eadric was later called Streona, the grasper, which is a clue. He has been named on lists of the worst Englishmen ever. Who doesn't love a good villain? Edward was famously pious; and Emma was certainly a manipulator.

The characters who aren't nobles, the Walts, the Fleadas, the Cudberts, and assorted headmen, thegns, ceorls, priests and peasants, are to a man, woman and child, necessarily invented.

As to Godwin, the main protagonist, although his early years are not documented, "the traitor's son" appellation is not controversial. He rose from that ignoble beginning to gain power equal to, if not exceeding, the King's. His son actually became King. He must have been a man of formidable ability, but to the delight of any author, history does not speak of Godwin the man, so I am free to recreate this mighty but neglected figure.

Place names

English place names and their spellings have changed over history. It is hard to accurately guess when one version mentioned, say, in a 10th century Anglo Saxon Charter, became another version in the Domesday book. I've tried to follow some indication from the records, but I've also used artistic licence. I've regularised most of the spellings of -caster, -caestre, -chester and so on, with a Latin-flavoured -caestr; and -borough, -bergh, -burgh to an admittedly cod early English -berh.

Some names, like Rye, appear to have survived unaltered through the centuries. I haven't wilfully changed these, although the recognisable form looks incongruously modern (Rye actually gets its name from old English Atter Ie, meaning 'on the island', thence Rie, until by the 11th century it had become Rye. The name of the wider area of Rameslege, which includes estates pledged to Normandy, is all but disused, but part of it is still known as Rye Foreign.)

I speculate that anyone in those times who was educated enough to have any geographical knowledge of continental Europe would use Latin forms, like Danuvius for the Danube, and the Germania Sea for our North Sea. English commoners more probably knew it as the East Sea; and the Danes, as the West Sea.

With a couple of exceptions, Norman towns seem to have had their current names, but for some I've found a Danish root. We will visit them in later volumes.

English towns, shires and provinces

Arun Dell	Arundel, West Sussex
Bernicia	The northern part of Northumbria, including modern Northumberland, Tyne & Wear, and County Durham
Bremesgrave	Bromsgrove, Worcestershire
Caestr	Chester
Caestrfeld	Chesterfield, Nottinghamshire
Cantenberh	Canterbury, Kent
Cantware	Kent
Ceorring	Charing, Kent
Cernwealas	Cornwall
Cicaestr	Chichester, Sussex
Coelmaersford	Chelmsford, Eassex
Comtyn	Compton, Sussex

Coventre	Coventry, Warwickshire
Cranboka	Cranbrook, Kent
Croming	Cromer, Norfolk
Defenas	Devon
Dofras	Dover, Kent
Eassex	Essex
Escancaestr	Exeter, Devon
Gegnesberh	Gainsborough, Lincolnshire
Glocaestr	Gloucester
Hrofcaestr	Rochester, Kent
Jorvik	York
Ledecaestr	Leicester
Lincylene	Lincoln
Lindesege	Lindsay, approximately modern Lincolnshire
Lunden	London
Lyccidfeld	Lichfield, Staffordshire
Meddestane	Maidstone, Kent
Northamtun	Northampton
Oxenford	Oxford
Plymentyn	Plymton, Devon
Readingam	Reading, Berksire
Rameslege	Lands west and north of Rye, East Sussex
Sanwic	Sandwich, Kent
Seletun	Selby, Yorkshire
Snotengaham	Nottingham
Somorsaet	Somerset
Soussex	Sussex
Stamsford	Stamford, Lincolnshire
Suthamtun	Southampton, Hampshire
Suthrige	Surrey
Swanawic	Swanage, Dorsetshire
Tamwerth	Tamworth, Staffordshire
Tenrige	Tandridge, Surrey

Tilberh	Tilbury, Essex
Ulwic	Woolwich, Kent
Weogorna	Worcester
Wiltun	Wilton, Wiltshire
Wintancaestr	Winchester, Hampshire
Wulfrunheaton	Wolverhampton, West Midlands

Geographical features

Ciltern Hills	Chiltern Hills
Germania Sea, West/East Sea	North Sea
Meduwaen	River Medway
Pen Hills	Pennines
Sabrin	River Severn
Tamys	River Thames
Trehynt	River Trent
Wihtware	Isle of Wight
Wrikin	The Wrekin, a steep isolated hill rising above the Shropshire Plain

Outside England

Byzantium	Istanbul (also known in the Middle Ages as Constantinople)
Cotentin	Peninsula in west Normandy, between Cherbourg and Mont St Michel
Deppa	Dieppe
Eirinn	Ireland
Flandra	Flanders
Huniflet	Honfleur
Sveoren	Sweden
Waelas	Wales

Glossary of selected old English words

Barghest	Evil dog monster believed to roam the north at night.
Berh	Fortified town.
Braies	Baggy shorts of linen or wool worn as underwear.
Byrnie	Chainmail armour, shorter than a hauberk.
Ceorl	Free man (pr. "churl").
Cild	Honorific title that predated Sir (pr. "child" or possibly "chilled").
Cofgode	House-imp, a mischievous creature that haunts households.
Collier	Charcoal maker.
Cullions/culions	Old French / English slang for testicles
Dokkse	Mistress or lover ('doxy').
Firouzeh	From the old Persian name for turquoise
Fyrd	Saxon army.
Glaive	A short sword-like blade on a spear's haft.
Hauberk	Thigh or knee-length coat of chainmail.
Husceorl	Member of a king's, ealdorman's or thegn's troop of personal guards.
Leech	Doctor.
Lem	Penis (old Danish, root of the word 'limb')
Merel	Stone or carved piece used in the game of nine men's morris.
Pintle	Penis.
Reeve	Senior administrator and tax-collector.
Scachis	Chess.
Sceatt	Silver coin. A half sceatt was literally the coin cut in half. In fact silver sceatts were replaced by silver pennies before the 11th

	century, but I have stuck with sceatt because to modern ears "penny" would imply lower value.
Scire	Shire (the post of scire-reeve later became the sheriff).
Seidh	Folkloric shamanistic system of magic (pronounced sithe – yes, George Lucas nicked it for the dark-side Jedi).
Seax	Small dagger.
Shaftment	Unit of measurement: width of the palm plus length of thumb.
Sheith	Sheath or scabbard; euphemism for vagina.
Slow fever	Thyphoid.
Spurtle	Stirring stick for porridge and stews.
Stade	Landing place.
Teorse	Boss at centre of a shield; a euphemism for penis.
Thegn	Formally appointed local leader.
Thuw	Slave.
Widdershins	Anticlockwise – literally 'other direction, (to the sun).
Witangemot / Witan	Gathering of nobles with the King. The Witan had the power to approve, and hence appoint, a new King.

Some key characters

Godwin, and his circle

From the village of Comtyn:

Godwin Wulfnothson

Wulfnoth Cild, Thegn of Comtyn, Godwin's father

Saehild, his mother

Saewin, his younger sister

Eagbert ('Eg') and Selferth ('Sel'), his friends

Cudbert, a ceorl, Sel's father

Gret, Godwin's girlfriend

Brother Snell, monk.

From nearby Bosham, on the coast:

Ham, a boat's captain

Arni, Ham's son

Odylia, his daughter

Hemming, a Danish boatbuilder

Nobles of Wessex

Aelfric, Ealdorman and Chief Thegn of east Wessex

Athelmar, Ealdorman of west Wessex

Ecfrith, Godwin's grandfather, Saehild's father

Soussex:

Gewis, Headman of the village of Brimclif

The English Royals, their servants and ceorls

King Aethelred ('The Unraed')

Children by his first wife:

Prince Edmund ('Ironside'), eldest son

Princess Eadgyth, married to Eadric of Mercia

Princess Wulfhild, married to Ulfcytel of East Anglia

Princess Aelfrith, living at Wherwell Abbey

Princess Ecfrida

Cynethe, Ecfrida's handmaid

Queen Emma of Normandy, Aethlered's second wife, sister of Norman Duke Richard II

Arsindis, Emma's maid

Emma's children:

Prince Edward, Emma's first son

Fulton, Edward's friend and companion

Theodric, Edward's guard

Prince Alfred, Emma's second son

Wilf, Alfred's friend and companion

Wendel, Alfred's guard, Wilf's father

Princess Goda, Emma's youngest

Hendi, Goda's friend and companion

Ellin, household maid

Wilmaer, the Royal Reeve

Ercenbert, Edmund's first husceorl

Deorleaf 'The Mown', Ercenbert's deputy

Father Trebert, priest serving Edmund's fyrd

Mercia

Eadric Streona, Ealdorman of Mercia

Terning, Eadric's Reeve

Marton and Dudric, Eadric's personal husceorls

Thyra, Eadric's dokkse

Brihtric, his brother

Aelfgifu, Eadric's ward, orphan daughter of Elfhelm of Jorvik

Fleada, Aelfgifu's handmaid

Nothman and Leofric, sons of Ledwyn, Ealdorman of Hwicce

East Anglia

Waltheof, shepherd boy of Croming

Ulfcytel Snillingr, Ealdorman of East Anglia

Wulfhild, his wife (Aethelred's daughter)

Father Stigand, Ulfcytel's emissary

Northumbria

Uhtred, Ealdorman of Northumbria

Ule of Stowe, a village headman's son

The Five Berhs

Sigeferth, Ealdorman of three of the Five Berhs

Aelswyth, Sigeferth's wife

Morkere, Sigeferth's younger brother, Ealdorman of two of the Five Berhs

The Danes

King Sveyn ('Forkbeard')

Prince Knut, his elder son

Prince Harald, his younger son

Clerics

Wulfstan, Archbishop of Jorvik and Weogorna

Aelfheah, Archbishop of Cantenberh

Cardinal Elfmar, head of Cantenberh Abbey

The Normans

Duke Richard II of Normandy ('The Good', 'The Pious') – Emma's brother

Judith of Brittany, his wife

Gunnor, his mother

Richard and Robert, his sons

Adeliza, Eleanore and Mathilde, his daughters

ACKNOWLEDGEMENTS

Many words of gratitude are due to many people. I'd particularly like to thank readers Jackie Carter and Sus Coupland, and editor Louise Buckley, whose sound advice I didn't always take.

I should also mention staff and volunteers at the West Stowe Anglo-Saxon Village, near Bury St Edmunds, for their insights into the Anglo-Saxon lifestyle. The Sutton Hoo museum near Woodbridge was equally inspiring. The Jorvik Centre in York, and the 878AD Centre in Winchester provided some irreplaceable visual insights into the period. All are highly recommended.

I could list the many books and articles I've read that have informed the narrative and the descriptions. I shall refrain, not because they are too many to mention, but to spare the authors complicity in my many departures, deliberate and accidental, from their writings. I'm grateful to them all.

But I will mention Academia.edu, which holds a mine of scholarly and accessible articles on the period. And Wikipedia. We can laugh at its errors, but it is a shortcut to information on, well, just about anything. If you use it at all frequently, please make a donation to keep this global resource, this wonder of the modern world, free, well moderated, and ever more reliable.

Preview

From *The Thegn* – the next book in *The Crown and The Arrow* series

The Filcher

(Godwin)

"I cannot vouch whether these paths are safe or lawless."

Trepidation marched with the fyrd like a grey pall. They knew that the march northeast took the very same route that Sveyn's army would take southwest, should he choose to attack Wessex. The Icknield Way might lead the men straight towards a battle, and it could be today or tomorrow. Songs died young, laughs faltered, and petty fights flared. Yet bonds were made on that march, whether men spoke their fears or shared them through silence, whether they boasted of their fine sons and daughters or prayed for their families to have no cause to mourn.

Godwin was now a hero, protected by Edmund himself. More immediately, he had Cudbert like a bear alongside him, so there was no resurrection of the bullying he'd suffered when he first joined the fyrd. He rarely saw Fordred, but if he did, as the men gathered for their daily ladle of stew or as they trained, they mutually looked away.

It was Selferth who noticed the tension, and drew the story out of Godwin. Fordred and his older brother Wystan had surrounded Odylia. Godwin had defended her, which allowed her to stab Wystan with a shit-smeared seax. Wystan had lost his arm, nearly his life, and Fordred blamed Godwin still. Then Godwin had shamed him, because he'd spurned an archery duel.

"Don't be fighting beside him," Eg said.

"Tell him the same."

Rumours spread of the mayhem being wreaked in Cantware and Soussex and Suthrige. The rumours mated and had children, and some of the children took after their parents while others were bastards of unknown ancestry: the Danish force was huge, no, it was small; it was Sveyn's main army, no, it was mercenaries bound for Wessex so we must stop it; no, it was headed for London which must be protected; no, it is there to lure us away from Sveyn in the north.

Men honed their swords again, checked their shields, and made more arrows. Those with no sword sharpened their pike or glaive or billhook, and more importantly, checked the fixing of blade to haft. Blacksmiths toiled.

A runner came for Godwin. Both he and Cudbert were to get themselves to Prince Edmund's tent at once.

Edmund welcomed them. "Men of Comtyn," he said with a smile, and poured ales from a flagon. "The brain, and the brawn. Cunning, and courage. Or luck, maybe? Best not look too hard, lest it vanishes like some faint star."

He bade them be seated. Godwin wondered at his tent's comfortable furnishings – there must be two waggonloads of stools, trestles, a low bed platform, cushions, furs, lamps, a writing lectern, and even a chair. Every day it all had to be packed and loaded, then unloaded and re-set in the tent every evening. Godwin supposed it was all necessary for a leader to meet his captains, to communicate with the King and Ealdors, to receive intelligence on the enemy. And to show he was Prince.

"You have doubtless heard the talk, rumours and

speculation. It is not healthy, and I am minded to do battle. A victory will lift the gloom that hangs over us. But it will not be the last battle, not by any means."

"We are ready," Godwin said, wondering why Edmund wished to share his thinking with him, of all the fyrd.

"I'm sure you are. Or if not, you know the words to say. But I fear your readiness is unnecessary. You will not be fighting."

Godwin looked up. Surely fighting was what he was here to do?

Edmund continued "You won't be missed, you're not full grown, and still no match for an axe-wielding Viking." He looked at Cudbert. "You'll be a loss, mind. The shieldwall is a place for brutes. It gives no value to initiative. Bravery, yes, but stupidity serves equally. If one brave or stupid brute falls, another can be found, until the other side's brutes turn to babies, and flee. We've always had the numbers, we just haven't marshalled them so well as the Dane, or been as brutal. But things are changing. Thorkell is with us now, and the gafol paid for Cantware will be the last time we raid our treasuries. Have you played the game of scachis?"

Godwin shook his head. "I don't know this game."

"No, I suppose not. It is played on a board, with figures that represent armies. The Vikingr play it, the Moors play it. Queen Emma brought a board and a set of figures here, a gift from some Count. She needed an opponent, but the King lacked patience, so she taught me and her sons. It is a game of strategy, and the winner is the one who profits most from his sacrifices. Very instructive, Godwin. Perhaps I shall teach you one day, although I suspect you'd soon beat me. Now, as a game reaches its conclusion, when few figures are left to guard the two opposing kings, it is vital to make no mistakes, for mistakes then cannot be undone. We are coming to that stage of our game against Sveyn, but the difference between scachis and real war, is that we cannot see all of the board, nor all of the figures. Do you see why I am telling you this?"

He couldn't imagine this game. "Um. No."

"Think, Godwin."

Two kings… We cannot see all of the board, nor all the figures... "You want to see more. You want to see Sveyn's figures."

Edmund slapped his knee and threw back his head. "I knew you wouldn't let me down!" Then he leaned forward. "Each player of scachis has some small pieces, small but important. Paons, they are called, and I have one hidden."

Godwin sensed that he was a paon himself, with all the men of the fyrd.

"You will journey to Northumbria with letters to Uhtred. Do you know of Uhtred? He is the Ealdorman of all the north. He speaks to King Aethelred of his allegiance and loyalty, but since the death of Elfhelm of Jorvik he has been Sveyn' s man. I don't blame him, he had no choice. You will have two letters, one from the King, one from myself."

"With terms for him? If he will turn against Sveyn?"

"You do not need to know. But essentially, yes, you're right. This errand is secret. If asked, you travel to seek old family ties. Invent your story while you're still in the south."

Godwin nodded.

"And there is a buggeration factor," Edmund added. "Unfortunately, it is important to keep Ealdorman Eadric of Mercia involved-"

"Brother to Brihtric," Cudbert growled.

"The same," Edmund said. "His time will come, I promise."

Cudbert grunted and wiped ale from his moustache.

"As I was saying, Eadric must be involved. Firstly, Uhtred will be more amenable believing that Mercia is part of the approach. More crucially, there's no saying how an excluded

Eadric might react, should Uhtred speak to him."

Edmund had no duty to explain his thinking to them. All he had to do was tell his pieces where to go and what to do.

Edmund was teaching him how this game is played.

"Those you trust least, are those you flatter with openness," Edmund said. "That is why you will have two of Eadric's men travelling north with you. You must divert them and keep them ignorant of your true purpose."

"It's not the letters," Godwin said.

"No. It's the paon."

Edmund wanted Cudbert to accompany Godwin, and Godwin suggested that Sel and Eg's presence would support the tale that they travelled on family matters. They were given horses: a strong punch for Cudbert, geldings for Sel and Eg that were too large, but well trained and even tempered, and a mule. Eadric's two men Marton and Dudric joined them at Coventre, and brought a second mule as well as their own horses.

The six rode in single file under low cloud, following Cudbert. His job it was to spot places where robbers might hide to waylay them, for Marton, the older of Eadric's men, had warned that they were coming into lands of uncertain jurisdiction between Mercia and the Five Berhs. "I cannot vouch whether these paths are safe or lawless."

"Must be pretty bloody lawless if you think six armed men are at risk," Cudbert said.

"Three men, three boys," Marton grunted.

Sel was set thick on his gelding's back, then came Godwin, tall on Ash, with Eg alongside him, followed by Dudric, the junior of Eadric's trusties, who took turns with Eg and Sel to lead the mules loaded with provisions, pots, traps, axes and the other essentials for travelling distances. Each carried his own blankets and oiled skins, tightly rolled and bound, a bag with their personal effects, morsels of food, and weapons.

Marton offered to bring up the rear, which was bold, for it was common for robbers to wait for the main party to pass before attacking from behind. But it also carried a risk that he and Dudric could retreat rather than fight with Godwin's men, should a skirmish arise ahead. When Cudbert pointed this out to Godwin, Godwin slowed and asked Dudric to pass himself and Eg. "It's safer to have the goods in the middle," he said. But the two Mercians seemed stout, Godwin thought, especially Marton, near as big as Cudbert, who spoke little but watched all.

Three days north of Coventre, and unassailed by robbers, they crossed the Trehynt at The Twyfords rope ferry. Marton demanded free passage in the name of his Ealdorman, although Godwin suspected they were clear of Eadric's lands by now. He gave the cowering and grateful ferryman a half of one of the sceatts Edmund had provided. Edmund had made it very clear to all that Godwin was to lead the group, and Godwin wasn't going to let Marton assert himself.

They rode on with sword hilts showing, and Godwin wore his chainmail hauberk despite its weight. The others had lighter chain byrnies under their surcoats, enough to deflect a blade away from the heart or lung. Godwin had told them all what to do in the event of threat: to draw their swords and follow Cudbert and to charge down any they might find in their way. Godwin agreed with Cudbert's judgement that such measures were unlikely to be needed: brigands would think twice about attacking a well armed group. Brigands weren't the worry, but Danes, for the six were southern Saxons entering the Danelaw.

Undergrowth flourished on each side, but the track itself was kept clear by usage. They stood aside for oncoming merchants' carts to pass, and Godwin professed surprise at the amount of trade in these reaches, away from the river, where villages were small and few. Or were these men buying and selling further afield? Were they headed into Mercia?

Where they came to a village of an evening, they bought bread, milk, and ale; and shelter too, if it was available. Little meat was for sale, but they had their own cured beef strips given to them by the Coventre Thegn's daughter, and the group kept themselves hale, if not exactly hearty.

This day there was no village or homestead to be seen, and dusk was nigh. Cudbert spotted a clearing where trees and the contours offered shelter from the wind. With the evening sky cloudless there was no need to spread the awnings. They gathered wood for a fire. Marton and Dudric went off on foot with light bows and cord snares, and returned an hour later with a fawn slung from a freshly cut pole. It would have ample pickings for the six of them, with some spare for the morrow. The young meat was so tender it needed little more than a couple of turns on the spit.

They sat chewing their venison veal, and passed a flagon of ale around, sharing tales from their homes. Marton still talked little, but Dudric entertained them with songs, and told a story of how his village's pigs, fleeing from a mad dog, had once herded his father into the Avon River, and how he'd then stalked the dog for days with a knife before doing it in. The story itself was not long, but Dudric digressed with descriptions of the people of his village who were all, according to him, crazed, stupid, fat, vain, or all four. "All villages have their idiot," he said. "Mine was made of them. It had just one sensible, so I left to be a husceorl to Ealdorman Eadric. Not that the other ceorls were much better. Let me tell you about one, name of Fram-"

Eg stood up, saying "My piss is about to pop its bung like elderflower ferment. If I'd known we were in for a saga, I'd have gone before you started, Mercian." He disappeared into the darkness behind the horses.

"The name is Dudric," Dudric called after him, then said to the others "If that's too hard to remember, I answer to Dudie." He shrugged, then also rose, saying "I too should have gone before I started. I always think, just a short tale, but it never comes out that way." He went off in the same direction as Eg.

"Tell us of your family, Marton," Godwin said, to fill the pause. By now, most of them knew each other's backgrounds. The Comtynians had related their histories, but kept the name of their village and the identity of Godwin's father carefully out of their tales, and omitted the confrontation with Brihtric. Dudric had told them more than enough of his past, but Marton had stayed taciturn.

He may have been about to reply when raised voices sounded from near the horses. Godwin glanced at Cudbert, who rose and strode immediately towards the disturbance. Marton followed him. "Oi, you two," Cudbert shouted, and the noise stopped. Talking came in tones too low for Godwin to hear.

Soon the four returned to the firelight. "Dudric accused Eg of stealing bread from his bag," said Cudbert.

Godwin said "Egbert does not steal."

Before Dudric could reply, Eg burst out "It is the Mercians who steal. My hood disappeared last night, from right next to where I slept, from under my very head! I was checking to see if it was hidden with his horse's tackle."

"And guess!" said Dudric. "It wasn't! But neither were there baked buns in my bag, where they had been before." Dudric's counter-accusation was heartfelt, Godwin thought. But then, Dudric was a good storyteller.

Marton said "I've lost two strips of dried beef. I thought I dropped them, though I could not see how."

Godwin looked at all the men. In the orange light from the slowly dying fire he could not see their expressions well enough, nor look into their eyes. "We shall sort this out in the morning. Cudbert, you and Marton will both keep watch tonight." He looked at the others. "They are watching you. Nobody leaves the fire. If you need to piss do it where you are. Crap, you can just hold in."

As they gathered themselves in their blankets, he whispered to Cudbert "We have a thief, or a mischief-maker."

"Ain't me, and it ain't Sel."

"No. But Eg? He can be impetuous. Whoever it is, he won't do anything tonight, but you need to stay awake to prove it so."

"I will not sleep."

"I know you won't. Wake me just after dawn."

Cudbert nodded.

Six hours later he felt himself prodded by Cudbert. The others still slept, save Marton, who had kept vigil with Cudbert, silent as ever. Hidden by his blanket, Godwin drew his seax from its leather sheath, and whispered to Cudbert "Mark Dudric, and follow my lead."

He sprang up, and before Marton could react Godwin crouched over him with the blade at his neck, saying "Undo your belt and lay down your sword."

Marton glared up, but did as he was ordered. Dudric awoke and hearing these words he reached for his sword, only to have his hand trodden on by Cudbert. Sel and Eg too went for their weapons, but Godwin said "Hold! Now, everybody, get up slowly, and stand in a line. All of you!" He turned to Sel and Eg. "I said all of you!"

Cudbert prodded them into line.

"Now," said Godwin, "Take off every piece of clothing. Yes, each one of you."

As they stripped, Godwin said "We are now in Danelaw.

People here serve Sveyn, whether they say so or not. I cannot have mistrust between us." He re-sheathed his seax.

Two men and two boys stood in a row, naked and goose-pimpled in the dawn's mist. Marton indicated Cudbert, standing just behind Godwin with his sword. "What about him?"

Godwin whipped the seax once more from its sheath. He grabbed Marton's manhood and balls in his fist, and held the knife to their root. Marton froze. "Not to trust Cudbert is not to trust me. And not to trust me is not to trust Prince Edmund or the King, who have put me in charge. Shall I send you back to Ealdorman Eadric as a traitor, with your bollocks as earrings?"

The Crown and The Arrow

Part 2: *The Thegn*

The book you hold is Volume II of *A Traitor's Son.* The two volumes form Part One of The Crown and The Arrow saga. Part Two, *The Thegn*, continues through 11th century England.

Godwin must undertake a dangerous task for Edmund. Eadric furthers his ambitions via a risky gambit in Waelas, then single-handedly reshapes history. Flaeda's return to her family brings unexpected problems. Walt is once again alone and lost. And Queen Emma finds an unexpected ally; while Prince Edward learns secrets that shake him to his core.

Like *A Traitor's Son*, *The Thegn* is divided into two volumes If you enjoyed this novel, you'll get even more out of the follow-ups.

Please rate and review them on Amazon. Thanks.

If you'd like to see more of my discoveries and thoughts about lives and events of 11th century England, have a look at **www.geoffcarthy.substack.com** (free)

For updates, and news about the forthcoming books in The Crown and The Arrow series, please sign up for an occasional newsletter on **www.geoffcarthy.substack.com**

Subscribe – it's free! – and I'll send you an exclusive fun freebie: a deleted chapter from *A Traitor's Son.*

Geoff Carthy, 2025

Printed in Dunstable, United Kingdom

64539356R00153